Triangular Prism
A = bh + 3ls
V = ½(bh)l
Sphere
A = 4πr²
V = 4/3πr³
Cube
A = 6a²
V = a³
Pyramid
A = 2bs
V = ⅓
Cylinder
A = 2πr(r+h)
V = πr²h
Cone
V = ⅓πr²h
Love is a quiet beast,
a poltergeist. It can convince
you it's not there, even when
it takes you by the hand
and pulls you in.
Dum spiro, spero.
Nil sine magno
labore.
Omne trium
perfectum.
I0823863

SIBYLLINE

ALSO BY MELISSA DE LA CRUZ

Cinder & Glass
Snow & Poison

The Encanto's Daughter Duology
Book One: The Encanto's Daughter
Book Two: The Encanto's Curse

The Queen's Assassin Duology
Book One: The Queen's Assassin
Book Two: The Queen's Secret

The Alex & Eliza Trilogy
Book One: Alex & Eliza
Book Two: Love & War
Book Three: All for One

Heart of Dread Series (with Michael Johnston)
Book One: Frozen
Book Two: Stolen
Book Three: Golden

Witches of East End Series

Blue Bloods Series

Beach Lane Series

The Ashley Project Series

Disney Descendants Series

Going Dark
The Headmaster's List
The Ring and the Crown
Something in Between
Someone to Love
29 Dates
Because I Was a Girl: True Stories for Girls of All Ages
(edited by Melissa de la Cruz)
Pride and Prejudice and Mistletoe
Jo & Laurie and *A Secret Princess* (with Margaret Stohl)
Surviving High School (with Lele Pons)

Sibylline

Book One

Melissa de la Cruz

putnam

G. P. Putnam's Sons

G. P. Putnam's Sons
An imprint of Penguin Random House LLC
1745 Broadway, New York, NY 10019
penguinrandomhouse.com

Created by Melissa de la Cruz and Michael Johnston

Design by Eileen Savage
Text set in Ashbury

Library of Congress Cataloging-in-Publication Data is available.

First published in the United States of America by G. P. Putnam's Sons, 2026

Manufactured in China

TOPL

ISBN 9798217002610
1 3 5 7 9 10 8 6 4 2

The authorized representative in the EU for product safety and compliance is Penguin Random House Ireland, Morrison Chambers, 32 Nassau Street, Dublin D02 YH68, Ireland, https://eu-contact.penguin.ie.

For Mike and Mattie, always.

Love is like the wild rose-briar;
Friendship like the holly-tree.
The holly is dark when the rose-briar blooms,
But which will bloom most constantly?

—*Emily Brontë*, The Complete Poems

Part One

Dum spiro, spero.

(While I breathe, I hope.)

–Latin proverb

Prologue

Know you her secret none can utter?
Hers of the Book, the tripled Crown?
Still on the spire the pigeons flutter,
Still by the gateway flits the gown;
Still on the street, from corbel and gutter,
Faces of stone look down.

—Sir Arthur Quiller-Couch, "Alma Mater"

SHE WANTED TO FLY.

Under the cover of night, the girl slipped out of the dormitory, darting between the gazes of watchful gargoyles perched on rooftops. The clock in Arches Tower chimed twelve times. Midnight. She was already late.

Like any great beast, Sibylline College slept when darkness fell. Like all living things, it dreamed. Though the cobblestone streets were empty and the wrought-iron gates stood like sentries, the night itself seemed to breathe. A deep inhale, the chill breeze prickling against bare skin. A deep exhale, the soft hush of leaves falling from the trees.

With the bell still echoing, the girl slipped through a door left open at the base of Arches and climbed the tall and spiraling stairs that took her to the top of the tower.

"Hello?" she called when she stepped out onto the narrow balcony at the top.

Only the wind howled in response.

Below, the Gothic campus rested, gray and stony towers poking from the darkness.

The steps had taken her near the top of Sibylline, to the highest balcony any student could reach by stair or elevator, but there was still one place that stood above it: a narrow platform that could not be reached by conventional means, where a single statue of an angel stood. Only magic could take you to it.

Touch the statue.

Claim its power.

Join St. Adolphus Hall.

Every freshman with ambition to be a part of the secret society completed the task. The moment you made contact, you were imbued with magic, and for days afterward, everything you touched would become enchanted.

From her pocket, she withdrew a single slip of yellowed parchment, the deckled edge rough beneath her fingers. The enchantment was simple. A single word, spoken. A single word, forbidden to anyone else who did not attend the hallowed halls of Sibylline. A single word was everything, and this one would carry her across the gap between the towers . . .

The moment she said it, she was changed. She felt lighter, her hair floating about her as if she were suspended in water.

She jumped.

One second, two. Air time.

Hanging in suspension. Freed from gravity. Leaping farther than humanly possible.

She laughed, throwing back her head and reveling in the freedom as she flew through the air, her feet landing on the distant balcony. She teetered, nearly falling, before she regained her balance.

Time to claim the prize.

She extended a hand, holding it out to touch the fabled statue, but her fingers did not make contact with stone. A shadow drifted from behind the statue. It coiled around her arm and spiraled down her legs, squeezing her bones in a suffocating embrace.

She couldn't move, couldn't breathe, as it pulled her into the darkness.

1 RAVEN

Thus strangely are our souls constructed, and by such slight ligaments are we bound to prosperity or ruin.
—Mary Shelley, Frankenstein

IT'S A TERRIBLE thing: wanting.

The envelope sits unopened in my hands. It's heavy, not with the weight of its contents but with its purpose. Acceptance or rejection? The letter will dictate my fate. My name glitters in silvery ink on the envelope, the wax seal for Sibylline College of Magical Arts still intact and tempting me to break it. It should be easy, like ripping off a Band-Aid. But I can't bring myself to do it. I've been waiting for this letter for what feels like my whole life, and now I'm not sure what to do with it. I both want and don't want to know what's inside. A purgatory of my own creation, and I've been trapped in it since the letter's unexpected arrival.

It appeared in between the pages of a library book I had checked out. Sibylline has no need for the postal service, of course.

I texted the group chat right away, sending a single exclamation point. I didn't have to say anything more than that. We all know when and where to meet. I'm still holding the letter tightly when I claim our bench on the Brooklyn Heights Promenade, with its picturesque view of the Manhattan skyline in the umber summer evening. People trying to capture the fading summer light with their phones walk past me, but all I can do is look at the letter in my hand.

A figure approaches. A dark-haired boy in a shabby but elegant tweed coat, hems and cuffs frayed from wear. A rare vintage find, like the wearer.

"Got yours, huh?" Atticus asks, flashing an envelope. It's identical to mine, save for his name: Atticus Edward Garcia. My relief upon seeing my friend is only a brief respite from the anxiety churning in my gut.

"I didn't want to open it alone," I say as he takes a seat next to me.

"Me neither," he says. A paper tray sits on his lap with three iced coffees from the nearby cafe.

"I don't think I should have any caffeine. I'm shaking already," I say.

"That's why I got you an herbal iced tea."

He knows me so well, even without his gift for reading people. He hands me my drink and a straw, and I accept it gratefully, though I don't take a sip. My stomach might just hurl it back up.

"Dorian?" I ask.

"On his way." Atticus sets down the tray with Dorian's drink on the bench.

"Where'd you get the letter?" I ask.

He takes a long sip and sighs. "I was doing line work in my sketchbook, and poof"–he flicks his free hand, mimicking a firework–"there it was, replacing the pen in my hand."

I nod, my insides still twisting with anticipation. I take a deep breath and set both the drink and my decision letter down to rub my throbbing temples. Meanwhile, Atticus at my side has one arm thrown over the back of the bench casually.

"How do you always seem so calm?" I ask. "Weeks of waiting, and you're just . . . fine?"

Atticus watches joggers passing by on the promenade, appreciating the last vestiges of summer. "Don't let appearances fool you." He talks around the straw in his mouth, lazily resting the tip of it against his teeth as he says, "Life's a façade." He swivels his head and looks at me with his deep brown eyes. "I read that on a fortune cookie somewhere."

He manages to get a smile out of me, which is exactly what he wanted. It does make me feel a little bit better now that *he's* here. When Atticus isn't drawing for the architecture firm where his mom works as a clerk, he scribbles in his notebooks and on tabletops, and sometimes, when there is no other surface available, he makes do. Ink covers his jeans. I can tell he's nervous now, especially since he's whipped out one of his fancy pens and started drawing crosshatches on his denim-covered thigh.

"If you must know, I'm terrified," he says, not looking up from his work. Each stroke of the pen is a delicate, practiced flick, each line perfectly spaced.

I like watching him work. I like watching him most of the time, but especially now. I love the way the sunset makes his brown skin glow. His full lips part as he sighs, his eyes dancing over his work, as if he's memorizing each line and shape he creates.

"If any of us gets in," he says, glancing at me from behind his shaggy bangs, "it'll definitely be you. You're the best of us. Plus, you're the only one of us who can afford it."

"Money doesn't matter," I say, trying to downplay it.

"Raven, I love you with all my heart, but people with money always say money doesn't matter. It also doesn't take away from the fact that you're a natural magician."

A hot blush rises on my face. My parents would say we're "comfortable," which Atticus has pointed out is code to mean *haven't a care in the world*, along with the "cottage" in the Hamptons (a ten-bedroom estate) and the London "attic" (a penthouse with river views). Dorian and Atticus don't have the same luxuries, and despite what many "comfortable" people want to believe, innate magical ability cannot be bought. A small percentage of the population has innate magical ability, people like us. Different. Special. Gifted. Everyone else can learn magic from spell books if they're accepted into a magical college, but for us, magic is like breathing.

I sigh, knowing it's best to drop the line of conversation, and notice a group of older tourists wearing matching backpacks, their expressions confused as they look around. Their rapid-fire German makes my ears perk. At first, I don't understand what they're saying. Then something clicks, like a camera lens focusing, and all at once, I do.

The leader of the pack is staring at a map and shaking his head. "*Ich*—don't know which way to go. Maybe we missed a turn?"

"Excuse me, do you need help?" I say in flawless German.

The tourists turn in my direction, then eyebrows shoot up. The man with the map stares at me, hopeful. "Oh! You speak German?"

I don't have to look directly at Atticus to know he's smiling. This is business as usual, even if he doesn't understand a word we're saying.

I answer them, providing the directions they need.

When I sit back down on the bench, Atticus is still smiling.

"Seeing you use your magic never gets old," he says, chewing on the straw from his iced coffee. He waves his hand over my head, passing his fingers through the aura only he can see. It's like he's trying to touch an invisible cloud. "You're shining."

I'm what's called a "situational polyglot," confirmed when I was eight by a specialist who studies magical skills in children. Our high school, Wellington Prep, had a dedicated track for kids like us. That's how I met Atticus and Dorian. We were the only kids in the program.

My whole life has been working toward this moment. The instant I heard about Sibylline's existence, my entire universe shifted. Nonmagical nerds can have Harvard and Yale. There's only one Ivy that counts for the magically inclined, and that's Sibylline.

It's not the only school in North America dedicated to the study of magic, but it is by far the oldest and best. Other magical schools teach rudimentary magic, or magic history. They'll help you pick up a minor spell here and there, but there is only one that instructs students in the mastery of the supernatural arts, one school with access to the oldest grimoires and the ancient wisdom they contain. In magic, knowledge is everything, and Sibylline guards its secrets closely. I want to know it all.

The envelope tempts me from the bench, so I slide it under my book.

"You're gifted," he says when he sees me hide the envelope. "They'd be absolute idiots not to let you in."

"Not really in my control, is it?"

The only problem is that getting into the most prestigious magical university in the country is one of the hardest things anyone can do. The odds are not in my favor, with only a one-in-three-thousand chance, they say, 0.03 percent. Might as well buy a lottery ticket while getting struck by lightning in the midst of a plane crash. And it's even worse for the three of us, not being the children of alumni. There's a rumor that Sibylline hasn't accepted nonlegacy admissions in generations, but the Supreme Court of Magicians ruled that there was nothing discriminatory in Sibylline's policies.

"I'm not special in the ways that seem to matter," I say. Even in the magical world, pedigree means everything.

"Well, you're special to me, so that matters," says Atticus. There's that heavy-lidded smile again.

My chest swells so much it aches. Having a crush on one of your best friends is a unique kind of agony that makes every atom of your being feel like screaming.

Atticus lifts his head, as if called to attention, and his gaze snags on something in the distance. He takes in the slightest breath. "He's here," he says.

I turn to see Dorian coming toward us on the promenade, wearing his signature navy wool peacoat despite the summer evening. Blond-haired, green-eyed, and straight-browed, the weight of the world pressing down on his shoulders.

When he spots us, he holds up his own envelope with a gloved hand. My stomach swoons at the sight of it, the anticipation before the drop on a roller coaster.

Atticus's eyes light up when he sees him, and his smile widens. "You open it yet?"

"Didn't even think to do it alone, Finch," he says, calling Atticus by his nickname, as in the hero from *To Kill a Mockingbird.* Dorian's voice is as buttery as the sunset sky. "I haven't been this afraid to touch something in a long time."

"If you touched it with a bare hand, could you intuit what's inside?" I ask.

"With something this magical, most definitely." Dorian drags his gloved hand through his hair, making it flop endearingly back into place, then he tugs at his kid leather gloves, making sure they're up to his wrists. It's a nervous habit. We're all twitchy.

Our lives are already defined by Sibylline, whether we want to admit it or not. It's the one chance we have of becoming real wizards. Otherwise kids like us get shuffled to basic magic programs and end up at some bank or accounting firm, using magic to sniff out whether people are lying on their loan applications. Boring and tedious work.

Atticus gets to his feet, replacing his pen and withdrawing his letter. "No matter what happens, I'm proud of us," he says, looking at me and then at Dorian, his smile for him even more radiant, so that I get a tiny twinge of jealousy.

"Together?" Dorian asks, holding up his envelope, glancing at the both of us.

"Nil sine magno labore," Atticus says. Nothing without great effort. It's our motto for the Oneiric Society, the geeky name of our little club of strivers. You have to earn your keep, nothing is given for free, something we know all too well.

Dorian's eyes linger on mine, sparkling in the setting sun like the flickering lights of the city. He looks at me like I look at Atticus. But that's not what I'm worried about now. I nod as I stand, repeating, *"Nil sine magno labore!"*

Dorian says it back, completing the circle. I'm a lot braver when I'm with my friends, but my hands shake as I wedge my finger under the envelope's flap.

"Three, two, one," says Atticus, and we all open our letters. "Here goes nothing."

None of us speak—I'm not sure we even breathe—as we read. The letter is written in a fine, looping script, and the sheet is made of yellowed parchment, the ink silver and glittering.

> *Miss Raven Chen,*
> *Thank you for your application to Sibylline College of Magical Arts. Unfortunately-*

Unfortunately.

One word.

It crushes my dream as easily as shattering glass.

I look up at Dorian and Atticus. They're both stock-still, staring at their letters. Dorian's face is white. Atticus blinks a few times, then finally he says, "Oh."

I don't have to be a psychic like Atticus to know what happened.

Atticus gently refolds the letter and slides it neatly back in the envelope, his mouth set into a grim line. Dorian crumples his up and throws it in the nearest trash can with a huff.

My knees give out, and I collapse back down on the bench.

I check and recheck the letter, hoping the words are different, that maybe my mind misread it. But no, it's real. I didn't get in. I won't be attending Sibylline. I won't achieve my dream. I might as well die. Right here and now. I don't even want to think about what I did wrong. I performed well on the written exams, scoring high marks in history and lore, and in the interview, I displayed my talents, transcribing in real time the text the assessor offered to me, a piece apparently written by an eighteenth-century monk in his own private dialect. I'd done well, but it hadn't mattered.

I want to leap off the pier or tear the letter into a thousand little pieces. I need to scream, but I choke down the urge. How can I not be good enough? Me? I worked so hard for this! How many sleepless nights did I spend studying for the MSAT, the arcane college admissions test? Was being the president of Manhattan's Youth Magicians Club not enough? What about my national award for excellence in sorcery? Did none of it even matter? My application was perfect, *perfect.*

The disappointment is numbing.

Atticus clicks his tongue. "Maybe it's for the better. It's just a school for a bunch of magic snobs and elitist wizards and rich enchanters. So what's even the point?"

"An education," says Dorian dryly, masking his hurt with humor. "And I think you need all the help you can get."

Atticus lets out a laugh. Dorian smiles back. That's what comes with being friends. *Best* friends. All of us. No matter what, we're together. We'd planned on attending Sibylline—so now what? Will we have to separate? My mouth feels dry at the thought.

"Well, there goes my one chance," says Atticus.

"You didn't apply anywhere else?" Dorian asks.

"It was either Sibylline or nothing," he says.

"Me too," I say, and Dorian nods. We all did the same.

I won't let this happen to us. I refuse. I can't give up. Not now, not ever. "What if we don't take no for an answer?"

Dorian's eyebrows rise, and he looks at me, as if trying to read my expression.

"What are you saying? Reject their rejection? We can't make them accept us," Atticus says. "Can we?"

I picture Sibylline's students on their first day of class: groups of eager young magicians walking the cobblestone streets, studying in the grand halls, and learning all that is worth knowing from masters of the craft. Everything that matters is there, nestled in the ivy-covered arches and the ancient tomes. I'd give anything to be there, at the center of it all. I'd do anything, any job . . .

It's then that an idea starts to form.

My entire world is books, old histories and tragic tales alike. Since freshman year, I've worked in the school library as an assistant. When I walk into it, I feel at home. But home isn't the same without my friends.

I can't say goodbye to Atticus. Or Dorian. Not yet.

"Maybe . . ." I say slowly, still forming the thought, "if we can't attend Sibylline as students, we can find work there instead."

"Work, you mean, like, get a job on campus?" Dorian asks.

"Oh, Raven. You *genius*," Atticus says. "Exactly! If the school won't teach us, we'll work in the libraries, museums, and anywhere else. The next best thing."

Dorian unfolds his arms and shrugs. "Sibylline adjacent. Huh." He glances at me, seeing how I'm feeling, his eyes hopeful. "It could work. If we're there, we'll have access to all the same materials as the students. Maybe we can teach ourselves."

"Get our hands on some books, eavesdrop on lectures, copy lesson plans. I'd even *pay* a student to do their homework for them, instead of the other way around." I laugh. "Maybe trick a wizard or two into meeting us for office hours. And maybe, just maybe, they'll let us in after they get to know us. Can't hurt to try, can it?"

I admit, my heart's racing. It sounds risky. It sounds hard, but it's a chance.

"We'll need to update our résumés, get references, write some letters . . ." Atticus says.

"Sacrifice a virgin under the full moon," jokes Dorian.

"So we're doing this?" Atticus asks. He looks at me and Dorian, his dark eyes glittering.

"We're going to learn magic," I say. "One way or another, at any cost. Agreed?"

Dorian's smile splits. "*Nil sine magno labore*, right?"

"*Nil sine magno labore*," Atticus echoes.

ATTICUS

Whatever our souls are made out of, his and mine are the same.
—Emily Brontë, Wuthering Heights

ON MY FIRST day of work, a black cat follows me across campus.

As I step out of the front doors to the redbrick town house—wearing my father's old tweed coat, tuxedo pants I found at a thrift store, a cable-knit fisherman's sweater, and a pair of shiny leather brogues I hunted down on eBay—the cat joins me, its tail curled around its feet, looking up at me with expectant yellow eyes.

"Hello, kitty," I say.

"What was that?" my mother asks, her voice warped through the phone.

I pinch it between my shoulder and my cheek as I open my umbrella with a snap. It's begun to rain lightly. "Hi, Mom. I'm talking to a cat."

This is not news to someone like my mother. "Oh, just one?"

"So far," I say, glancing up and down the street to try to catch a glimpse of any more darting out of sight. Animals sometimes shadow me, especially when I least expect it. Cats, dogs, birds, even a fox during a school field trip to the Hudson Valley. When I was in elementary school, I was sent to the principal's office because a swarm of frogs had crawled through the window and, for whatever reason, had chosen to gather and sit on my desk. My teacher thought I was somehow responsible.

Animals have never bothered me; they're quiet and often uncomplicated emotionally, and I greatly appreciate having the company. I don't have to be anything other than myself when I'm with them.

The cat slowly blinks and flicks the tip of its tail. It doesn't seem to mind the rain, but then again, neither do I. Autumn in Vermont is cold and dreary and gray. In other words, perfect. The last vestiges of summer have long faded, the air dominated now with chilly mist and dead leaves. Rain clouds hang low in the sky, draping the mountain skyline like a shroud.

"You're settling in, then?" my mom asks. I can hear her at the breakfast table in our apartment in Brooklyn, the groan of the wood as she slides her chair back, followed by the clink of silverware on porcelain. I picture her sitting with a mug of hot coffee and a stack of expense reports spread out in front of her before work.

"Yep. My apartment is just off Sibylline's campus. You should see it." Luckily for us, Sibylline is in a sleepy, small rural town and most off-campus housing was cheap and available.

"Draw it for me," she says. It's a game we play, describing our surroundings with ink instead of words. Mom wanted to be an architect, but her family never had the money for graduate school. So she works at a firm as their secretary, keeping track of accounts and blueprints.

"I will, but I can tell you about it, too. The buildings are colonial-style town houses, lined with the golden leaves of sugar maples, just like home." I've only been gone a week, and I'm already a little homesick.

I extend the umbrella to the cat. The cat seems appreciative and matches my stride as we make our way down the puddle-strewn sidewalk.

"Sounds perfect. Do you have your portfolio? And your drafting pencils? What about your new architect's scale?"

"I'm just the new admin assistant at Mansart Hall," I say. "I doubt they'll want me doing design work for them, but . . ." I smile. "I brought them anyway." It hurts to think that after all her sacrifice–scraping by so she could send me to Wellington–in the end I've landed just where she has. Working as a secretary. The irony doesn't escape me. I hope this plan works, that somehow, some way, being so near to Sibylline will lead to being accepted one day.

"Good boy," my mom says. "You're going to blow them all away. You're . . . –y son, after all . . . –oud of you."

"What? I'm getting too close to campus," I say. "You're breaking up." A veil of woven spells covers all of Sibylline, rendering cell phones and internet useless, as they want the students to focus on studying magic. I won't be able to text my mom, email, or FaceTime her whenever I'm on campus. It's one of the school's many charms.

My mom raises her voice and enunciates as best she can. "I! Am! Proud! Of! You!"

I swallow a lump in my throat. I haven't done anything to make her proud yet, but I swear I will one day.

The call ends before either of us can hang up.

The magic of Sibylline waits for no one.

I stuff my phone into my bag, and the cat silently slinks next to me, creeping over wet autumn leaves with its tail held high as we make our way west down the block toward the old campus. We take the path around the cemetery, where a moss-covered building rises above the others, a strange symbol carved into the pediment. It looks something like an eye surrounded by a pentagram. My curiosity spikes, and I make a quick sketch of it on the back of my hand.

I round the corner, and the cat and I join the students entering the wrought-iron gates of Sibylline's main campus. I can't help but feel a jealous longing, seeing them in their billowing apprentice wizard robes, juggling wands, books, and bottles of potions.

I'm early for work as I climb the steps to Mansart Hall, the architecture building, and walk through the front doors, the black cat stopping at the entry, guarding it like a Sphinx. "Wish me luck," I say, bidding it farewell.

I find my way to my employer's office on the first floor, but when I come to the waiting area, no one's there. The front desk is empty, though I do notice there's a still steaming mug of coffee on the table where an old-school typewriter sits by a rain-streaked window, the gray sunlight illuminating its black keys.

"Hello?" I call into the back hallway, but no one answers. Maybe they stepped out.

So I hang my coat, leave my umbrella in the rack, and take in my surroundings.

Forest-green damask wallpaper lines the upper walls, bordered by dark hickory wood paneling. An ornate Persian rug covers the polished wood floor, flanked by miniature models of buildings from the Sibylline campus: the Rosette, the iconic library with its gargantuan medieval stained-glass windows; Old Bones, the Gothic-style museum of magical items, artifacts, and even human remains; the historic Piranesi Auditorium, said to have been inspired by Piranesi's own designs and made real by the legendary architect Anna White—all protected behind glass cases, each model more beautiful than the next. Shelves of architecture books line almost every available surface. A part of me wonders if this might be the most diverse collection of architectural knowledge in the world, a veritable museum on its own.

I think about texting Dorian, knowing he would love this, and my hand automatically moves for my phone; then I remember it won't work here.

Disappointment makes my stomach twinge. I dreamed about him only last night, and it felt as if he were right next to me. I still recall the dream.

His lips touched mine.

It happens a lot. Dreams about Dorian. We've known each other since ninth grade, but what started out as friendship turned into something more for me. I don't know when, exactly, my feelings for him changed. It was gradual, like the dawn turning to day. It crept up on me. Then something just clicked. When we weren't admitted to Sibylline, I realized that I could lose him forever. Our paths might diverge, and the thought of not having Dorian in my life scared me, but I kept my fears to myself. I didn't know how to tell him what I was feeling. How could I expose my heart to a friend and not be afraid? There's a certain radiance about him, like the flashbulb from an old-fashioned camera. It lingers after he's gone.

He's the only person I've ever liked in that way.

Whom I dream of in that way.

It's torture, knowing him as a friend but not knowing if he'd want more than that.

I walk into the office, and the moment I do, I'm overwhelmed with noise. Not just audible sound, but mental noise. The air is thick with it, so thick it stops me in my tracks, and my eyes close like I've been met with a sudden, brisk gust of wind.

People aren't like cats; they're so damn loud.

The cacophony thrums hard in my skull, vibrating like I'm pressing my ear directly against a concert speaker. My own thoughts are drowned out, and I forget to breathe. I have to take a moment, reeling with the force, my hand held in front of me as if seeking to grab on to something.

See, I have this thing, a sort of psychic thing. My aunt has it, too, and I think I got it from her. She works as a phone medium, talking clients through work and relationship problems. I can sense people, their emotions, at times even their thoughts. My power manifests often without my control. I have good days and bad. Some days I can see hazy colors floating around people's heads; other days I can feel their moods as if they're my own. Once in a while, I see people's moods as colorful auras: pink or red when they are angry or agitated, blue when they are calm, sometimes all mixed up like a kaleidoscope, as it so often goes with the complexity of human emotions. I've had this power ever since I can remember, picking up on the energy of those around me, maybe to an unnerving degree. I think I knew my parents were getting a divorce before they did.

Being here at Sibylline now, though, it's as if my power is dialed up to eleven. Maybe it's the magic that's collected in Sibylline amplifying my ability, but it takes me by surprise just how loud it is all of a sudden. Like I've had earplugs in my whole life, and now they're gone.

I ground myself, blocking out the noise of other people, and begin to count. *Zero, one, one, two, three, five, eight, thirteen, twenty-one*... The Fibonacci sequence. It's an old trick I adopted when I was young. My aunt used to do the same thing, blocking out the noise of other people with knitting, counting her stitches.

It's meditative, and I've always liked numbers. There's no room for confusion or interpretation. Numbers are literal, predictable, safe.

The counting does the trick, and once the shock fades, I gain my bearings. I've found the right office. Twenty or so architects crowd the room, all of them hard at work, moving quickly about, the air alive with chatter. It's an open floor plan, with antique mahogany desks, large stained-glass windows, wall-long filing cabinets with drawers full of papers, and a chalkboard packed with diagrams and measurements.

There's a big table at the very center of the room, brightly illuminated by a low-hanging suspended lamp, and everyone's gathered around it. Their faces glow, their eyes sparkling, the lights from below blessing them with an otherworldly appearance.

And that's when I realize it's not just light beaming up from the table. It's magic. The blueprint is literally glowing.

An older woman, with dark gray hair tied up in a neat bun on the top of her head and a pencil sticking out of it, looks up and notices me standing in the doorway.

"Atticus Garcia?" she asks.

"Yeah," I say, then correct myself: "Yes, ma'am." Sibylline doesn't give off "yeah" energy.

"You're late," she says, marching over. She wears low-heeled retro wingtips, a long tan skirt, a white blouse, and a man's black necktie hanging loose around her neck, stylishly unkempt. She's quite short, but she walks with authority.

Heat rises in my face. "I wasn't, I—"

"You and me, let's go," she says, grabbing a coat from the back of a chair.

For an instant, I think she's kicking me out, but then she thrusts a thick binder into my arms, giving me only a brief moment to catch it before she's moving toward the exit, beckoning me to follow. I barely have time to grab my coat, forgetting my umbrella in my haste to keep up.

Her heels clack loudly down the hallway, sharp staccato taps that match the clip of her accent. *One-two, one-two.* "We've got a lot of work to do, so let's not waste time, shall we? I'm Professor White, lead architect for restoration and preservation, your supervisor."

I'm struck then, realizing I'm walking with a living legend. I know all about Professor Anna White's legacy. She's spent most of her esteemed career researching how magic was used long ago to create Sibylline's whole campus. I have all of her books on my shelf, and I've watched her in countless online interviews. I once attended a lecture by Professor White with Dorian on a Sunday at the Cooper Union. She's an absolute icon and the chair of the architecture department at Sibylline. I didn't think I'd be actually working with *her.*

I almost have to jog to keep up, and she leaves the building without an umbrella. The cat is still waiting on the steps, its tail flicking curiously, watching us go.

Despite the rain, Professor White remains dry, not a drop on the shoulders of her tan overcoat. Any other mundane person might think it's a coincidence, but I know the truth. She's using magic. As I shield the binder with my body, Professor White glances at me and mutters a spell under her breath, and suddenly I'm also protected from the rain.

"At Sibylline," she says kindly, "we make magic work for us. We are the architects of this world–never forget that."

All I can do is nod. I won't let her down.

Professor White's eyes linger on the back of my hand, where I sketched the symbol I saw in the graveyard. "Is that a tattoo? Are you interested in St. Adolphus Hall?"

I glance at my hand. "Oh, no, it's just a drawing. I saw the symbol and liked it. What's St. Adolphus Hall?" I ask, curious. There is so much I don't know.

"A secret society," she says. "Kids call it St. Ad's."

"Ah." A secret society, only for students, not lowly minimum-wage workers like I am. Emphasis on *secret*. Even someone like me who's obsessed with Sibylline doesn't know about it. One more privilege I've been denied.

"Watch out for them—they have strange ideas." She waves her hand, and the evil eye I sketched vanishes from my skin. I'm not sure I'll ever get used to seeing magic used so casually. It's thrilling. Then she sets off at a march and I follow, my stomach twisting in knots. Professor White crosses the diamond—the grassy quad now empty—and marches us through the music school, cutting through the lobby that's full of the sounds of violin and cello. Butterflies made of light dance out of the practice rooms, conjured by the music. We exit, crossing the street and heading straight for a tower whose top is crowned in dewy mist. I realize it's part of a greater structure, cathedral-like, with a main atrium occupying most of the block. I follow her inside and find the interior mostly empty, like it has been carved out, and there are no lights, even of the magical sort. What remains of the interior is covered in drop cloths, so it looks like great ghosts of giants linger in the darkened hall. Dust clouds the air.

"Arches is one of the older buildings on campus. We're in the process of restoring the structural systems, but there's a problem with the renovation," Professor White says, gesturing to the building as she begins her ascent, climbing the switchback stairs of the scaffold as she leads me higher and higher through the center of the tower.

Something rumbles in the distance, and the ramp beneath me shakes. I sneeze when dust fills the air. Professor White bids me gesundheit, then continues, "Since you have experience with mundane architectural practices, you should know that the buildings at Sibylline are different. Arches was designed, developed, and constructed with magic, and therefore it must be maintained with magic." She pauses when yet again a soft rumbling echoes afar. "You may find the job difficult or overwhelming. This sort of work requires a skill set that some do not exhibit. From foundation to finial, this entire tower resonates with the power of Sibylline. In times past, wizard architects who possessed great magical ability erected entire buildings"–she snaps her fingers–"like that, crafting their architectural visions by harnessing the spirits of the natural world."

The way she says it, I sense something beneath her words, a kind of reverence, maybe even envy. It's like a whisper, the deep desire radiating from her, and I yearn to know her thoughts. Too bad I can't read them today.

"To build something like this . . ." Professor White's face turns up toward the inside of the tower, her head shaking in awe.

"Even a brick wants to be something," I paraphrase.

Professor White's gaze shines with mine. "Louis Kahn," she says, naming the famous architect. "You understand, then."

She doesn't know the half of it. Maybe in this metaphor I'm the clay yet to be shaped. "There's power in creation."

The way Professor White looks at me, I wonder if I've overstepped, but the smile on her face gives way to a question: "What does this work mean to you?"

It's easy speaking from the heart. "Creating, to me, is like breathing. I have to do it, otherwise it feels like I'm dying. So to build something like Arches . . ." I gesture upward. "It's a testament to life."

Maybe it's cheesy, but Professor White seems pleased. "Very good, Mr. Garcia. But that is only the beginning of what we do here. There are no living architects that still possess the talents required for the job. Magic of this sort has dwindled over time, similar to how we've moved beyond inventions like Gutenberg's printing press in favor of modern innovation. So we must preserve what we have of this lost science of building with magic just like we would preserve a site of historical significance. But this particular task is difficult."

"How so?" I ask, my feet trembling. Or is it the scaffolding that's shaking?

"The builders cannot use modern technologies or materials, lest we upset the balance of the magic that thrives within Arches. So our task is twofold, to maintain the history as well as the power within. But–"

The scaffolding shakes once more, harder this time, and I reach out for something to hold on to. Professor White stumbles, nearly falling, as the floor beneath us trembles. Then all at once, a great hunk of stone shakes loose from the structure above and comes crashing downward, breaking and tearing the scaffold, ripping apart the wooden planks in its path. It strikes a spot that's only a few feet from where I stand.

I fall to my knees, gripping the boards beneath me, hoping they won't crumble, tumbling along with that hunk of stone to the distant floor, three or four stories below. I freeze, hoping the floor won't collapse beneath me.

I count numbers to maintain my calm as the air clears, the dust fading until once again I can see Professor White, her face caked in dust.

"You see what I mean?" Her tone is calm, as if she'd half expected that stone to fall. "There's something wrong with Arches. And if we don't find out what it is, we may lose the tower completely."

DORIAN

Nowadays people know the price of everything and the value of nothing.

—*Oscar Wilde,* The Picture of Dorian Gray

THE BENOIST MUSEUM is as dark and silent as a tomb. The only source of illumination comes from arcane spotlights beaming down on the artifacts protected in their glass display cases. The cases are lined like headstones, forming a natural aisle for me to walk toward the rear of the atrium, and I glance into each as I pass by. Gilded swords, suits of armor, enormous textiles, cuff links, even fountain pens. The vastness of the collection is breathtaking.

The air here smells of wood polish and old leather, and the dark wood paneling mutes the sounds that echo in the space. It looks like I'm the only one here. The silence of the room is broken by my quiet footsteps on the polished stone floor. Calming my nerves, I breathe as deeply as if I'm at the lacrosse pitch underneath all my padding as the goalie. But there's more at stake here than the mid-Atlantic championship. I'm breathing in the scent, the smell of history, their air of wealth and prestige. The Benoist Museum is the most famous magical museum in the world, and it's my first day on the job.

I pause and check my reflection in a nearby display case. Annoyed that a lock of hair is out of place, resting too casually on my forehead for someone who works in a serious institution like this one, I comb it back with my fingers, ensuring that I look the part. I adjust the cuffs of my jacket and smooth out wrinkles in my slacks. I have to force myself to stop fidgeting, but I'm excited and eager to get started, so I take out my pocket watch and hold it in my gloved fist. I like how solid it feels under my grip, solid and trustworthy. I never leave the house without it. It doesn't work anymore, not to keep time. But I don't use it as a watch. My mom gave it to me when I was younger, because she said I looked so much like its previous owner, her grandfather. She'd said I reminded her of him. Now it serves as a reminder of her. She's why I'm doing this, after all.

"Oh," a voice coos. "Is that a full Hunter, Wehinger & Brahms skeleton pocket watch?"

I turn and see a slender man of about fifty standing behind me. There's no sign of gray in his pitch-black hair, and he's dressed in a dark suit jacket and white shirt. He's smiling at me, his light eyes crinkling behind square glasses looped with a thin golden chain.

"Am I correct?" he asks.

"Yes. It was my great-grandfather's." I raise an eyebrow.

His eyes light up. "A rare antique! May I?"

He holds out his hand, and I set it in his palm. He pushes his glasses up his nose and raises the pocket watch to the light. "Yellow gold casing, good condition, well-loved, clearly. Original leather strap, too. I'm guessing 1930s or so—maybe 1932, to be precise, based on the reddish stain, as they discontinued that color soon after. Oh, what delicate craftsmanship on the front, so wonderful. Are these your great-grandfather's initials?" He points to the engraved letters on the back of the casing.

I nod, admiring his skills in observation. I had no idea this model was so rare.

He presses the button on the casing, flipping it open to look at the watch face. "Ah, but it's broken." The glass is cracked, all of the gears and mechanical dials in permanent stasis, stuck at 3:33 exactly. His expression falls as he closes the pocket watch. "Shame."

"My great-grandfather dropped it on the deck of his ship crossing the Atlantic. It hasn't worked since." Even if it was worth millions, I don't think I could ever bring myself to sell it. It'd be like selling a part of my soul.

With a tilt of his head and a smile, the man returns my watch and extends his hand to me. "I'm the head curator here at Old Bones, and chair of the art history department, Nathan Evander. You must be our new junior curator, Dorian Winthrop."

I pocket my watch once more and shake his hand. "I am indeed. Good to meet you, Professor Evander, and happy to be here."

"And we're happy to have you." The professor gestures for me to follow, leading me deeper inside. "Welcome to the Benoist Museum. Everyone calls it Old Bones, for reasons all too obvious." He gestures casually to a human skull encased in glass with emeralds set in the unblinking eye sockets. Its toothy grin is like a taunt from the dead.

Evander begins to lead the way to a set of doors at the end of the atrium. "Behold, our esteemed collection. You're going to become all too familiar with the artifacts, from paintings to relics, ceramics to busts–"

As we pass it, the skull seems to be watching me, its grin permanently stretched. "Is that real?" I ask.

"The human bones? Of course they're real," he says. "All of the artifacts here are part of arcane history, often displayed alongside remnants of their dearly departed. Skulls, mummified hands, tanned human skin preserving tattoos, all of it is meticulously cataloged by my team. The residual magic left over from a wizard's life still permeates the physical form long after the spirit has left this plane, making the wizards as useful in death as they were in life, for the greater cause that is Sibylline. Magic is all around us, Dorian."

I put my hand in my pocket, brushing my fingers against the watch inside. It's a habit, a security blanket. Even though I can't touch it with my bare hands, I like to know it's there.

He slows his pace, glancing at me. "Cold, are you?" he asks, noting I haven't taken off my gloves.

"No, sir," I say.

"I've been told that you possess a magical ability, is that true?"

"Psychometry, yes." That's the clinical term. "When I touch something, I see flashes of its history, of the person who carried it, the emotions poured into it when it was being held." The talent works with people, too, but results are unpredictable, dangerous even.

The professor's eyes gleam. "Psychometry, is that right? And you never take them off? Your gloves?"

"Never," I tell him. My mother called what I have a gift, but it can be embarrassing somctimes and inconvenient. When my magic first manifested, I used to open doors with clothed elbows or use my sleeve to push buttons, because the visions can be overwhelming. Most people thought I was a germaphobe or had some kind of obsessive-compulsive disorder. No one knew the truth of it. No one else could understand. Except for Atticus and Raven.

It was Raven who got me these gloves for my sixteenth birthday. I don't go anywhere in public without them now. Like a half-remembered dream, I can still feel the gloves' faded memory of the moment when she picked them out for me, a hazy but pleasant reminder that she's always with me.

"It's difficult to control my magic," I tell the professor. Touching is a problem for me. When I was eleven, I touched a person—not in that way—but it was the first time I had touched someone skin-to-skin since my magic manifested, and it didn't go well. The memory still rattles me. It's so bad, I can't even bring myself to kiss my mom on the cheek when she's in the hospital for more chemotherapy. I'm too afraid to feel the pain she's in. It's a shame I carry.

I clear my throat. "Sometimes my visions can be distracting." Professor Evander looks slightly disappointed, so I add quickly, "It won't interfere with my work, I promise."

"Interfere? It's why we hired you! I was hoping we could make use of your gift."

Intriguing. I've always been curious about what I can do—when the gloves come off, so to speak. "I'm eager to help."

The professor smiles broadly. "Splendid. Someone with your talent will thrive in this institution. I'm certain of it. Would you be so kind as to give me a little demonstration?"

The collar of my shirt suddenly feels too tight as he studies me, like a butterfly pinned in a glass case. I get the sense that this is some kind of test. If I decline, I'll disappoint him, and I'll throw away this one chance to learn more about my magic.

"Sure," I say, my heart pounding in my chest, a drop of sweat forming on my brow.

He guides me down a darkened hallway and into the back rooms of the museum, where the curators flit in and out of the preparation rooms. It's like being backstage at a play: busy but quiet. Hardly anyone glances my way, they're so focused on their tasks, handling statues and sculptures as if they're priceless. Maybe they really are.

Evander stops at a room stacked with wooden crates stuffed with straw.

"We're quite busy sorting through all of the recent donations, organizing, and cataloging."

I stare dumbfounded at the stack of crates. "Are there usually so many?" I ask.

"We're bringing together a large exhibition. It's called *The Procession of Time*. It honors some of the first benefactors of the institution. The museum is hosting a fundraising gala. It'll be the party of the year, but the schedule is tight, and we're behind on the work." He turns and gestures to the back of the room. "Come. Perhaps you can settle a little predicament."

He brings me to a large wooden crate where an oil painting in a gilded frame sits propped on its side. The image depicts Dante descending into hell.

"Is this a Hubert?" I ask, stunned. Francis Hubert was one of the most famous magical artists of the nineteenth century, imbuing his paintings with enchanted paints.

The professor nods. "Good eye. A certain high-profile art broker in London, I shan't name who, acquired this for me. They claim it's a lost piece, once thought stolen and now recovered. They've had it authenticated by their finest in-house detectives. I, however, would like a second opinion before adding it to the show."

I'm still staring at the painting, enthralled by the movement in each stroke of the brush. Atticus, the artist of us three, says Hubert is one of the most inspiring artists, making paintings literally come to life. Dante actually blinks on the canvas. I can't believe I am here right now, close enough to smell the paint. I'm this close to history. I'll have to make sure Atticus sees this, too.

"If you'd be so kind," he says, gesturing as if letting me pass.

"You want me to touch it?" I ask, awed at what I'm about to do.

"I would like to see your gift in action. To touch literal history is one of the only ways we can fully grasp the scope of the human condition, I always say. Go ahead. Don't be shy."

"Are you sure?"

The professor's eyes sparkle with intrigue. "You wouldn't have found your way here if you weren't special," he says. "Please."

But I'm not special, I want to argue. I wasn't accepted into Sibylline.

Slowly, I take off one of my gloves and flex my bare fingers. I hesitate, a little apprehensive about what comes next. When it comes to my visions, I never know what to expect or how it'll feel. The intensity can be staggering. But Evander frowns almost imperceptibly at my hesitation, forcing me to gather my nerves. Steadying my heart, I reach inside the crate, touching the tips of my fingers to the canvas.

Instantly, the vision comes to me. I'm transported into a dusty warehouse. A television hums in the corner as a hand–my hand, *ours*–holds a paintbrush, putting the finishing touches on the canvas. That's definitely not Hubert and not the fifteenth century.

"It's fake," I say, removing my hand and pushing back a strand of hair that had fallen onto my forehead.

"You're certain?" Evander asks. He seems more excited than disappointed.

"Yes, I saw him. The forger. Another wizard, not Hubert. Besides, he was using a particular shade of blue paint that didn't exist during Hubert's time."

"I had my suspicions. I guessed this acquisition was too good to be true." He sighs, but he seems relieved. "It appears we have our own in-house art detective."

I burn with pleasure.

"I see a great future for you, Mr. Winthrop. Now let's put you to work. Keep those gloves off." He leaves me alone in another room, where the curators have arranged objects for inspection. It feels like a closet, lit dimly by candles burning behind red glass and cramped with shelves full of boxes of artifacts.

There are dozens: gilded chests from the Ming dynasty whose contents change every time you open the lid, porcelain dolls from Paris that have beating hearts, heirloom rings from Cairo that glow with magical light.

I pry open a lid and push aside the straw to find a necklace of carved beetles and an onyx ring with snakes entwined around the band. Next to them is a thin piece of wood about as long as my forearm. It looks like it was picked up off the beach, the bark having long ago been stripped, leaving the wood smooth, revealing the knots and whorls. I've never seen one in real life before, but I know what it is: a wizard's wand.

I reach to touch it, then hesitate. It has a strange quality, a kind of dark aura. Almost as if the memories within it are so strong that I can feel them before I make contact. Something deep within me tells me not to touch it, to move on to the next object. I ought to listen to that voice, but instead I push it aside. I came here to take risks and to learn. So I extend my index finger nervously, my whole body twitching.

It's just a piece of wood, I try to tell myself, but I know in my soul it is something far more potent. The instant I touch it, my eyes roll back into my head. I'm pulled, drawn downward, deep into myself. It's like I'm being dragged underwater, falling to the bottom of the ocean, my feet heavy, the water dark and silent.

I am subsumed in the blackness of space.

And then the memories come, rolling over me like tidal waves, pushing me down deeper. These images don't belong to me, but they consume me, haunt me. They are ghosts of a past belonging to someone else.

The visions arrive in bursts. Rolling thunder. Crack of lightning. Roaring fire. A glyph on a marble floor. A pointed star, drawn in blood. The coppery smell in my nose. Red staining my hands. Burning incense. Cloying smoke. Candles. A voice chanting. Another screaming.

"Adelina! Adelina! Please!"

There's a body. Wearing a Sibylline cloak. Spread-eagle. Chained. Dead. And then *something's* here, a shadow.

The vision is over in an instant, but it feels as if hours have passed. And when I release the wand, my knees lock up and I keel backward, darkness taking me.

Then I wake, hearing Professor Evander speak some sort of incantation, his voice low and soothing. My head aches, and my whole body is sore. I try to move, but I'm sluggish and dazed. Professor Evander's face fades in above me, looking concerned. Light hovers around his hand, and he gently lowers it as my eyes open fully.

"There you are," says Professor Evander softly. "Are you all right, Mr. Winthrop? What happened?"

I try too quickly to sit up, and the world spins. The professor calms me with a gentle hand on my shoulder and then helps me to my feet, slowly this time. He guides me to a nearby chair before my knees give out.

"I touched this," I explain, motioning to the wand. "Who owned it?" I ask, shaking, the vision still swirling in my thoughts.

He frowns. "It's a wand said to have belonged to the goddess of witches, Hecate. It's supposed to contain great magic."

I say nothing for a moment. Memories of the vision choke me.

Someone used it far more recently. They were wearing Sibylline robes. But what they were doing . . . I lift my hand, almost expecting to see it covered in blood like in the vision, but it's not. My stomach sours at the thought it might be.

"Is there something I should know? Is it a fake?" Evander asks, waiting, his eyes expectant. He doesn't seem to know its history.

I shake my head. "No," I say. The visions were real. The wand, whether it belonged to Hecate or not, is certainly powerful.

4
RAVEN

This pure little drop from a pure little source was too sweet: it penetrated deep, and subdued the heart.

–Charlotte Brontë, Villette

A LIBRARY IS like a dream made of endless possibilities.

I push the wheeled cart down the aisle and slot a book into its place on the shelf.

"*Eighteenth-Century Techniques for Conjuration* . . ." I whisper to myself, reading the title. I shelve the next book. "*Fundamentals of Standardized Sigils* . . ." I continue down the aisle, scanning the spines before I find the right place for the next book. "*Practical Uses in Applied Arcana* . . ."

Since it's my first day of work, I'm shelving books. I don't mind. Of course, it was tedious, having to memorize an entire new cataloging system, one that still utilizes aged card stock smeared with ink from a century ago, but I quickly got used to it and soon settled into a comfortable rhythm.

Atticus, Dorian, and I used to spend countless hours together in the library when we were in school, tearing through books in a day, side by side at a table we claimed as our own in the back of the reading room. I've always felt at home in the library, so it was only natural that I would find work here. I've taken a position as an archivist in Sibylline's Rosette Library. It's not much of a job, but I can tell I'm going to like it. Being surrounded by words has always made me feel at peace, and it's no different here. I like the calm of the silent stacks. The whispers of the patrons soothe me. There's an obvious reverence in the air, a silence that's reserved for worship. It is almost as if I were working in a temple dedicated to the written word, and that might not be too far off the mark. The Rosette was once a cathedral, and it's one of the oldest buildings on campus. But in more recent years, they've converted the chapel into an archive for magical texts, one of the largest on the continent. It houses the school's exhaustive collection of rare and magical books and scrolls—some secret, some powerful, some (I've only heard) too dangerous to leave the premises.

I glance around to see if anyone is watching.

The rain taps gently along the towering stained-glass windows that make up every wall, streaks of water cascading down across depictions of knights slaying fire-breathing dragons and golden-haired maidens leaning out of towers to gaze at their saviors. The candlelit chandeliers overhead warmly illuminate the atrium, pouring golden light upon thousands of rows of books, all of them meticulously categorized by the archivists. Whispers carry great distances in the open chamber, and footsteps echo around the great hall. I have a full view, back to front, of the library and occasionally catch glimpses of students and faculty as they move from one aisle to the next, disappearing behind the seemingly endless rows of oak bookcases. While no one watches, I scribble a letter to my parents.

Paris is gorgeous this time of year. Vivienne says hi! We took a walk along the Seine and ate lunch at La Terrasse. We'll be going to Versailles tomorrow. I can't wait.

My pen hovers over the page as I think about what to say next. I can't. So I go back to shelving books. I'm lying to my parents, ruining the mood and making the atmosphere less romantic. The ceiling, crisscrossed with gold and blue arches, depicts a starry night, but it hangs darkly overhead, mirroring the sky. And my heart.

After I was rejected by Sibylline, I told my parents about our plans to find work here instead. They thought it was a bad idea. They ranted and criticized. They lectured me endlessly. They wanted me to move on, wanted me to look at going to other schools, maybe to one of the lesser magical universities. *What's wrong with State Magic,* they'd asked, *or even the local magical trade schools?* But I couldn't bring myself to do it.

I know they love me, but they've never really understood me. I'm not sure if it's because I'm magical and they're not, but I've always felt different from them. I didn't want to fight, so I told them I was taking a gap year and staying with my cousin Vivienne in Paris, unplugging from my normal life as I figured out what I wanted to do next. No phone, no internet, total digital detox, just Europe and a wayward spirit. They were more than thrilled that I was letting Sibylline go. Vivienne agreed to the scheme without question. Lying buys me time. I know I can't keep it up permanently–my parents will have to find out eventually–but I'll deal with it when the time comes.

I shelve three more books. "*Encyclopedia of Dream Symbology . . . Inventions of the Arcane World . . . Guide to Arithmancy.*" I read the titles aloud as I slot them into place, then I flip that last one open and find pages full of mathematical equations. This is something Atticus would love.

"*Ahem.*" An elderly archivist stares at me from the far end of the aisle, offering me a stern look over half-moon spectacles.

I snap the book closed and place it back on the shelf, smiling apologetically.

She disappears down the aisle, her glare disapproving. I'm not allowed to read while on the job, and I've already been told that only the students and teachers are permitted to scan these books, but I can't help it. I'm like a child in a candy shop. With the archivist gone, I scribble the last lines of the letter.

> *I'm having so much fun here, but I miss you both already.*
>
> *xoxo Raven*

I read, and then reread what I've written. At least that last part is true. I am having fun at Sibylline so far. Still, it feels odd lying to them. I fold the paper into thirds and stuff it into an envelope with my parents' address on it. Then I place it into another envelope with my cousin Vivienne's address in Paris so she can mail it for me, and I seal it shut with wax.

With my letter in hand, I go to the mailbox in the lobby and give it a kiss before slipping it into the mail slot. When I look inside the box, the letter is already gone, whisked away on the winds of magic to its destination. It's out of my hands now, and I finally take a breath.

When I come back to the circulation desk, a tall stack of books waits for me on the counter. I search the spines for titles but find only worn fabric covered in stains that blot out the titles. Opening one of them up, I find no half-title page or author listed, but there is elaborate handwriting, made in what looks to have been a quill and ink, on pages made of vellum. The book smells of mold and rot, and it makes my nose wrinkle.

I'm about to ask my coworker on the opposite side of the circulation desk what I should do, but I stop myself. I came to Sibylline to learn, didn't I? The knowledge within them is strictly controlled by the school, but there's no harm in taking a peek, right?

I leaf through the text. The book isn't written in English; it's in Welsh. But as my eyes scan the page, shapes become letters, and letters become words, and words become language. Like water rippling on the surface of a pond, the characters on the page shift, and before I know it, I understand Welsh. For me, it's as natural as breathing.

This is a book of ancient incantations.

Conjurations, divinations, evocations, even necromancy—an entire manuscript filled with everything one needs to know to perform magic. My mind races. This is exactly the kind of thing that the Oneiric Society would love.

"What are you doing?"

A voice startles me, and I jerk my head up.

My deskmate, Pippa, another junior archivist and a proper first-year Sibylline student, looks at me, her brow knitted with intrigue. She's my age, with a smattering of freckles on her nose, silky blond hair, and a rosy complexion. Her well-manicured nails curl over the back of her chair when she's turned to me, the glossy red catching the light like blood. When we were first introduced, I recognized her instantly. She's the daughter of a famous Sibylline alumnus—a wizard who uses divination to expand his hedge fund.

Pippa is one of the few people who was accepted to Sibylline this year. Unlike me, she's working here as part of a student employment program. I don't think she's doing it for the money, though.

I scramble for a reasonable explanation. It's no use pretending

I wasn't reading, so I might as well tell the truth. "I can't figure out how to catalog these," I say. "There's no identifying information."

Pippa's gaze flicks to the books, then back to me. "The archive is closing soon," she says.

"I know. I just want to get these done."

"Fine," she says. "What does it say?"

"It's a book of incantations."

She notices the intricate Welsh cursive. "You can read that?"

"Yeah."

"You're so interesting," she says, laughing like I've told a joke. "Do you, like, study languages or something?"

"No, it's part of my magic." Before I can stop myself, I add, "What's yours?" I know it's a bit rude to ask a fellow magician directly about their capabilities, but I'm curious. What made Sibylline accept her and not me?

Pippa looks at me like I've asked if she likes eating slugs for dinner. She spins back around in her chair, stands up, and starts gathering her things: a series of reference books, her journal, her scarf, her coat, and her book bag. They don't need names for me to know they're designer. "I can always tell the time, without looking at a clock," she says coolly. "I know, it's kind of trivial."

"Not at all," I say, to be polite. I know it's not her fault that her father's name and reputation probably got her in, but it stings a little. That's all she can do?

Pippa doesn't seem bothered at all as she slings her bag over her shoulder, turning to an archivist who's pushing a wheeled cart toward us. "Raven needs help," she says.

I blush, especially when the archivist glances my way as Pippa leaves. He's cute, and that somehow makes it ten times worse.

"I don't need help," I say to the archivist.

"It's not a problem," he says. He's a little older than me, maybe twenty or so, with shoulder-length brown hair that's a little scruffy for such a charming face. He reminds me of a Labrador, with cheerful dark eyes and a friendly smile. His name is embroidered in gold thread on the breast pocket of the blazer that all senior archivists wear: Aspen. I'm not sure if it's his first name or his last.

He picks up the book I've been reading. "Well, now, how'd you get up here?" he asks the book amusedly, as if it might answer. And then I almost think it really might. "I know just where these go. Would you help me carry them?" Aspen glances at me. "I'm Aspen, by the way, Aspen Franklin. And you are?"

"Raven Chen," I tell him.

"Cool name," he says. "Your parents were into Poe? Quoth the raven, Nevermore?"

I laugh. "Nope. I wish it was that cool. My real name's Clarissa, but it never stuck."

Aspen's smile is contagious. "Are you a first-year? What house are you in?"

"No . . . I . . . I'm not a student here. I just work here," I say, trying not to sound too embarrassed. "You?"

"I'm a third-year," he says easily. I can tell he's wondering what I'm doing in Sibylline. Probably thinks I'm a townie. I guess I am a townie.

I take half the stack while Aspen takes the other, leading me away from the circulation desk and toward the back of the hall. Invisible at first until we make a turn, the shelves are actually a narrow, manufactured alley, hiding a large wooden door that Aspen unlocks with a brass key from a chain on his belt. The air shifts, turning stuffier and more humid, when we step into a long hallway. Offices and lounges for the archivists border either side of the hall as Aspen takes me through another locked door. It leads us to a narrow, winding stairwell, spiraling down into the dark.

Aspen waves his hand in the air, and a trio of small lights burst to life in front of us, leading us like little fireflies.

"I hope you're not afraid of the dark," he warns.

I try to laugh, but it comes out like a hiss. "The dark? No. Tight spaces, though?"

"Oh, me too! I eventually got used to it, and you will, too. I promise, it doesn't get too bad," he says. He's sweet. The way he's reassuring me is making my face red. I hope he can't see it. "Think of the tunnels under campus like a big basement. Nothing to worry about."

I have no choice but to trust him as we climb down and down. The air grows heavier, smelling mustier as we go, and I'm getting dizzier by the second. I don't want to think about how far underground we are, but I can't help it. It's getting harder to breathe, but I don't let it show.

"So!" Aspen's voice rips me away from my spiraling thoughts. "Do you have a boyfriend? Girlfriend? More-than-a-friend friend?"

"Are you trying to distract me?" I ask coolly.

He swivels his head to look at me, grinning. "Is it working?"

No, I want to say. *I'm not interested. I'm in love with one person and one person only.* "Anyway, to answer your question: No, I don't have a boyfriend." I think about Atticus, though, and only slightly choke on my words.

"Huh," says Aspen.

"What?"

"Just surprised, that's all." When he looks at me again, a glimmer of something is in his gaze.

Before he says anything more, the stairs end at another hall, where we pass through more locked doors and more branching tunnels. My thighs burn. I try not to make it look like I'm huffing with exhaustion, but it's taking everything I have just to keep moving. My arms shake with the weight of the books. Small conveniences like elevators are sorely missed. Before I can ask if there's much farther to go, Aspen opens one final door. "Here we are," he says as the floating lights vanish. "The Eastern Archive."

We're deep underground, but the archive is bathed in golden light reflected off the silvery arches that span three stories overhead, the polished surface gilding the room in a warm glow. Frescoes on the walls depict scenes from Greek mythology, like Persephone journeying into the underworld, Orion hunting the Pleiades, and Athena cursing Arachne. On the ground floor, glass display cases with books propped open on pedestals reveal illuminated manuscripts that look so old, they might crumble to dust if I stare at them too long. Three levels of mezzanines circle the room, accessible via iron spiral staircases, each section locked behind wrought-iron cages. A roaring fireplace blazes at the far end of the room, burning without any visible fuel.

Aspen scales the steps, climbing up to the mezzanine, where he opens one of the iron cages. I obediently follow, even though all I want to do is stop and read everything I can.

"What are these books we've been carrying?" I ask, waiting patiently while Aspen tidies the shelf.

"These are some of the most important books in our collection, and their access is strictly controlled. The spells contained in them can be . . . dangerous, you know. The books are rare. You can't find spells like these anywhere else on the planet."

"Is that why you need to lock them behind cages?"

Aspen nods. "Otherwise, they might escape. Although they usually don't make it too far . . ."

The shock that's apparent on my face makes Aspen laugh. "It's true. They like to wander the archive. We can't let any of them leave the premises, otherwise who knows what might happen. They might be lost forever."

"The books have a mind of their own?"

"Don't we all?" He considers it for a moment. "We all have a desire to be free . . . but I guess it's safer this way, for everyone."

I fall silent as Aspen sorts through the books, putting them back into their places on the shelf. Another thought occurs to me. "Are they dangerous? These books?"

"Aren't all books dangerous? Knowledge is power, isn't it?" he says matter-of-factly.

I nod, my mind racing. If only I'd had time to translate what I read earlier. I can't remember what the Welsh incantations said exactly, but if I could just get another look, then I could translate them into English.

When the last book is set back into place, Aspen locks the cage and checks the time on a candle clock. "The archive's almost closed. Sorry I kept you so late. Let's lock up and head home, shall we?"

We exit the archive, and he seals the room behind us with a brass key from the chain at his hip. I glance at the door, and a pang of regret shoots through me. Everything we want to know is beyond it. The whole history of magic rests in that room. I try not to stare at the keys as they dangle from his belt, but I wonder what would happen if I took one.

As I journey back to the surface, my thoughts race, a plan

slowly coming together in my head, thinking of what Aspen told me about the books. It was my idea for the three of us to come here, and if we are going to teach ourselves magic, we're going to have to be unafraid to break into rooms we're not allowed in and use everything we have in our arsenal.

5
ATTICUS

There is something at work in my soul which I do not understand.
—*Mary Shelley,* Frankenstein

I BALANCE TWO trays of coffee as I climb the scaffolding around Arches up and up, the early morning light cascading downward through distant windows as I wind my way around right corners, following the trail of voices above. I'm already higher than most of the buildings on campus when I spot the Rosette's great glass windows through the gaps in the iron clock. It makes me think of Raven, and I look over, hoping to catch sight of her at work, but the window is unoccupied.

I pass clockfaces mounted on each side of the tower, with a bell ringing out the top of the hour from the highest peak. Seven members of the architecture department, all of them older than me by several decades, barely glance in my direction as I offer up coffee and breakfast, doling out the napkins. The mood is tense, their voices raised.

"It's not the sigils! I checked and double-checked the readings," says a woman flipping through the pages of a book on sacred geometry. She's dressed like the archetypal academic, wearing a tweed jacket with patches on the elbows.

Another architect peers through what looks like a glass telescope pointed toward the ceiling as he asks, "You used a Solomon sphere?" He jots down some notes with a wave of his hand, the numbers appearing magically on the paper as though inked by an invisible pen.

"Of course I did. I'm not some dilettante."

"I'm just saying, with the position of Mercury, you may be missing something if you haven't calibrated it correctly."

"Please," interjects a woman in a navy blazer, taking a sip of her coffee and looking bored. "A Solomon sphere can only do so much. The root of the mess may go deeper than the sigils."

The others erupt into more arguments, talking over one another, until it's just a swarm of noise, and I have to blink back the cacophony of energy that pulses through me.

I count out the Fibonacci sequence until the noise passes.

It sounds like they still haven't figured out what's causing all the trouble, including that stone that fell from the ceiling. I listen and don't ask questions.

I interrupt only when I notice I have one coffee left. "Where's Professor White?" I ask, glancing around, and I realize she's missing.

"She's at the top. She'll want her coffee *hot*," says the woman in the tweed jacket, tilting her head toward the stairs.

I don't have to be told twice. The arguments fade as I make my way up. Professor White doesn't seem to notice my arrival. Her back is to me, and she's muttering to herself as she flips through a book. When I clear my throat, she turns and shoots me an angry look. "Oh," she says, her expression softening. "I thought you were one of my incompetent juniors who can't tell a Greek from a Roman Doric."

"Sorry, Professor White, I didn't mean to disturb you."

"No, not at all." She gratefully accepts the remaining coffee and pastry, making certain the sugar doesn't fall on her clothes.

"This is just what I needed," she says, sighing. "How did you know how I take it?"

I stammer over an answer. I don't think I should tell her I caught a whisper of it in one of the other architects' thoughts. "Uh, one of the architects downstairs mentioned it," I lie.

There's a flash of an impish smile on Professor White's lips. "I imagine the team is still arguing down there."

"Not *too much*," I say.

This time for sure Professor White knows I'm lying and chuckles. "You don't have to defend them. I have half a mind to wonder if they're not trying to undermine each other on purpose."

"Anything I can do to help?" I ask.

For what feels like an eternity, Professor White stares down at me, and I offer her a small, hopeful smile, wishing I'd remained silent. To my relieved surprise, she juts her chin toward a leather-bound folio resting on one of the balustrades.

"You may peruse the binder, if you're so inclined . . ." she says, watching me as if her gaze can pierce my thoughts, revealing what I'm made of. "Though I wager you already know what I'm thinking."

"No, I'm not–"

She quiets me with a raised hand. "No need to worry. Your secret is safe with me."

I'm too excited to say anything, not even a thank-you.

Before she can change her mind, I flip open the book and riffle through the notes. Pages upon pages of arcane analysis and theory, schematics and diagrams, all of them signaling that there's a misalignment somewhere in the tower. Finding it, however, has proven elusive. After all, the building is enormous, almost three hundred feet tall, and the issue could be anywhere.

Professor White places her fists on her hips, inspecting the stone ornamentation and embellishments, all of it covered in pigeon waste and feathers. "If you need me," she says, "I'll be dealing with the cacophony downstairs."

That's code for *don't bother me unless it's necessary*. I've only known Professor White for a week, but I understand this much: She doesn't like to be presented with a problem unless there's already a solution. I'll try to find one. This is what I've always wanted, right? To prove my worth.

She leaves me to go over the notes, and I walk the scaffolding, mulling over every detail, every design. My head swims with arcane geometry, and the desire to know it all practically burns a hole right through me. In the vastness of the space, sounds echo off the stone walls in unexpected ways, making it seem like my own footsteps are following me as I walk. So I find a place that is quiet, and I breathe deeply, grounding myself in the space.

There's a hint of something in the air. It's a sensation similar to the one you might feel when entering a room someone's just left. There's a faint energy or, rather, the ghost of it, lingering in the space. Like a ripple on a pond.

I reach for the building with my mind, the way I would if I wanted to feel a person's thoughts. I've never tried to read a building, so it feels like I'm moving a new muscle. I open my mind, and when I do, I sense it: the disharmony. Where there should be equinumerosity, equipollence, equipotency, there is disparity.

This isn't like when I read people. There's an immediacy about their energy. This . . . this is something older and stranger. I've never been able to sense the energy of a building before. But this isn't any old building. When Professor White first brought me to Arches, she'd mentioned that the original architects had harnessed the spirits of the natural world to build it. Maybe I'm sensing those same spirits, hearing the latent energy of their sleeping consciousness. It's like I'm in the belly of a great, sleeping beast.

I'm hit with how natural this is to me, how easily I sense the imbalance in the fabric of magic. It's like I've always known it was there. Just like math, it's always existed, but now I have the equation to understand it.

I can *do* this. I really can.

The ancient spirits talk, their words distant and unintelligible. I follow the sound. In the southeast corner a few levels up, there is a place where the voices howl in dismay. The source. The stone here isn't visibly damaged in any way. But after inspecting it, I realize the problem isn't here but on the small entablature above me, a decorated cornice that rims the interior of the tower like bracers.

To get a closer look, I would need to step off the scaffold and cross a thirty-foot drop.

I don't even pause to think as I set the binder down, climb on the scaffold railing, grab on to a double-bellied baluster for support, and step off. There's a brief moment where my stomach swoons, and I look down at the straight drop below me, then my foot touches the cornice, and I step fully onto the ledge. My heart pounds with excitement as I run my hands over the carvings in the frieze, feeling the lion, ivy, and snake designs in the stone with my fingers. The attention to detail here is incredible.

And that's when I see it, or rather feel it, both magically and with my fingers: jagged marks. They seem recent. I have to lean my head over the edge to get a better look at them, and I realize they aren't random marks. It's a sigil in the shape of an insect. A fly, maybe. The magic imbued in the marks seems to buzz, too, droning in my head. I hate bugs, but I have to remind myself it's not real, even though it sounds like it is.

"Professor White?" I call.

She appears on a scaffold below me and looks up. Her eyes go round when she sees where I am, and I realize how dangerous this is, but I don't care. "I found something."

Professor White comes up to see for herself, and I point out the sigil. She's forced to stand on the railing to get a better look, too, holding on to the balustrade like it's a lifeline. Her knees shake, but she only needs to glance at what I've found.

"Oh my," she says, stumbling back to the safety of the scaffolding. She isn't surprised by what I found. Her face shows only resignation, a sigh in her shoulders. "This whole time I thought my team was misreading the symbols."

"What is it?"

"It's a symbol of undoing. A sign of Beelzebub, the prince of demons."

Professor White holds out a hand and helps me back onto the scaffolding. She looks at me with an expression that appears, dare I say, impressed. "Atticus, relegating you to administrative duties is clearly a waste of your talents. I'm putting you on the team. Apparently, we need your help."

"Help?" I ask. "Really?"

"Yes, it looks like someone is sabotaging the project."

DORIAN

The day lingered and the last calls of the last birds sounded, in a flushed sky, from the old trees.

—*Henry James,* The Turn of the Screw

"ADELINA! ADELINA! PLEASE!" The ghostly voice rings in my thoughts. I'm still haunted by what I saw when I touched Hecate's wand. It's been days, and it persists, far longer than any vision I've had before. It's leached into me like a red wine stain, and I can't scrub it from my mind. *The body . . . symbols in blood . . . red candles . . .* I blink the vision away. But just like the setting sun, I know the vision isn't gone. The memories will return like the dawn, whether I want them to or not.

"Just relax, Dorian," I say to myself. "It's a memory. It can't hurt you." I force myself to believe that as I open the door to the coffee shop. Briefly, I want to share what I saw with Atticus and Raven, but the memory is still too raw, too violent to discuss, so I push it from my mind. I don't want to think about it. I just want a moment's peace.

The Acroteria is a dusty but cozy building nestled into a corner of the old campus, and it already feels like home. It's easy to forget the rest of the world when you walk through these doors. It is a winding, labyrinthian shop, known for almost every inch of the place being covered in books. They are piled so high they form walls. The whole place is organized chaos. There are hallways that lead nowhere and paths that wander like the alleys in a maze.

Atticus and Raven have already claimed our table. We've been using the same one all week. They've burrowed in, marked their territory, acting like they belong here. We're in the cafe area, in a section right in front of the showstopping arch made of books that leads into the bookstore proper. Atticus spots me from his seat next to the window and waves me over.

When Raven glances my way, a soft smile curves her lips, like the sun coming out after the rain. My breath hitches. Today, she's wearing a diamond-patterned sweater vest over a collared shirt, looking just like one of the students. As I sit down across from her, she slides a ceramic mug toward me.

"Well, well, well," says Atticus with a grin. A half-eaten cinnamon roll warms the plate in front of him. "If it isn't Indiana Jones himself."

I know he's teasing and give him a withering look. "You flatter me, Finch."

But in truth, I'm pleased. Atticus is just like his namesake: fair, brave, and just. My best man, my best friend.

"Hey," Raven says with a smile, and my skin tingles. "How was the museum? You look like you've had a long day."

"I'm fine," I say. I tug my gloves higher up my wrist. "Old Bones is the shit, actually. They had me cataloging their inventory today."

"You mean you touch the old bones?" Atticus asks, a wicked grin on his face.

"Yeah," I say. "Tons of skulls."

Atticus makes a *yeugh* sound. "Gross."

I shrug as if it doesn't bother me.

Raven nudges her hand toward mine but stops short of touching me. "Would you like another pair of gloves to celebrate your success?"

"I'm good," I say. It takes effort, what with my heart feeling like it's lodged in my throat. I'll probably keep these gloves until they rot off. These gloves changed everything. The moment Raven gave them to me–hiding them behind her back and asking me to guess what they were, and no, I couldn't use Atticus to cheat–was the moment I fell in love with her. But I've never told her. That was my sixteenth birthday. Two years ago. That might not be a long time, but carrying such a secret weighs on a person. "These gloves are the only thing keeping me sane these days."

I notice Atticus is staring at me, and I rake the foam from my upper lip with my bottom teeth. Atticus's gaze flicks to my mouth momentarily before his eyes go back up to mine. They're brown and bright like sunlight.

"Atticus and I were just talking about work before you came," Raven says, filling me in. "I have so much to do, it's crazy. But I missed you guys."

"We haven't gone anywhere," Atticus says, pinching a piece of his cinnamon roll with his thumb and index finger and slipping it into his mouth. His fingers are still covered in sugar. Has he always had a dimple on his chin? I've never noticed before.

"What's up with you?" Raven asks me. "You seem distracted."

"I'm okay," I say, taking another sip, my tongue absorbing the sweet flavors of cocoa and cinnamon. "Same as always."

Atticus doesn't buy it. "You're having visions?"

My right eye twitches when I tell a lie, and he often notices. Even without his abilities, he can read me. With them, he can probe my thoughts and feelings, and hiding anything from him is next to impossible. I know he can't shut it off easily; it's not his fault. Hiding gifts or surprises from him requires Fort Knox levels of mental control.

"Yeah, it's just getting harder for me to control my magic."

"What happened?" she asks.

I'm not sure what to say. I'm not even sure *what* I saw in Old Bones. "You know how I have to touch items in the museum to verify their origins? Well, it makes me super tired. I haven't used this much magic in . . . *ever*."

A line appears between Atticus's eyebrows. He knows I'm not telling them everything, but he lets it pass, saying, "I've been wondering. Do either of you feel like you're . . . different here?" He licks his lips and shifts in his seat, almost excitedly. "Like, do you feel . . . stronger?"

Slowly, I nod. It's like this whole campus is teeming with magic, and it's flowing through everything and everyone here.

Raven nods, too. "Being surrounded by all these people who live and breathe magic . . . Maybe it's rubbing off on us."

Steady but soft, Raven's dark eyes hold mine. A lock of her straight, shiny black hair has fallen across her shoulder, and the desire to tuck it behind her ear makes my hands burn. The gap between us is almost unbearable. I wonder what it would be like to touch her, to feel her skin, and slot my fingers in between hers. What it would be like to kiss her. But I can't remember the last time I let anyone touch me, even a loving kiss on the head from my mother.

"Our plan is working, then," I say, changing the subject. "Being at Sibylline even as staff *is* doing something to us."

"Yeah, well, but I want more," Raven says as she peels apart her cinnamon roll. She doesn't mask her resentment. She's still angry we've been denied, and desire has burrowed deep in all three of us. We want to learn, we want to know, we want to be who we're meant to be.

"So do I," Atticus says mildly. "Any ideas?"

"There's a recitation on magical theory tomorrow morning at Piranesi Hall. I saw a flyer in the library," Raven says. "What if we slip in, catch a little lesson?"

"What if we get caught?" asks Atticus.

"What are they gonna do, fire us?" Raven says.

"Yes," I say. "That's exactly what they can do."

Raven's eyes sparkle mischievously. "Then we don't get caught."

IN THE GRAY light of dawn, we join the mass of robed students pouring through the central gates and into the square. My heart pounds with anticipation as we stride through the arch toward Piranesi Hall. It's a three-story-tall brick building, with large stone steps flanked by stone lions on either side. The lions seem so lifelike, I half wonder if they'll spring up and maul trespassers. But we walk with our heads down so the hoods cover our faces and we blend in with the crowd. No one around us speaks, as if it's part of some ritual, a somber occasion that requires the utmost focus and respect. But I can practically feel Atticus vibrating with excitement next to me. He catches my eye, grinning, and a surge of something like joy spreads inside of me.

The moment we step into the auditorium, Atticus's hand tugs on the sleeve of my robe.

"This way," he says, pulling me aside. I barely have enough time to grab on to Raven's sleeve as we split apart from the rest of the students, taking red-carpeted stairs up to the higher levels, checking over our shoulders just in case someone's spotted us.

The auditorium is dark except for the single spotlight shining down on the center of the dais, the lecturer waiting in the wings. Red velvet curtains frame the stage. The mezzanine is empty, but we keep low as we crouch along the balcony wall. The student body below us buzzes quietly, anticipation permeating the air. Atticus stops in the middle of the row, making Raven and me pause, too, and he lowers his hood to peek out above the railing. A strip of light illuminates his eyes, and I can tell he's smiling.

"Perfect view," he says.

On my other side, Raven kneels to also look over the balcony. "Someone's coming," she says.

It's my turn to look. Sure enough, a lone figure walks onto the stage, clad in dark robes like everyone else, the hood raised high. My heart pounds when I realize this is it, this is what we've been working toward. We're actually going to learn a little magic. The figure onstage lowers their hood, and the room falls quiet.

"Good morning." The lecturer is a man whose face I recognize: Jeremiah Stone, warden of Sibylline. The highest-ranking administrator. He's an older man, his face lined with age, hair long. A ruby earring glimmers in one ear. He wears dark robes, making it look as if he's made of shadows interrupted only by the whiteness of his hair and face. Even from this distance, I can tell his eyes are blue as Arctic water. "Welcome to the first recitation of magical theory."

"He's hot," jokes Atticus. "*Please* tell me he's single."

"Ew, he's like a hundred years old," replies Raven, sounding annoyed. "If we get caught, he's the one who'll throw us out. Don't try to be funny."

"Shut up, it's starting," I say.

Below, Warden Stone continues, "Goetia is an ancient type of witchcraft, the study of spells contained within grimoires, or in common terms, 'spell books.' Unlike other esotericist practices taught by our contemporaries, here at Sibylline, we have gone to great lengths to ensure that goetia remains one of the most powerful applied forms of magic in the world. Those in this room will join the ranks of some of the greatest wizards in history. Through rigorous practice and intense study, you will achieve powers known nowhere else in the world. The task is not without its challenges and dangers. Fortunately, you're in good hands."

His words elicit polite laughter.

"Let's begin with a demonstration, shall we?" Warden Stone holds out his empty hands. He stands up straighter and says something in a language I don't understand.

Raven pulls herself up a little higher to get a better look. The lower half of her face is in shadow.

"He's speaking Latin," she whispers. "I understand him."

"What's he saying?" Atticus asks.

"It's an evocation, a summoning spell."

And before our eyes, there's a burst of light, and a book falls into Warden Stone's empty hands. There's once again polite applause as the onlookers realize he's just conjured a grimoire from thin air.

Warden Stone holds up the book, an ancient-looking leather-bound text. "All magic stems from the knowledge within these books. Every grimoire is a key to metaphysical understanding, but without training, you're simply stating the words without invoking the magical components inherent in them. Basic spells don't require more than one's will, and I know you're already thinking it—advanced spells require the right equipment, like wands and sigils. Though let's not get ahead of ourselves. Let's practice together a simple incantation. You'll find under your seats a single red rose. Your job is to wither it into dust, using these words."

He begins his lesson, referring to a chalkboard behind him, reciting the words, explaining how they are spoken, describing the ways in which a spell caster can elicit power from the words in a book. He speaks at length, and we listen. The students–with varying success–change the roses, some of them withering into dust. Most just seem to turn gray. There's lots of hand waving, and stumbling pronunciation, and not much else. The room is full of frustrated murmuring and sighs. I'm almost embarrassed for them.

"This is supposed to be the elite of the elite?" Atticus asks, voicing my own thoughts. "It can't be that hard, can it?"

"Wish we could get our hands on one of those roses to try it out," I say.

Raven's lips are twisted in a pensive frown. "Does that mean our magic is different?" she asks. "Is it really only just words that have power? Or is there something else?"

Atticus waggles his fingers at her. "Abracadabra! Is it working?" He cuts his playful demeanor short as the color drains from his face and he whips around to face the rows behind us.

Someone's there. It's almost as if they appeared out of nowhere. They clear their throat, but I can't tell who it is. The figure is shrouded in darkness. My stomach drops. All three of us are frozen with shock, surprise, and maybe a little fear.

When the figure leans forward, catching the ambient light, Atticus recognizes them. "Professor White!" His boss.

The woman stands with her hands behind her back, her shoulders level, her face slightly upturned. "This recitation is for students only," she says flatly. "I'll have to escort you out of the auditorium."

THAT'S IT, THEN. I'm already mentally packing up my things, ready to move back home, as Professor White leads us out of the hall. We're all nervous. I keep dragging my hand through my hair, Raven worries her lower lip, Atticus hangs his head in shame. Professor White, however, doesn't look angry or frustrated. She sighs and adjusts the cuffs of her robe, as if she's more bothered by its fit than the sight of us.

She stops when we reach the front steps to the building, and Atticus has the bravery to speak up.

"Forgive me, Professor White. It was my idea to come here," he says, taking the fall for Raven. "I just wanted a peek to see real magic. Please don't punish my friends for me being stupid."

Raven stays silent, her hands clasped tightly in front of her. I follow Atticus's lead, ready to jump in anytime.

But Professor White sighs deeply, still frowning as she looks at all of us. "Understand me clearly, Mr. Garcia. If I catch you or your friends intruding upon a private recitation again, I'll have to take action." She straightens her robes and turns to leave. "Now, go enjoy your day off."

"Wait . . ." says Atticus. "You're not firing me?"

"No, Mr. Garcia. I have enough trouble finding competent assistants. I'm not interested in losing you now."

Atticus lifts his head, shocked that she might have just given him a compliment. I have a hunch that she's someone who's hard to impress, like a coach who wants you to run that one millisecond faster.

Professor White almost smiles. "I suggest you find what you're looking for *elsewhere*." She says the word with enough emphasis, I realize she's giving us a hint. "Might I suggest a library?"

It's almost a welcome invitation.

She walks back to the recitation hall without another word. All Atticus does is stare after her with an open mouth.

Shocked, Raven asks, "I thought she was going to chew us out. Why didn't she turn us in? We should all be fired."

"Absolutely," I say.

"But she didn't," says Atticus. "A warning is enough."

"She likes you," I tell him. "Seems like she needs you."

He beams. "She called me 'competent.'" Dreamily, he strips off his black robe, revealing his clothes underneath—a Fair Isle sweater and pleated slacks. He bundles his robe up into a mass and tucks it under his arm. "Right," he says, "so that means we won't get many more chances."

There's a hardness in his eyes, and I can tell he's thinking of what to do next.

"We do what she says. We can't learn in public," he says at last, gesturing to the closed auditorium. "We need to study in private."

"Then we need one of those books," I say. "We can't just wait for one to magically appear in our hands, right? Not like what Warden Stone did onstage."

Raven takes off her robe as well and neatly folds it over her arm. "What if we steal one of the books from the archive?"

"Steal one." I nod as Atticus jumps on the idea.

"Perfect! You already work at the archive."

Nervously, I tug at my leather gloves. "I like your idea, except I don't want to put Raven in danger. They'll notice if one of their books is gone, won't they?"

"Apparently some of the books have a mind of their own. In this restricted section called the Eastern Archive, they move around all the time, by themselves, and they have to be locked in cages. If we're fast, they might think one of the books wandered off, giving us just enough time to bring it back before anyone raises an alarm."

"Cages?" Atticus asks. "Like zoo animals?"

"Yeah. I can steal a key, I think, and we can return the book as soon as we copy its contents."

"We're liberating the books," Atticus says, his smile growing.

I brush my fingers against the watch in my pocket. It's annoying being this close to learning about the nature of our powers and not being able to learn how to use them. "All right," I say. "Let's plan a heist."

7 ATTICUS

You too shall know, what it is to love without hope!
—Matthew Gregory Lewis, The Monk

"AM I THE greatest, or am I the greatest?" I ask, finding Raven and Dorian after work in the Acroteria, sitting across from one another at our usual booth, leaning over mugs of steaming hot coffee.

"Is there a third option?" Dorian asks dryly. He looks particularly handsome today, in an emerald-green sweater vest, brown tie, and dark jacket. The green really brings out the color of his eyes.

"What did you do?" Raven asks conspiratorially. She looks like she just came straight from her shift at the Rosette, with ink stains on her hands and a small paper cut on the tip of her finger.

I produce a large piece of paper, rolled up and tied with a cotton yarn. "*Voilà.* Our plan."

It's been three days since we were caught at the lecture by Professor White, and we finally have what we need to move forward. Raven and Dorian clear off the table as I unroll the paper. He slides over to make room, and the cushion is still warm from his body heat. I catch a whiff of him: leather and aftershave. God, he smells good.

"Blueprints?" Raven asks, looking at the curling paper.

Right. Focus.

"I copied them from work," I say. "Stayed late at the office yesterday. See these?" I run my hands over the lines, a labyrinthine network of dizzying twisting and turning corridors, like an upside-down Christmas tree. "These are the underground tunnels beneath the Rosette. You said that's where the archive is, right, Raven?"

"Yes, exactly."

The tunnel layout reminds me of this video I once saw of an artist pouring melted aluminum into an anthill, filling up the tunnels, all invisible from above ground. Once the metal hardened, they pulled the cast out, preserving the complexity and pure engineering of the colony forever. I'd love to build something as beautiful as these tunnels someday.

"Wow, good work, Finch," says Dorian, sounding genuinely impressed as he gazes at the map.

I love that he calls me Finch; he's the only one who does. If only he knew how much it means to me.

"There will be risks—we're trespassing—but I think it's worth it. A room full of magical texts seems like the perfect place to start our education, right?" I ask.

"No doubt," says Dorian. "But these tunnels are a maze."

"I mostly remember the path we took," says Raven.

"'We'?" Dorian asks.

"Me and one of the senior archivists, Aspen. I can retrace my steps, and there isn't a lot of security—it's a library, it isn't a bank or anything like that. But we'll need the key to get into the restricted archive."

"Can you get it?" I ask.

Raven folds her lips nervously. "Maybe? Aspen had it on a chain. I thought about taking it when we first visited the library, but I've never done anything like that."

"We just need it for one night," I say. "Take it for a few hours, return it before he knows it's gone?"

It's the best plan we've got, and Raven seems like she understands that. Resolve hardens her eyes. "I'll try to get it tomorrow," she says, tapping nervously on her mug with the tips of her manicured fingers. *Clinkity-clink–one-two-and-three,* like a rallying drum. "Then we can slip into the tunnels at night. There won't be many people. We can be quick."

"Raven," I say, and glance at Dorian for support, "actually, maybe you should stay behind."

Dorian nods gravely. He's with me–I knew he would be. He cares about her too much.

Raven looks crestfallen. "What do you mean? Why?"

"You should be conspicuously out in public when the book goes missing so they don't suspect you."

"Finch is right," Dorian says softly. "It'll be better this way."

Raven's lower lip juts out a little, but she nods in understanding. "I think Aspen was hitting on me, so maybe I can get close enough to him to get the key. Distract him. Ask him out or something."

"Raven, you don't have to do that," says Dorian. One of his eyes twitches, and the air around his head shimmers and turns green, but he smothers it like pinching a candle flame, and the aura vanishes.

"It's fine," Raven tells him. "It's for us. I don't like him like that anyway, I like . . ." Raven trails off, eyes on me, suddenly looking like an animal trapped in a corner. She stiffens, straightens up, and rubs her hands together. "Never mind."

I think I hear Raven say something, so quiet it's like it's under her breath.

I like you.

"Excuse me?" I ask.

She stares at me, startled.

"Did you say something?" I ask again.

"What? No." She looks genuinely surprised I would even ask. "I didn't say anything."

Then it hits me. She didn't *say* anything. She was thinking, and I heard her thoughts. Clear as day. *I like you*, she thought plainly.

Hearing her thoughts feels like spying. My gift means I sometimes hear people's deepest secrets. People's feelings are sometimes so loud, they're screaming in their own heads. Being gay myself, I know how it goes. I used to think it was just raging hormones for me to be attracted to boys like Dorian–tall, athletic, smart–but the more I've thought about it and the more my feelings have grown, I think a better way to put it is: I'm not straight. The scope has become broader, more fitting for how I feel.

I don't know what Raven sees in me, though. Does she not care that I'm not straight? Sometimes the heart ignores reason. I guess I can't talk, what with my just-as-hopeless pining for Dorian.

"Right, my mistake," I tell her.

Raven bites her lip, looking at the map for a long moment and then at me. Her cheeks turn pink, and I wonder if she's starting to think about backing out, but finally, she grabs a pen from her bag and begins to draw on the map. "Let's find the best route."

Raven plots out the path we will take, telling us where there are locked doors, and we plan our work around them. We consider various options, tunnels we should or should not take. When the last line is drawn and the work is complete, it's closing time at the cafe, and the baristas behind the counter are wiping down all the tables, stacking chairs, and shutting down the machines.

"We'll break into the archive tomorrow night, yes?" Dorian asks, keeping his voice low. Even though it's late and we've been working all day, he doesn't look tired anymore. "Does that give you enough time, Raven?"

Raven shifts, playing with the ends of her hair. "It has to be. Try to be at the archive by midnight, but not any earlier. The staff should all be gone by then."

Dorian nods, and I can practically feel his anticipation next to me; his knee is jangling up and down under the table. I refrain from putting a hand on it to still it, but I'm sorely tempted. Raven rolls up the paper and hands it to Dorian. We stand, the light turning off as we shuffle out into the cold night.

As we walk, I think about what Dorian said. Raven is putting herself at risk for us. And I really don't want her getting hurt. "You sure about all this?" I nudge Raven.

"*Nil sine magno labore,*" she says firmly.

8
RAVEN

She had beauty that endured, and a smile that was not forgotten. Somewhere her voice still lingered, and the memory of her words.
—Daphne du Maurier, Rebecca

PIPPA, MY COWORKER, is already gone for the day, the library is closing, and the only people left are the overachieving archivists setting the last of the books in place. I pretend to be one of them, sorting through piles of old books, putting them on carts, staying busy while the library empties. From the circulation desk, I see Aspen approaching, and I quickly lift the stack of books I've prepared, an inkwell balanced on top. I plot a course that will run right into him, then I raise the books in front of my face, listening to his footsteps tapping on the old wood floors. As we cross paths, I *pretend* to trip, and the inkwell tips, emptying its contents onto his jacket, the books sliding out of my hands, falling haphazardly onto the floor, and making a terrible racket.

"Oh!" I cry as Aspen lets out a surprised yelp. "I'm so sorry!"

Aspen raises his arms as I rush in, patting my hands frantically over the ink stain setting into the fabric of his jacket. In the chaos, I take note of the keys, which look heavy in the pocket of his jacket. "Let me help," I say, real tears burning my eyes.

"It's okay!" he says. "It's all right!"

Aspen slips off his jacket, and I take it, swiping the keys from the pocket and putting them in mine as I fold his jacket over my arm. I fuss over the ink and try not to think about what I've just done. The keys feel heavier than they ought to, as if they're made of lead, my guilt weighing me down.

"I'm so clumsy," I say. "I wasn't thinking–"

"Don't worry about it." Aspen kneels, helping me pick up all of the books and setting them back into a pile.

"I don't know what came over me," I say, putting the books on the desk.

Aspen grasps me by the arms, capturing my gaze, and says earnestly, "It's just ink, Raven."

"I know, but your jacket is ruined. Let me try to clean it for you, please."

"Don't worry about it. I promise, it's okay."

"No, it isn't. I'll take it to the dry cleaner's for you and everything."

But Aspen just smiles and presses his hand on the stain and murmurs an incantation in Latin, removing the ink from the fabric.

"Good as new," he says, still smiling.

"Wow." I'm genuinely impressed.

"This kind of thing happens all the time. Trust me, I spilled a dozen in my first year."

I tuck a lock of hair behind my ear. "I guess I'm still getting used to working around magic."

"We all start somewhere. No one's holding it against you, especially not me."

From the way he's looking at me, the intensity in his eyes, I realize this is going to be easier than I dreamed.

"It won't happen again."

A small, charming smile appears on his lips, making him look even more like a Labrador, eager to please. "Maybe you can repay me by joining me for coffee. How's tonight?"

"Oh," I say, blinking. I didn't even have to ask. His smile is warm and hopeful, and it makes me feel all the more wicked for using him. He truly has no idea that he's doing the work for me. I swallow the lump in my throat. "Sure, I'd like that."

"There's this place, the Acroteria. Have you heard of it?"

"Yeah, it's one of my favorites."

Aspen beams. "Then it's perfect. Let me just pack up my things, and we'll go."

"Sounds great," I say.

When he's gone, I take the key to the Eastern Archive from the ring and stuff the rest of the keys back into his pocket.

And not a moment too soon.

"Ready?" He's back, his messenger bag thrown over his shoulder and his eyes bright with expectation.

"Yeah!" I say, a little breathless.

I extend his jacket toward him, and he slips it back on, patting his pocket and checking that his keys are still there. My heart leaps into my throat, and I expect him to pull them out and check if any are missing, but he doesn't.

Outside, the sky is clear but the air is cool, and my warm breath makes icy-white clouds drift from my lips. I stuff my hands into the pockets of my coat to keep them warm and finger the stolen key, trying to maintain my composure as Aspen and I walk down the stairs to the street. At the bottom, there's a small group of people with handmade signs sitting on the sidewalk. They don't look like Sibylline students; they're wearing puffy parkas, not student robes, and when they see us, one woman rushes forward, brandishing a cardboard sign. She stops me at the bottom of the stairs, blocking my path.

"Do the right thing!" she says, a wild look in her eye. Her placard says the words BLOOD ON YOUR HANDS. "Please, you have to listen to us before–"

"That's enough," a deep voice says from down the sidewalk.

A group of glowering security guards are marching toward us. Leading them is Warden Stone. He was the one who had spoken. His icy blue eyes are narrow as he glares at the woman. They glint with an otherworldly glow.

The woman's eyes widen, and her mouth closes. Panic creeps across her stiffened face. She lets out a kind of wail behind her closed lips, and I take a step back, suddenly fearful. Growing up in New York, I'm used to people acting strangely on the street, on the subway. It's just a part of living in a big city. But there's something about the look on her face that makes my blood freeze.

The woman moans, gripping her head in her hands, and her friends hurry to her side, asking her if she's okay as the guards rush in and break them up and Warden Stone's gaze turns to us, eyes cold.

"Come on," says Aspen, touching my arm. "We should go."

I hesitate, watching as the woman and the other protesters are forcefully led away by the guards. It doesn't feel right at all. I want to speak up, to say something, but Aspen is adamant. "We're not allowed to talk to them," he says. "It's policy. They could fire us if they see us engaging with them."

"Fired?" I ask, stunned. "For having a conversation?"

Warden Stone calls out instructions to the guards to escort them from campus as he gathers up the protesters' signs. His gaze moves toward us, his features hardening.

“Come on,” Aspen says again. “There’s nothing we can do.”

I follow him down the street, remembering how the woman looked at me, the unnatural way her mouth was snapped shut, the effort she made trying to open it.

“What was that back there?” I ask as I catch up to Aspen. “Was that magic?”

He cringes uncomfortably. “A simple spell. It’s not permanent. Warden Stone silenced them. I’ve seen him do it once or twice.”

“So this has happened before? Why haven’t I heard anything about these protests?”

“That’s the point. Sibylline is good at keeping things quiet.”

Literally, I think. I glance over my shoulder, hoping to catch a glimpse of the protesters again, but they’re gone. What was that all about? I can’t shake the image of the woman’s face, frozen in fear, her mouth held closed by magic. Aspen and I barely talk. I hardly notice him when he stops at the Acroteria, where he buys us drinks to go. He offers me tea, and we walk, strolling the campus green. By the time we loop back to the Rosette, there’s no sign of the protesters or the guards or Stone. The sidewalk is empty, illuminated by squares of orange light from the nearby buildings. My tea is too hot, and I haven’t taken a sip.

“What are they protesting?” I ask. “Why did her sign say ‘blood on your hands’?”

His lips pull back from his teeth as he winces. He seems to be uncomfortable about what we saw, too. “There are people who think the books in the Rosette were stolen.”

It’s like I’ve been punched in the gut. “What?”

“Yeah. Since its founding, Sibylline has made it their top priority to preserve magical texts. In places all over the world where there is war, or unrest, or even natural disasters, Sibylline has rescued thousands of texts and brought them here for safekeeping.

Some people, however, think they stole the texts, or otherwise acquired them illegally, and that the university is hoarding them for their own gain. Certain spells and rituals can only be found in those books, so it makes them priceless. And by working at the archive, we're complicit."

I shake my head in disbelief. "I remember reading about some scandal with some stolen scrolls that Egyptian magicians demanded back. I heard it was resolved, though. I thought they were returned."

"Lots of people think so. There was an investigation some years ago. The government got involved and everything, lots of hearings—it was a big deal at the time, but people moved on. Or forgot. Stone does a really good job at keeping these kinds of things out of the news as much as he can."

"What about the hearings? What did they find?"

"They just sort of fizzled out, I guess. The board ruled that all of the acquisitions were legal, so . . . nothing happened."

"But people are still protesting. Everyone hasn't forgotten," I say.

"We see a few pop up now and again, but Warden Stone is quick to shut them down. I don't like the way he treats them, but I guess there's really nothing we can do about it. We're just employees, right? We're not the ones calling the shots."

"No, I guess not. But is that a good excuse?"

Aspen shrugs. "I like my job. I think we do good work. Whatever happened in the past, right or wrong, I know I'm at least keeping the books safe. I'm doing them justice, and that's what matters to me."

"But I mean, why would Sibylline ever rule against its own self-interest? Just because the board says something's legal, doesn't mean it's right."

Aspen studies me for a moment, a curious curve in his brow. "I mean, yeah. You're not wrong. You've got spirit, I like that." He laughs.

I blush. I should keep quiet. I shouldn't draw attention to myself, but then again, does that make me complicit in Sibylline's corruption, like that woman's sign said?

"Hey," Aspen says, making me look up. He stops me on the sidewalk with a gentle touch on my wrist. I notice we're in front of the Benoist Museum, situated near a small row of ornate potted plants leading up to the entrance. Dorian should be getting out any moment. I tuck my hand into my coat pocket, as if staving off the cold, but my fingers curl around the key.

Aspen steps in closer to me and dips his head a little to even our gazes. "I mean it," he says. "I really like you."

"Thanks." I'm still blushing. I don't know what else to say.

"You can say no if you want, but I'd kick myself if I didn't ask. Can I kiss you?"

It's such an earnest question, it catches me off guard. The key in my pocket feels even heavier now.

Behind Aspen, the front doors to the museum swing open, and I catch sight of Dorian leaving. He pops the collar of his coat to shield his neck from the chilly autumn air, and then his eyebrows rise when he notices me. There's an ache in his gaze I can't ignore, a longing I know all too well. None of us in our little trio is in love with the right person. We are each an arrow pointing the wrong way.

My gaze snaps back to Aspen. He's close, soft-eyed and smiling. He's waiting for an answer.

Without a word, I lean in, pressing my lips to his. He's warm and soft, tasting like blackberry tea. It'd be a nice kiss if my heart were in it. My mission is more important. I palm the key and take my hand out of my pocket to wrap my arms around Aspen's shoulders, pulling him closer to me. He lets out a pleased little sigh, and I raise the key behind his head to show Dorian that I have it.

Then, without Aspen being any the wiser, I drop the key into an ornate planter. Our date is only just beginning.

9 Atticus

I am tired of myself tonight. I should like to be somebody else.
—Oscar Wilde, The Picture of Dorian Gray

AT MIDNIGHT, I arrive at the agreed-upon spot, near the main gates of campus in a walled-off garden darkened by the moonlit shadow of the hulking administration offices. Stone statues are scattered about the garden, and the fountain is quiet, the paths neatly raked. At first I think I've beaten him to the rendezvous, but then I sense a presence nearby. One of the statues isn't a statue at all. Like a piece of art coming to life, Dorian steps into the slanting light of the streetlamps. He's been waiting for me, silent as a cat, wearing all black: a hoodie, sweats, a baseball cap, and as always, his gloves. The ones Raven bought him. I wish I had thought of them. I wish I'd been the one to give them to him. Still, they're convenient, especially for not leaving fingerprints.

"Hey," I say, my heart racing as usual. He looks dressed for the lacrosse pitch, and a memory of watching him—years of watching his graceful, athletic body run around the field—floods my vision. "Fancy seeing you here."

"Waiting around in the dark made me feel like a creep," he says, coming to my side.

"I mean, that is textbook creep behavior," I tease.

In the warm glow from the gas lamp above, I can just make

out the hint of a smile. Affection radiates off of him. But he only thinks of me as a friend. I know that, and I've accepted it. I'll pine for him forever. My heart sinks when I look at his gloves. The gloves he never takes off, to feel closer to *her.*

"Did you get the key?" I ask, masking my churning feelings.

Pulling it from his back pocket, Dorian holds it up. "Raven did her job."

"Then let's put it to good use."

Without a minute to waste, we make our way toward the student union, Dorsia Hall. According to the map, the underground tunnels are all connected, and the entrance in Dorsia Hall is the closest access point outside of the Rosette. Raven said the library will be locked at this hour, so this is our best bet. We navigate to the basement of the Palladian-style building, slipping between the white columns of the portico at the side entrance, and enter the mostly empty atrium, where only a handful of students linger in the lounges, their faces illuminated by soft candlelight as they study in silence. The map says there's an entrance to the tunnels in a closet behind the boiler, so we make our way as casually as we can toward the rear of the building, where there are fewer people.

No one crosses our path as we descend the stairs to the basement, but my heart feels like it might burst out of my chest. Nervously, I tap out a paradiddle on my thighs as I walk, *one-two-three-four, one-two-three-four.*

At the end of the hall, we find the janitorial closet unlocked.

Slowly, I push open the door, careful not to make the hinges creak, and Dorian slips in past me. The room is dark, the air humid and warm, and the boiler hisses. It takes everything I have not to bounce on my toes, giddy with excitement. This is the most rebellious thing I've ever done.

"Behind there," I say, pointing to the boiler.

But when Dorian rounds the corner, he stops short.

"Where is it?" Dorian asks.

All that's here is a solid brick wall.

"It has to open somehow," I say.

"I don't see a mechanism."

He's right. No door. "Maybe the map is out of date . . ." I say. It's rolled up against my back, tucked safely into a cardboard tube, and I pull it out to check the route again.

But Dorian steps toward the wall. "Let me try," he says.

He takes off one of his gloves, and my gaze latches on to the smooth milky-white skin of his hand, the tendons moving as his fingers twitch, like they're eager to touch. He takes a deep, calming breath before he places his palm on the cold brick. He closes his eyes and traces his hand over the rough surface, searching. A line appears between his eyebrows, and his mouth turns down into a small frown.

Watching him use his power is a thing of beauty.

It's like he's his most true self, his armor stripped away.

A small intake of breath, and Dorian's eyes snap open. "Got it." He keeps his palm pressed to an unassuming brick, one of hundreds. "The last person who used this tunnel. A teacher, I think. I can see them. We just need to say the secret word: *pateface*."

Just then, the bricks rumble and grind, moving on their own, forced by an invisible hand. Then they crumble away, and a hole appears, revealing a dark, echoing tunnel.

Dorian slips his glove on, acting as if what he's done is no big deal, but it is.

"You just used magic," I say, impressed. "Successfully, I mean."

Dorian looks at the hole in the wall as if it only occurred to him. "I know." Then he smiles at me, a big toothy grin, and I can't help but smile back.

Sibylline was *so* wrong about him. He and Raven are incredible magicians. They should be students here. We all should.

I step into the tunnel first, and Dorian closely follows. When we're inside, there's a rumbling sound again as the bricks rearrange themselves back into a wall, sealing up the tunnel once more. We're plunged into darkness, but I can feel Dorian's body heat, his breath on my neck, the shape of him beside me.

I wonder what it would feel like to hold his hand.

I have to force the thought from my mind as I reach into my bag and find the lantern I brought, igniting the wick with a lighter. The warm flame illuminates the area around us, throwing Dorian's face into a ghostly version of itself. But his eyes are bright. He's excited.

"Shall we?" I ask, and hold out the lantern.

He takes it with an amused smile, and my fingers slide against his gloves briefly. "After you," he says.

Cobwebs brush against my face as I head down the tunnel. It's clear this passage hasn't been used in a while, but I'm still careful to keep my footsteps light, just in case there is someone up ahead. Even Dorian's sneakers barely make a sound as he follows close behind me. The glow from the light makes the shadows on the walls shift, and for a moment, it's easy to think we're disappearing into the belly of the underworld, walking into unknown danger.

"If we're caught, what do we say?" I whisper.

"You sound like you've got an idea."

"We were kidnapped? Thrown into this dungeon against our will?"

I can hear the amusement in Dorian's voice. "You really think that'd work?"

I whip around, making him stop in his tracks. "Or we can lie and tell them we were making out."

"Good lie." He lets out a laugh and his white, perfectly straight teeth peek out for only a moment. He's so pretty, it makes my heart ache. "But let's just plan on no one catching us," he says, nudging me onward with his gloved hand.

I exhale.

The tunnel opens up into a massive space. Even the light from the lantern can't reach the farthest end. We're standing on a high platform, and stone stairs in front of us wind downward, disappearing into lower tunnels, spiraling into the blackness below us. Wooden beams crisscross each other to hold up the structures around us, and ropes dangle from pulleys and wheels. Faces carved into rock decorate the walls, their stony eyes watching over the cavern like guardians. Ominous.

"Whoa," says Dorian, too amazed to keep his voice down. It echoes in the cavern, multiplying as it fades. The sound of running water comes from far below us, maybe an underground river of some kind. A person could get lost in here if they didn't know where to go. Suddenly I'm thankful for the map.

We plunge deeper into the bowels of the labyrinth, the light from the lantern illuminating our path. We follow the map, trudging through more tunnels, more stairs, more ramps. My knees are shaking when we reach the door to the archive.

Dorian takes out the key, but when he puts it in the lock, he pauses.

"It's already open," he says.

Something is wrong.

Dorian douses the lamp before he opens the door. The lights in the room are off, save for a fire roaring in the fireplace. Raven mentioned it might be magicked, to preserve the books, so I'm not surprised it's still burning. In any case, the magical fireplace is not the most impressive element of the room. There are thousands upon thousands of books packed into towering shelves. Dorian gazes upward, taking in the scene with a kind of slack-jawed amazement. I, too, stand in awe. A place like this, hidden underground, only accessible to the elite? What a waste.

Where do we even start? I'm paralyzed with choice.

But before either Dorian or I can start browsing, footsteps echo in the distance.

There's someone here.

Dorian and I stare at each other, frozen in fear, then he grabs me by the wrist and pulls me around the corner. Desperate, we search for somewhere to hide as the footsteps draw closer.

Hurry, I mouth to him.

He grimaces, but then his eyes go to the fireplace, and he pulls me toward it. There's a small opening, a gap behind it just barely wide enough for us to slip through. It must be where the attendants go to check the fire. It's just big enough for the both of us to hide.

A shadow passes in front of the opening, the footsteps growing louder. Dorian and I are pressed up against each other, chest to chest. I don't breathe. We stand frozen, watching, waiting. Then a person appears. His iconic ruby earring glints in the firelight.

"That's Warden Stone," I whisper. "We are so fucked."

"Shh," says Dorian. "I don't think he can hear us. Just stay calm."

"What's he doing here this late?"

Dorian shrugs. His guess is as good as mine. "Warden things? Must be why the door was unlocked. Guess we're stuck here until he leaves."

Warden Stone looks tired, weathered and aged like a crumpled-up piece of paper, as if he never went to bed in the first place. Whatever work he's doing, it must be important.

"We might be here for a while," I say.

Dorian sighs, and his breath curls against my cheek. He's taller than me, but only by a little. We stand, touching just slightly, our bodies meeting, coming together, then parting awkwardly. In the narrow space it's impossible for us not to touch.

I wonder, is this the closest he and I have ever been?

"Comfortable?" he jokes, his whisper drawing my gaze up to his eyes. They're green flecked with gold, and it's dizzying to see them up close.

I shrug. "As comfortable as one can be hiding behind a fireplace in a secret room full of magical books."

The corners of his mouth curl into a smile. "Maybe we can make that making-out lie true."

He's joking. Right? Dorian's straight. He's in love with Raven. He'd never think of me like that . . . would he? Even he must realize what he said, because his smile falls and his eyes drop to my lips, and he looks away.

We fall into awkward silence, watching Warden Stone's shadow moving slowly around the room. It's like he's looking for something and can't find it. He looks angrier with each passing minute. My hands are bunched up against Dorian's sweatshirt, and I can feel his heart beating beneath the fabric. I try to move my hands away, but I can't. We're too cramped. Dorian senses me trying to shift, and he lifts his arm above my head, bracing himself against the wall to give me space. We twist and turn; I'm amazed Warden Stone doesn't see us. I tuck my arms to my sides, breaking a brief, accidental embrace.

The urge to touch him is overwhelming, but I don't because of how he feels about Raven. Every time he catches her eye, he looks like a lost puppy. When she's around, his aura goes pink and orange, like the most brilliant sunset.

I get it, Raven is beautiful. They would make a great couple. I don't blame Dorian in the slightest. And I can't bring myself to tell him how I feel. I don't want to lose either of them because of something I said. I don't want to break up our trio.

By now, Warden Stone has moved far enough away, I know he can't hear us. I have to change the subject, or I might say something foolish, like tell Dorian how nice this moment is. "What you did back there, though, seeing the past by touching the wall, it's amazing."

"Is it?"

"Always has been," I say, feeling dizzy on my feet.

I breathe in his cologne. It's subtle, and it mixes with the scent of his body, his soap and a dash of perspiration. It fills my nose, making me feel as if I've pressed my face directly into the nape of his neck. They say that scent is tied closely to memory, that the aroma of one thing can trigger a hundred recollections, so I drink in that scent, hoping to recall this moment.

"You know, I've always wondered about your power," I say. "You've never told me what happens when you touch a person."

Dorian takes a deep breath, half his face lost in shadow. He hesitates, somehow nervous. "I've only touched someone once since my powers manifested. It was an accident."

"You never told me about that."

"That's because it . . ." He winces, and I stare at him, wondering what ails him. We've always been friends, but there are some things he likes to keep to himself.

This is one of them.

We're alike, I suppose, in that regard, keeping secrets.

But maybe because it's me asking the question, or maybe because he's feeling brave, he says, "During summer break, right before sixth grade, I was on the subway, and this old man . . . He collapsed, right in front of me. No one else did anything. And I didn't think about it, I just reached out, tried to shake him awake, and when my hand touched his . . ."

Dorian shudders. "My heart stopped when I touched him. Actually stopped. He was going into cardiac arrest, and so was I. It hurt so much." His lips twitch, tears forming in his eyes. "It's hard to explain, but I think maybe I died. For a second. With him. I somehow absorbed what was happening to him."

"Oh, shit," I whisper. "What happened next?"

Dorian shrugs. "He woke up, and the paramedics took him away, but . . . I can't be certain, but I think he lived. I don't know, but I might have saved him. When they lifted him to his feet, he was talking, and his face was no longer gray." He looks haunted, his gaze distant. "It's one of the reasons why I wanted to come to Sibylline. If there's anyone out there who can help me, this is the place–right?"

I nod slightly.

Dorian focuses his gaze on me, those green eyes of his dancing as he does. All I can think about is him, wanting to touch him, to feel him.

"Do you want to try again?" I ask.

Dorian stiffens, shoulders raised, and his Adam's apple drops when he swallows. It's almost like I can see him building a wall around himself.

"As friends," I quickly add.

"You want me to try to use my power on you?"

"Why not? I'm not going into cardiac arrest, not yet."

Dorian's breath comes out a little shaky. He clenches his hand into a fist, still braced against the wall above me. He has the strong hands of an athlete. I wonder what it would feel like to grab his bare hand. To feel his skin on mine.

"What would you like me to do?" He's nervous. I can sense it. The nervous energy is rolling off of him in waves.

"Whatever you want."

His gaze drops to my lip again, pausing for the span of a heartbeat, before it snaps back up to my eyes.

I ache with desire.

"Finch, it's . . ." His gaze roams the space around my lips, and he bites at his lower lip.

I sense the rejection coming, and I bat it away before it can hurt me. "Right, I know, it's stupid," I say. "Forget I mentioned it."

"I didn't say it's stupid."

Hope can be like hunger. Once you've gone long enough without what you want, one bite can make you sick. But there's something in his eyes, a hunger of its own kind that reignites the hope I've grown so used to starving with. It leaves me to wonder what he truly desires.

Dorian, do you want me?

The question hangs between us, the air alive with tension. Just then he moves closer, and my breath catches. His lips part as he presses his chest so close to mine that I can feel the beating of his heart, pounding like a drum, each beat sending shock waves through my skin. I lean toward him–

A loud crack reverberates throughout the tall chamber. I turn, catching sight of Warden Stone lifting a book from the floor. He must have dropped it a second earlier when I wasn't looking. Dorian withdraws, flattening his back against the wall, shifting so our bodies no longer touch.

Warden Stone tucks the book beneath his arm and moves behind a tall tow of shelves. A door closes, banging shut.

"Is he gone?" I whisper.

Neither of us knows the answer.

We wait, listening, but the room is silent, save for the crackle of the fire, Dorian's soft breathing, and my own heart beating out a plaintive rhythm.

"Let's go," I say. The morning shift will likely be here soon.

I peek out from our hiding spot. Warden Stone is gone.

Dorian follows behind me as I dart into the room. I look for a book, any book that looks interesting, and point to one.

"There, that one, with the blue cover," I say.

Using the key to unlock the cage, Dorian slips the book from its shelf.

We make our way to the door, lock it behind us, and then we're sprinting down the darkened tunnel, Dorian with the book in his hands, and me still wondering if he almost kissed me.

10
RAVEN

Who has not, a hundred times, found himself committing a vile or a silly action for no other reason than because he knows he should not?

—Edgar Allan Poe, "The Black Cat"

WAITING FOR ATTICUS and Dorian is an exercise in patience, and I am not patient. Back at home, I rotate between sitting on the couch or the breakfast table downstairs, or on the bed upstairs, and finally end up standing in the landing, hoping for the door to open. I check the window, but all I can see is wet pavement glinting beneath the streetlamps. The clock on the mantel tells me it's three in the morning, and the street remains infuriatingly empty except for the occasional headlights of a slowly rolling car, or a stray cat darting across the lanes.

I jump when there comes a sharp triple knock.

On my feet in an instant, I rush to the door and yank it open.

"We did it, Raven. Holy shit, we did it!" Dorian's voice carries as he holds up a leather-bound grimoire. He and Atticus look flush with excitement, their identical smiles lighting up the dark hallway.

"Shh. You'll wake up my landlord," I say as they slip inside. I have the top two floors of a town house, but the building is old, and the walls are thin. "What took you so long?" Dorian passes a look to Atticus. I get a strange feeling; something's changed between them. "I was starting to worry."

Then Dorian grins at me. "You weren't kidding, the tunnels under campus are massive. It's basically an underground city." He sounds a little breathless, like the adrenaline is still pumping through his system. His cheeks are rosy, his hair windswept, eyes bright and clear. Next to him, Atticus looks similar, although in his eyes the look of triumph is laced with something else I can't quite identify. Is it disappointment?

"You have to come next time," says Atticus.

"Next time," I say, trying to smile but failing. The invitation somehow doesn't feel so special now that it's over. "So, what did you get?"

Atticus hands me the book before throwing himself down on the couch. "We grabbed whatever we could."

"It's in Latin; you'll know what it says." When Dorian plants himself next to Atticus, he gives him a lingering look that he hides with a sweep of his glove through his hair. Atticus returns the glance, a kind of half-lidded wink. Something passes between them, and I'm not quite sure what. Suddenly, I'm feeling left out all over again, and the loneliness is like an ice pick to the heart.

"Did something else happen?" I ask, probing, though hopefully not pressing.

"No, nothing," says Dorian, shifting in his seat.

I know a lie when I hear one.

Sweat blooms across my palms. Jealousy takes hold. Do I even want to know? I try not to look at Atticus. I know. I know. It's so silly to love a man who can't love me back, but as they say, the heart wants what it wants, and I've always wanted Atticus.

Atticus explains, "Warden Stone was in the archive when we arrived, so we had to hide until he left."

"Warden Stone." Hearing the name, I feel foolish. After dealing with the protesters, he probably went to check on the archive, making sure the books were secure. I should have warned them after I saw him. "I wish you'd told me you'd be late," I say stupidly and regret it immediately.

"How?" Atticus asks, confused. "It's not like I could have called or texted."

"No, I know, but . . ."

Dorian's gaze slides to Atticus. "It won't happen again," he says. "Right, Finch?"

Atticus straightens up a little, shoulders back, and tilts his head as if listening to a distant sound. "Yeah," he says. "We'll have to find some other way to talk to each other across distances."

It feels as though I'm not privy to something. Like I haven't seen them in years instead of hours. I want to ask about it, but it's probably nothing and Atticus is already opening the book and paging through it. The writing is faded, the paper thin and fragile, yellowed and frail with age. It cracks when he runs his finger across the surface.

"I vote we see what's inside," he says.

"I'm too awake to go to bed anyway," I agree, taking a seat.

We gather around the ancient book as Dorian offers to make tea. While he fills the kettle, we prepare ourselves, making room to work. The coffee table is actually just the old trunk that I packed my belongings into, and he clears it of everything but the book, brushing away dirt and a few odds and ends.

"How did it go with Aspen, anyway?" Atticus asks.

"Fine."

"Just fine?" he teases.

"What are you getting at?"

He glances in Dorian's direction before replying. "Your energy is . . . off."

I bat my hand through the air. "It's nothing."

Atticus presses his mouth into a line. "Still. You can tell us anything, you know that."

I can't. I really can't. I like Atticus too much. And I know he won't ever like me in the same way. I can't help wanting him, wanting him the way he wants Dorian. I've always wanted things I can't have. It's like I torture myself on purpose, even when I know it makes me miserable.

Atticus watches me, and for an instant, it feels like he can see right through me. I almost want to hide, but Dorian returns with the teapot, steeping with bags of black tea, a trio of mugs balanced in the other hand. We arrange ourselves on the floor around the trunk. Dorian sits opposite me, Atticus at my side. I welcome the warmth of his body next to mine.

I close the book and study it. The cover is made from blue leather, the texture soft beneath my fingers. A cross flecked with gold decorates it. I trace my fingers over the leather, feeling the grooves and indents made by the script, letting my eyes unfocus and my mind relax. Something shifts, and the words make sense. Nothing about them changes, but I do. I morph myself around the language, taking its shape, embracing it.

My tongue tingles as if I've touched it to a small battery.

"It's written by a wizard by the name of Apuleius. There's a stamp here. This book belonged in the Library of Alexandria."

Dorian straightens, anticipation making his muscles grow taut. Atticus lets out a shuddering breath.

"Really?" he asks. "*The* Library of Alexandria?"

"Yes," I say. "It must have survived the fire, probably brought to Sibylline for safekeeping." Maybe Aspen was a little right. If not for Sibylline, it would have been lost. The book feels ancient, like a tree with a million rings in its trunk. Somehow touching it feels sacrilegious. I want to be respectful, but at the same time, I want to know everything it contains.

I open the cover, and the words practically leap off the page.

"It's a book of incantations, all of them meticulously detailed, as if the inscriber was documenting them for future generations. A step-by-step guide to the arcane wisdom within the ancient language."

Atticus and Dorian look at me, waiting, unable to do any of this without me.

Satisfaction worms its way inside of me. They need me. Without my power, they would have no idea what this book contains. When I flip another page, there's a diagram of a man, naked, impressed upon a pentagram. His head and splayed arms and legs make up the points of a star, and each point is labeled with an astrological symbol.

When Dorian sees it, he stiffens at my side. "What's that?" he asks.

"It's a ceremonial ritual, the invocation of a spirit."

Dorian leans forward, his forehead creased.

"Do you recognize it?" Atticus asks.

"I've seen something like it," he says soberly. He tugs at his gloves.

"What's an invocation again?" Atticus asks.

"Calling forth a spirit into our realm, manifesting its energy," I say. "It's different from an evocation, where you call a spirit into the material world. In an invocation, you call a spirit into *you*."

A worried expression crosses Dorian's face.

"We don't have to do anything like that," I say. "We should start small, try something easy." We take performing our first spell seriously as we meticulously go through each page of the book for at least an hour until we unanimously agree on one: a simple conjuration to light a candle. It was one of the first things a young magician learned back then. There's little room for error. Either the spell works or it doesn't. It's reasonable for us to start small, after all.

Dorian seems more at ease with our choice at least.

"What do you need us to do?" Atticus asks me.

I check and double-check the instructions. It's a straightforward spell. "This one only requires a vocal command and a sigil."

"Sounds simple," says Atticus.

"Atticus, can you fetch the candle from the windowsill there? And hand me my journal, please, Dorian," I say. They do, eager to begin.

I open my journal to a blank page, where I copy the sigil as it is in the book, a simple triangle–the alchemical symbol for fire–writing the same Latin phrase on each of the three sides, exactly as detailed in the grimoire.

I explain as I work, "It says that the upright triangle is the symbol for fire, a representation of rising energy, of reaching above, whatever that means. The triangle is also the strongest of the basic shapes, or so it claims. Every line supports the others. Without one, it falls apart. Some sort of ancient logic."

"Makes sense, I guess," says Atticus, shrugging.

Dorian kneels on the other side of the coffee table, opposite me, and Atticus now hovers behind me, leaning over to look at the book. I can smell his aftershave, that familiar scent that brings me back to the days we spent in his room, poring over books late into the night, moonlight breaking through the window. It was a time of possibilities, of promises, of the future. I want to impress both of them. I want to impress *him*.

"So what now?" Atticus asks.

"Just watch," I say, placing the unlit candle over the paper where I drew the sigil. I push the book away and get up on my knees, stationing myself so I have a clear view of everything involved in the spell.

"I think I'm ready," I say, but I hesitate. Something holds my tongue. I want to do this, but I don't truly know what is going to happen. I could be doing this wrong. There could be a thousand things I don't understand about this spell. The anticipation sits like a stone in my mouth, preventing me from speaking. This, right here and right now, is everything I've been waiting for, so what's holding me back?

"Are you okay?" Dorian checks on me, concerned.

"I don't want to mess it up."

"You won't." Atticus touches my elbow, sending goose bumps shivering across my skin. Dorian offers an encouraging smile, a lifeline to latch on to.

"Okay. Give me a minute." I take a deep breath, set my shoulders, and straighten my spine, staring at the symbol.

Lighting a candle seems so simple. Too simple. What if I did more? What if I could show Atticus and Dorian what I can really do? I notice Atticus watching me, and a swell of determination bubbles inside of me, like a pot ready to boil.

I clap my hands, the sound ringing out in the silent apartment, then I read the words aloud from the page: "*Vocare . . . ignis.*"

The air between my hands gets warm, like invisible sunlight cupped in my palm. It feels so good. Magic flows through my hands and down my fingers, tickling my skin. This is nothing like I've ever felt before. Power. Pure power.

More. I can do more. The sensation in my chest simmers. I imagine myself turning up the heat. Just a little more. Only a twist of the wrist.

There's a blinding flash. The air crackles. Then everything explodes.

A bolt of what looks like lightning, white-hot and impossibly loud, hits the room.

A searing heat strikes my face, and a force throws me backward. All I can do is cover my eyes and cower, waiting until the heat and the light fade.

My ears are ringing, head spinning. Someone's screaming.

"Raven!" It's Atticus.

I look around me. The candle is on fire, but so is everything else in my apartment. The room is alive with flame. It dances across the carpet and up the curtained wall to the second floor. The heat stings my eyes, and the smoke is everywhere. Flames roar, almost to the ceiling, and a thick gray cloud chokes the room as the fire alarm shrieks to life.

The spell book burns, too, and the pages turn to ash. "Shit!" The precious book that once escaped a legendary devastating fire now burns before my eyes. I slam the cover shut, but it's too late. Much of it is already gone, the ancient paper consumed in mere seconds.

More screaming. Dorian's shirtsleeve. It's on fire. He falls to the floor. Atticus throws a blanket on top of him to snuff out the flames.

"Oh my God! Dorian! No!" I scream as I grab a pillow and try to extinguish what's left of the fire.

There's a voice in the hall and a fist pounding on the door. Furious bangs. "Hello? What the hell's going on in there?"

I try to make it to the door, but it's too smoky. Dorian's face is tight with pain, teeth bared, his eyes squeezed shut. Tears stream down his cheeks. Atticus is yelling. Everything is burning.

Then Mr. Benson, my landlord, bursts through the door, a fire extinguisher in his hand, and he sprays the walls, the carpet, and the furniture. White mist fills the room, dousing everything. I settle beside Dorian. His shirt is ruined, the skin beneath it red but not burnt. He's okay, thankfully. The same cannot be said for my apartment.

It's been almost completely consumed by the fire. What's left is mostly ash, embers, and smoke.

"What happened?" Mr. Benson demands. He must have heard the commotion and come running. If it hadn't been for his help, we'd likely be dead.

"Cooking accident," I say. "Left the stove on after making tea. Thanks for, uh, putting it out."

Mr. Benson just stares at me, a look of fury on his hardened face.

I'll need to find a new apartment and pay for the damages on this one, but I don't care.

I summoned *lightning.*

11
DORIAN

I love, and am in despair—yes—despair.
—*Ann Radcliffe,* The Mysteries of Udolpho

THE SOFT AUTUMN morning outside draws the world downward, brings gazes to the wet pavement, shadows into inky spills, gold and red leaves to the grass. I pass customers writing in journals, sipping chamomile tea, or chatting over cupcakes and cookies. The Acroteria at this late hour is quiet. It was the closest place to the hospital. I wasn't in the mood to go back to my apartment on the southern side of town anyway.

When I come out of the bathroom, having just changed the bandage on my arm like the doctor said to, and return to our booth—the one by the arch made of books—a steaming blueberry muffin waits for me on a small, slightly cracked ceramic plate. Atticus's doing. He's always taking care of us.

Raven watches me approach, a feverish glint in her eye. It bothers me a little that she doesn't seem at all shaken that she practically set me on fire. She almost looks . . . excited.

"I'm so glad you're okay, Dorian," she says when I slide onto the bench. I think it's the thousandth time she's said it.

"Yeah," I say. "Me too. I'm just a little freaked out."

"I'm really, really sorry," she says. "As sorry as I am that the book is destroyed. Ugh!"

She's been apologizing nonstop since we jumped in a cab to the hospital, all throughout when she sat with me in the emergency room, and especially when the nurse smeared gel on my pink and tender skin and wrapped it in gauze. To be honest, Raven's constant stream of apologies only reminds me that she set me on fire. By accident. But still. Maybe I'm being harsh. Maybe she's just freaked out like we all are.

Atticus clears his throat and leans in toward us. "What we just did . . . It was dark. Potent. Frankly terrifying." He stops, glancing around the cafe again, maybe fearing he's been overheard, and whispers, "That was nothing like the stuff we've seen on campus. They're struggling to turn roses to ash, and we're . . . summoning lightning? Why can't anyone else do what we can do?"

"Good question." Raven's eyes never break away from my arm, even while my hand is hidden. "It felt . . ." She trails off and doesn't finish. I almost think she's going to say "good."

"What happened afterward wasn't your fault, Raven," I say. "It was—"

She nods, her gaze distant. "Power is what it was."

She's right, and we're messing with things we don't understand. I worry it could have been worse—much, much worse. But I don't want to say it.

"Maybe we didn't do anything wrong. What if the spell worked and we just didn't know what it was supposed to do?" I ask, but the words ring hollow.

Raven doesn't buy it. "The instructions were clear. I was just lighting a candle, nothing more." She shakes her head. "No, something was off. Maybe I mistranslated the grammar or got the dialect wrong."

I point to the table for emphasis. "There is one other possibility. Maybe, in your hands, the spell reacted differently than it might have with any normal person. Listen, what if the spell worked exactly how it was meant to? It was an evocation, right? Words change the material world. That's what Warden Stone said at the recitation. Maybe in less talented hands, the change is quite small. A tiny flame. Coming from you, though, the words had power. *You* have power, and you summoned something far more potent than a little flame to light a candle. In your hands, the spell is able to call lightning."

"You think?" Raven meets my eyes, her black ones matching mine, a curious look in hers. It's like I've said something she's always been waiting to hear, but no one's ever said it before. It's true, though; we're all powerful, aren't we? Our strength is magnified by learning the spells, or perhaps the spells amplify the strength within us.

"It makes some sense." Raven looks troubled. "I asked my deskmate, Pippa, what kind of magic she can do. Get this–she can tell time without looking at a clock."

"That's it?" Atticus is indignant.

Raven rolls her eyes. "Yep, that's it. I can tell the time without looking at a clock either. I have Google Home."

I'm completely irritated by this news. "How on earth did she get in, then? Sibylline students are supposed to be the best magicians in the world! I thought they all had *something special*."

"Yeah, that something special is money," says Atticus archly.

Raven blushes. She's always a little sensitive about her background.

A resigned laugh escapes me, and Atticus's eyes flash delightedly at the sound of it. I look away, suddenly feeling hot under the collar.

I wanted to kiss Atticus back in the archive . . . But I couldn't.

Touching him—touching anyone—is like asking me to grip a hot stove or a bolt of lightning. It's not that I don't find Atticus attractive, it's that my crush on Raven is all-consuming. I'd never really noticed him before in that way. And I did find him very appealing last night. I'd never really thought about whether I am attracted to men or women. It's not something that worries me, thinking I might like Atticus. Curious. I'd always thought I'd wait as long as I needed for Raven to come around.

But what if—what if I was waiting for the wrong person?

"Could we try any other spell?" Atticus asks, shifting focus back to the matter at hand.

"You'd really want to?" Raven looks nonplussed.

Atticus sighs. "I'm not ready to give up. Are you? If we don't try, we can't learn. We came here to learn about magic, didn't we?"

"I guess, but the book was ruined in the fire," I say. A part of me is almost relieved when I recall how the book burned, but the other half wishes that we could have had another chance. Maybe, with time, we would have been able to control the lightning itself. "We're back to square one."

"Plus," adds Raven, "my landlord is kicking me out. I have to pack up my things—what's left of my things, anyway—by tomorrow."

"Is that legal?" Atticus looks appalled.

Raven shakes her head and says, "I don't know."

"Where will you go?" I ask.

She shrugs half-heartedly. "I could check in to a hotel for now, I guess."

I would offer her my apartment, but it's a hovel compared to what she's used to, and I'm too embarrassed. Thankfully, Atticus speaks up. "You can move in with me," he says. "I'm closer to campus anyway."

"Are you sure?" Raven asks.

"It's not a problem. Just so long as we don't start any more fires," Atticus says.

He meant it as a joke, but Raven hides her face in her hands and lets out a small groan.

"We need another book in the meantime," says Atticus.

"Won't they get suspicious if a second one goes missing?" I ask.

Raven lifts her face out of her hands and glances around. "One going missing might not raise alarms. Two? I don't know if we can risk it. And after being the cause of its demise, I don't really want to risk stealing another."

She has a point, and Atticus knows it, too. I see it in his eyes.

We fall into silence, my head spinning, a hundred different theories colliding in my thoughts. Maybe that book really *was* dangerous. After all, it was locked up. Maybe there was a reason why it was hidden away in the basement. It contained a drawing that looked exactly like what I saw when I touched the wand. I've been reliving that dream ever since my first day of work, and now I can't get it out of my thoughts. The image of the man on the pentagram comes back to me. Again, I hear screams, and I can almost smell the incense.

"Adelina! Adelina! Please!" screams the voice.

I wanted to forget, to push the images out of my mind, but I can't. Finally I say, "Have either of you ever heard the name Adelina before?"

It's a unique enough name. I'd hoped they would know any association with Sibylline, but they offer blank stares, and Atticus shakes his head.

Raven says, "I haven't, no. Why do you ask?"

I lick my lips and take in a deep breath, mustering the nerve.

I don't want to frighten them, and yet I can't keep this secret to myself.

"My first day at the museum," I say, "I touched an artifact, this old wand that she used. It belonged to Hecate."

Both Raven and Atticus seem impressed, though about different things.

"The goddess of magic," Raven says, amazed, at the same time Atticus asks, "You had a vision?" His eyes are bright with curiosity.

I nod. "I saw a person, a Sibylline student, chained up on the floor, lying on a star just like the one drawn in the grimoire. There was blood, fire, and screaming. I think Adelina was using Hecate's wand to cast a spell, a deadly powerful one, and it may have involved a murder that was somehow a part of the ritual casting."

Raven leans forward intently but neither of them says anything. A hush falls over the table, making it seem as if the air itself is holding its breath.

"There's more . . ." I pause, uncertain of what to say. "I'm not completely sure what I saw, but there was another presence in the room, something they'd summoned. I saw a shadow, but nothing else. It was alive."

Atticus and Raven glance at each other, confused.

Atticus asks, "Like an evocation? They summoned an elemental? Or a spirit?"

I shrug. "It wasn't human."

"How do you know it was summoned?" Raven asks. "Did you see it happen?"

I shake my head. "No, I didn't see everything. I witnessed flashes. It was like a dream. I somehow knew that's what was happening, but everything seemed as if it was happening at once."

"And you think it was some sort of ritual, like the one we saw in the grimoire?"

"Possibly . . ." I shake my head. "I don't know. Honestly, I haven't seen a lot of nightmare rituals." I try for a joke—something to cut the tension—but it doesn't hit.

A second silence falls over the table as Raven and Atticus exchange glances. A part of me wishes I'd never brought it up. I don't want to scare them away from using their gifts. But maybe there are things in this world that truly are frightening. I wonder if we should change course and try for something smaller and less dangerous.

Maybe the book should have burned a long time ago.

Atticus lets out a heavy sigh. Raven simply stares at the empty plate in front of her, her brows knitted in concentration.

"I've read most of the histories written about the school," Raven says, "and I've never heard of anything like that. Ritual murder? Summoning? Wouldn't everyone have heard about it? Wouldn't it have been all over the news? If some student died . . ."

"I know," I say, understanding what she's getting at. "It doesn't make sense, not yet. But I do know what I saw. And unless my power shows me things that aren't true, which I doubt . . ."

"You've never had issues with your magic—right?" Raven asks. "It shows you the past, and it's never been wrong?"

"Never," I repeat so it sinks in. I've never been wrong.

Which means a student died on the pentagram, summoning the shadow I saw in my vision.

12 ATTICUS

But hers also was the misery of innocence, which, like a cloud that passes over the fair moon, for a while hides, but cannot tarnish its brightness.

—Mary Shelley, Frankenstein

I SENSE RAVEN before she knocks. I know she's in the hall. My power, it's growing. I open the door and she stands, fist raised in the air, frozen for a moment before her eyes land on me. "Atticus," she says, recovering from her surprise.

"I knew it was you," I say, smiling.

I step back, waving her into my apartment.

She arrives with only a backpack and a singed antique trunk on a small cart. I push it inside and close the door behind us. Raven follows. Her gaze slowly moves through the room, and I watch her carefully, gauging her emotions.

"What do you think?" I ask. "I've tried to make it my own."

"It's perfect," says Raven. "Like your taste."

She isn't wrong, but I can't take credit for the apartment, not entirely. It was furnished when I moved in. It's on the second floor of a brick walk-up, with a living room, a small kitchen, one bedroom, and a bathroom, but it's the design itself that spoke to me, called to me. Crown molding, wood-coffered ceiling, a bespoke fireplace, William Morris wallpaper, built-in bookcases filled with the previous owner's old books, tall casement windows, original wood floors. It even smells like history. Musty, in a good way. And age.

She lets out a little gasp when her attention falls to the books. "Is that a first-edition Louisa Elmore?"

Louisa Elmore was a famous apotropaic wizard, a nineteenth-century scholar who studied the art of good luck symbols to ward off evil spirits. Of course Raven would find the rarest one in the collection. I laugh as she takes it off the shelf and moves to the couch to read. The dark corduroy love seat is a leftover from the previous tenant, and it still smells of rose perfume and fresh linen.

"This is incredible." Raven flips through the Elmore book, shaking her head and smiling. "Why didn't you tell me?"

"And spoil the surprise? The person who lived here before left a bunch of cool stuff behind."

I sense Raven's emotions swirling around her, not a tumultuous storm but a settling breeze. She was excited about coming here, eager to leave her old apartment behind, but she's also nervous for some reason. When she looks up from the book, her dark eyes capture mine. "This place is so you," she says. "So Paris Left Bank."

"Really?" I beam. I'm inordinately pleased about the reference. "I was worried it looked too try-hard."

Raven shakes her head and admires my thrift-store valuables—antique lamps I found at Connecticut estate sales, a collection of miniature marble obelisks (a symbol of Paris), velvet curtains, and throws.

"Are you hungry?" I ask. "I'm cooking pozole." The scent of stew fills the air. It's my grandmother's recipe, a dish that has to simmer for eight hours for the meat to melt, but it's worth every second.

Raven looks over the linens I've prepared. "You've already done so much," she says. "I wish I'd brought *you* something."

I wave her off. "Please. It's no problem. I was cooking anyway, and it *is* bad luck if you don't have a little housewarming when someone new arrives. Elmore will tell you that." I point at the book still in her hands, and she grins, relaxing in the chair.

I plate our dinner in large soup bowls. The rain's started up again, and it taps lazily on the glass.

"Where's Dorian?" Raven asks. "Is he coming tonight?"

"He's working late at the museum," I say. "They're running behind on that big gala they're having in a few weeks. A big shipment of donations came in for that exhibit, so his boss asked him to do some overtime."

I hand over her bowl, and she holds it close to her chest. When she looks at me, her mood has turned somber. "About last night, when you two were . . ." Raven watches me, as if gauging how best to ask.

Raven seems to know something happened between us, something more than we've told her, so I deflect.

"You're coming with us on our next book stealing mission," I say. "We missed you."

Her shoulders relax a little.

"Don't feel like you're a guest here," I tell her.

"Thanks. I'm not sure I'll be able to find another apartment this close to campus."

"That's why I offered it." I smile, and she finally smiles back. It's one of my life's missions to see it. I sense a warm feeling rising up in Raven, a kind of swoop of pleasure that I embrace as my own.

We eat our dinner, perched across from each other on the bay window seat, our knees tucked up and our ankles slightly touching, as she tells me about her day at the library. The dinner, while excellent, hearty and robust, is nothing compared to the feeling of Raven being here. She's a steadying presence, like a fire crackling away in the same hearth for years, its light and warmth a constant comfort. This is the perfect picture of a cozy life. It's the safety of being near someone who knows me, maybe even better than I know myself.

When she's done eating, I take her bowl and put it in the sink, saving the washing up for later. "Do you want to take a shower or . . ." I pull a bottle of red wine from atop the vintage fridge. "Do you want a nightcap first?"

"Sure," she says, eyebrows raised in surprise. "Where'd that come from?"

"Another gift from the previous tenant," I say, holding it up for her. It's a little dusty, but I brush it off with my sleeve and inspect the label. "It's a Bordeaux, bottled in 1913."

"Wow, that's probably incredibly expensive," Raven says.

"Then that's all the more reason we should drink it."

Raven doesn't argue as I uncork it. Immediately, an aroma of spicy black pepper and star anise wafts out of the bottle. I manage to find two glasses, pour for us both, and take a seat across from her again.

The wine is so red, so dark, it almost looks like blood in the dim firelight. I hold the glass up, peering through it. Time, literally bottled. There's something magical about it, otherworldly and esoteric. If I had to guess, the vineyard was owned by a wizard. Probably a Sibylline alum. The aroma is seductive, like lips brushing against my skin. I suppress the urge to shiver.

The last time this wine breathed, a world war was just about to begin. How much it's missed since then. I notice Raven looking at me, but she turns away again, tucking her hair behind her ear. She puts her nose in the glass and takes a sniff, and something changes in her face, a kind of relief, like she hasn't taken a deep breath in a long time.

"Toast?" I say, holding out my glass.

She holds out hers, the rim hovering inches from mine.

"To good friends," I say. "And good wine."

"To best friends," says Raven with a rueful smile. "Thanks for having me, man."

The wine is dry and tangy, with a little bite. Warmth rushes into me, and I let out a soft sigh, the taste lingering on my tongue before it fades into a pleasant tingling in the back of my throat.

"Nice." I nod, approving. As if I know anything about wine.

"It could breathe for a bit," Raven decides.

"You think?" I ask.

"Maybe." She shrugs. "I'm no expert. My parents are wine lovers. They say the tannins need to be exposed to the air to fully develop the flavor. To be honest, I've never been able to tell the difference."

She's lying. She's rich and sophisticated and has always been comfortable among the finer things, unlike me, who's just pretending. The aura around her head shimmers, like a mirage.

"The wine's been waiting to be enjoyed for so long, you're telling me it needs even more time?" I tease.

"Time makes things better."

I tip my head to the side. "If you can't enjoy things now, it's a waste."

"Maybe some things take time because they need it," she says.

Her cheeks are already pink, and I'm not convinced it's the magic wine's doing.

The rain pelts the glass. The wind howls, making the window creak and whistle gently. These old buildings talk, but all I can hear is Raven. I can hear her heart. Not the beating but the aching desire, yearning for me, pulling at her.

I realize how close we're sitting. Our heads bowed together, just as we used to when I'd spend the night in her room. Funny how her parents never minded that I was a boy. I think it's because they knew about me even before I knew myself.

But do I know myself?

She wants me . . . and I . . . I'm struck by how earnestly I want her, too. The realization sits like a lump in my throat.

"Atticus," she whispers. "All we have is right now, this moment."

She waits for my reply, her eyes locked on mine, her features as rigid and still as a statue. Her gaze drops to my lips, and I feel what she's feeling: *You, you, you, I want you.*

Her desire for me is so strong I'm overwhelmed by it. I used to think not being straight was simple. Instead of knowing what I was, I knew what I wasn't. Or I thought I did. But this gravitational pull toward Raven is bending the curve even more. The borders of my identity have smeared, like water spilled on an ink drawing. I am attracted to her. Have been. Maybe I never let myself recognize it before, out of fear. Maybe it was never about what was on the outside to begin with. Maybe I want to be with people who make me feel alive. Raven and Dorian make life worth living.

My body warms as if I've been basking in sunlight while I look at her. Beautiful, lissome, brilliant. What if I want to touch the lips that speak a thousand tongues, to taste the wine as she tastes it? I listen for her thoughts, but they're too jumbled to comprehend. Like whispers from another room, distant and soft, they mumble in my ear, and I lean in as if to hear them more clearly.

"I want you, Atticus. I always have," she whispers.

Raven's full lips part. I can see she wants me to answer, but somehow, I can't seem to find the words. Love is a quiet beast, a poltergeist. It can convince you it's not there, even when it takes you by the hand and pulls you in.

I narrow the gap between us, our mouths inching closer together. But Raven's so still, I can tell she's holding her breath, like she's afraid that if she breathes, the illusion will shatter and the moment will end. I sense her fear, her anxiety, at finally getting what she wants. Me.

"May I?" I ask. The alcohol makes me feel bold.

"May you . . . ?" Her words are strained. Her shyness is so sweet.

I smile. "May I have this moment? With you?"

My question hangs in the air between us, Raven practically vibrating with anticipation, the tension rising, unfurling, begging to be eased.

"Y-yes," she stammers.

And I kiss her.

Her lips are tight at first. Then, as the second stretches and the warmth between our kiss spreads, her mouth relaxes. Her shoulders drop, her eyes flutter closed, and she lets out a wonderful sigh. Emotions rush as our lips press, like a cup overflowing, pouring onto the table. They wash over me, threatening to drown me.

She was holding herself back, but no longer.

All of the tension in her body releases when we touch.

More, she begs, *more,* as I kiss her.

I move over her, and her teeth scrape my bottom lip, tugging it down and sending a thrill of pleasure through my spine. She's growing more confident with each second. She releases a small whimper of pleasure and squirms underneath me. Her hands roam my body, like she's exploring, too, reading me like she can braille, cuneiform, carved graffiti in Pompeii. Her nails draw lines across my skin.

She pushes me backward into the cushions, dragging her tongue across my jaw, my throat, tasting my skin as her fingers undo my buttons. It's so good.

Her thoughts in her own voice ring out, clear as day. *Yes. Yes. Atticus. Yes. More.*

I respond to her touch, arching into her when her warm fingers wrap around me. It's like she's the one who can read minds; she knows exactly where to touch, where to stroke, how to make me shiver. My hand cups her breast and squeezes it. I kiss her so tenderly. I don't want her to stop. And God help me, I'm ready to explode.

And then I think about Dorian . . . His name bolts through my mind so fast, I actually gasp.

"No," I say. "No." I push her away, pulling her hands off my groin. I can't do this.

Raven's eyes are cloudy, dazed, and she stares at me. "No?"

Dorian loves her. This is all wrong. If I let this go on any longer, it would destroy him. How could I ever do that to him? To us?

I shake my head, zip, and button. "I should go."

13 Raven

Virtus tentamine gaudet.
(Courage rejoices in challenges.)
–Latin proverb

As I shelve another book at the Rosette, sliding it into the gap between two faded leather tomes, I tremble with the memory of Atticus's lips on mine, kissing me, his warm hands on my back as my hand slipped into his pants. I'm dizzy, as if the wine is still flowing in my veins, Atticus's lips gliding over mine, the two of us a mess of entangled limbs. But then he pushed me away. Went to his bedroom and slammed the door.

I'd wanted to blame the wine, to say it was a mistake, and salvage what remained between us, but it would have been a lie. A lie to save our friendship, but a lie all the same. Then this morning, when I finally rallied to talk to him, he had gone to work before I even woke up. He obviously hates me. What now? And what about Dorian? What would he say if I told him? Would Atticus tell him? All I have now is my own shame and hours of silent work in the library feeling sorry for myself.

"Hey, Raven." Aspen's friendly voice cuts through my thoughts like a silver blade. I startle, turning on him, and Aspen holds up his hands. "Whoa, sorry. I didn't mean to scare you."

I laugh, knowing I must look silly, jumping for no reason, my heart thumping like a fist against my chest. "It's okay," I say, a little breathless. "I didn't hear you."

"Apologies," he says, glancing at the stack of books that still needs to be shelved. "Do you need any help?" He appears concerned.

"No, I'm okay. Thank you, though."

"Anytime," he says, his gaze tender and warm. I'm reminded of the way Atticus looked at me last night. Before he stopped what he'd started. Ugh.

"I actually wanted to ask you something," I say.

The way Aspen's face lights up with expectation makes me rush to say, "Do you know where I can find any information about a former student named Adelina? Could be from a long time ago."

That wasn't the question he wanted me to ask, and he tries to hide his disappointment with a curious tilt of his head. "Adelina Ward?"

My heart hammers. I never doubted Dorian's vision, but now it feels real. "Yeah, maybe! Do you know about her?"

"I remember seeing the name way back when I was starting out here and we were collating some old records. I think she came from some big donor family. Why do you ask?"

I can't let him know about Dorian, so I lie. I'm doing that a lot lately. "A student was asking at the circulation desk. I think for a family tree project or something."

Aspen seems to buy the lie. "Well, don't let me stop you. I may be well-versed in the archive, but I'm not all-knowing. Maybe try the alumni records, see if you can find her there."

"I'll do that. Thanks," I say, hoping he'll depart, but he doesn't budge.

Aspen only smiles, then he steps in closer to me. He glances around, checking if anyone is nearby. "You know, I had a really nice time with you the other night," he says, his voice barely a whisper.

Heat rushes to my cheeks. Here's this guy who actually likes me, who's showing genuine interest in me, and all I can think about is Atticus—someone I can't be with. What is wrong with me?

When I don't reply immediately, Aspen continues awkwardly, his voice cracking. "And I really thought about what you said, about the protesters and doing the right thing in the face of injustice."

"Yeah?" I say.

"Sure," he says. "You're right, I was being defeatist."

"Glad to hear that." I'm happy to have the subject changed. I know Aspen means well, and I feel like I'm cruel for using him. He left his key chain on the desk this morning, and I slipped the stolen key back into place easily. Will I ruin the one good thing I have left?

"I care," he says, "so of course I listen." He looks at me bashfully, his brow furrowed. "Listen, before I get back to work, I was wondering if you wanted to come to a party with me."

"A party?" It hadn't occurred to me that we'd hang out a second time.

"It's nothing formal. You can invite some friends if you want. It's a Halloween party thrown by St. Adolphus Hall."

"What's that?"

"Sort of a secret society. Like Skull and Bones at Yale or the Sphinx at Dartmouth. I know it sounds snotty, but we do know how to have a good time."

"Am I allowed?" I ask. "I'm not a student."

"I'm a member. It's just a party, and you're my guest. I want you to be there. All you need is the password." He draws an X in the air with his finger. It lingers, glowing like embers from a long-dead fire. "*Omnes una manet nox.* 'One night–'"

"'Awaits everyone,'" I finish for him, knowing the phrase without needing my magic. "Horace the poet."

He raises an impressed eyebrow and laughs. "Of course you'd know. You're incredible. So is that a yes?"

I chew on my lip, debating. I don't want to lead him on too much, but . . . what's the harm? Atticus and Dorian would die to go, and we *are* here to learn and to experience all that Sibylline has to offer. I'd be selfish not to invite them to come with me.

"Yeah," I say. "I'm happy to go . . . with you."

Aspen grins for an instant, then he catches himself, as if embarrassed to show his emotions. "Awesome. I mean, good. I can't wait. Oh, and it's a masquerade, masks required, so be prepared. Come dressed for the Carnevale."

"Got it." My parents used to go to Save Venice parties all the time.

Humming quietly, Aspen leaves, but not without looking over his shoulder at me as he goes. One last glance.

I finish shelving the books on my cart, then make my way to the catalog room. It's almost empty. My Mary Janes click noisily on the marble floor, echoing as I walk down rows of cabinets that stretch ten feet overhead. The white ceilings glow orange in the soft candlelight of the chandeliers, and the cabinets are made of polished oak stained dark with weathered brass plates attached to every drawer, the knobs sagging with age, the wood worn smooth by human hands. There are thousands of drawers, and I guess it'll take some time finding Adelina's alumni record, but my work is done and I am mostly alone. There's only one other person in the room, another archivist, standing atop a rickety stepladder, a drawer pulled out, flipping through the yellowed cards nestled inside it.

I search for any record that includes the last name Ward, or Warde, or any other phonetic variation, but come up short. I can't find any proof that someone named Adelina Ward went to Sibylline.

Weird. Don't big donors love having their names plastered everywhere they send money to? I'm left wondering if this is just a dead end, but then I think maybe I'm looking in the wrong place. What about student papers?

The student archive is a slightly less formal space than the primary atrium. It's small compared to the main archive, with only a few cabinets full of notable student papers. Sibylline loves to keep records of its students' work. And, just like I hoped, I find a listing for an undergraduate thesis by a student named A. L. Ward. It's a treatise published in 1924. The card claims it is a paper outlining the summoning of matter from chaos. This is her. It has to be.

I check the shelves to read her completed treatise but come up empty-handed. I search the surrounding shelves and double-check, just to be sure I didn't miss it.

Nothing.

It seems like the paper no longer exists.

I make my way back to the circulation desk to see if I can track down the paper in some other way, but I find its section of the library is roped off. Inside the roped area, an instructor speaks in hushed tones, conducting what appears to be a class involving several of the library's texts. The books are chained to heavy wooden desks, preventing them from wandering, like Aspen told me they could. The teacher is lecturing in the middle of the library instead of some classroom. It's amazing, the lengths this school will go to in order to keep the knowledge in their books locked tight and secure.

"Enunciation is key," the teacher says, walking down the row of seated students. "Any slight variation in accent or intonation can lead to improper results."

I wonder, once more, if I might have made some small error in either one when I called the lightning, mispronouncing a word or maybe even just a syllable. Maybe then I wouldn't have made such a mess. I don't know, and hearing the professor talk about the very subject that concerns me makes me more jealous of the students than ever.

I wish I could try it again. My fingers itch to do it. I know I hurt Dorian, but I want to make fire again. I want to be better. I *know* I can be better. Sure, I might make little mistakes along the way, but it's what we came here for, isn't it? To use our power?

A small voice in the back of my mind wonders if that's true. Is setting one of your best friends on fire a "little mistake"? But I don't listen to it.

I have power, and I can prove it. I need to.

Instead of going back to my desk, like I should, I stop and listen, watching as the students practice repetition and spell construction. I open my journal, thinking I might jot down a few notes, but a gust of wind kicks up, fluttering the book's pages. I slap my hand down to stop it, before realizing how strange that is. Wind indoors?

I glance toward the class. A gentle breeze ruffles everyone's hair and clothing. At the center of it all, a girl leans over her own book, chanting an incantation. All at once, I understand the words. I know she's speaking in Mesopotamian, and I translate in my head.

"–call forth thee, in thy name, to manifest, in form, and freedom–"

"An evocation." I realize the words and phrasing are similar to the spells I saw in the book I accidentally burned. From what I can gather, she's evoking a wind spirit, bringing it into this realm. I called energy to light the candle, but she appears to be summoning a living thing, a magical creature. I watch, amazed, just to see it happen, magic wielded by language. There is something beautiful about it.

The student's voice is soft at first, measured and controlled. Her brow knits with focus, her hands holding the pages of the book down against the rising wind. The class watches with languid interest, but the professor is pleased.

"Well done," she says, clapping her hands, signaling for the student to conclude the spell. "You may dismiss the elemental spirit."

"I *am* done," says the girl. She's leaning over the book, her voice trembling. Sweat blooms on her brow, and she grimaces, stumbling over the words as she repeats them.

"Ms. Claremont," the professor says sternly. "Conclude the spell."

The girl shakes her head. She can't, and worse yet, she's losing control of the spell.

She stutters, repeating the words over and over, but the elemental does not vanish. Instead, the wind thickens, gathering dust, dimming the light in the room. A low and rumbling sound tears through the room, making the very floor shake. Students sit up in their chairs, watching with growing apprehension. They glance at one another, unsure about what to do.

"Ms. Claremont!" The professor rushes forward and grabs the book, reading the spell aloud in the ancient language: "'In thy name, thou art free from this summons.'"

The wind grows stronger. It blows books off the shelves. Students shield their eyes. Some even scream.

The professor mistranslated, used the wrong form of the word *summons*, but only I seem to know this.

Overhead, a great black cloud appears, growing darker and thicker with each second, looking like something over a volcano. Puffy black clouds roll up to the ceiling, choking the air with ash and sulfur, and block out the light from the stained-glass window. People are starting to panic.

I gag on the smell, and tears blur my eyes, but I just manage to see a shape inside the cloud—bright orange, like a moving flame. It almost hurts to look at it straight on, but I make out its glowing white eyes and its bright white mouth. Lightning crackles through the cloud. You can't mistake it for anything else. It's the elemental spirit the professor mentioned. And it's angry.

The fire elemental rages, toppling books from shelves, knocking over chairs and upending tables. Fire burns the pages, turning them to dust in an instant. Students flee as the sulfuric cloud washes over them, whipping through the tall stacks, pulling books from the shelves. Papers scatter, ink spills, crystal balls crack on the marble floor. Every candle burns even brighter as flames fill the room.

At first I think it's a fire alarm, but it's too high, too long, too loud. Then the great stained-glass window of the Rosette shatters, a thousand shards of glass falling to the floor and melting into a puddle.

The fire demon is going to burn everything to the ground.

I run toward the chaos.

Everyone else is fleeing. Panicking.

Students knock into me in a desperate attempt to escape, but I push through. Tears fill my eyes as ash threatens to blind me. The heat stings my skin.

I lift the abandoned book from the floor and find the evocation. The student mispronounced the words, and the teacher mistranslated. But the words come to me easily.

A simple revocation isn't enough, though. The book says I need to reverse the spell.

Without thinking, without questioning, I act. "*Erehem oc lewton erauoy!*" I recite the spell backward, my own words sounding foreign on my tongue. This is a language of undoing, and I'm forced to shout it over the howling inferno. The sulfur burns my eyes, but I need them to read, to keep the words of this ancient and dead language flowing out of me, so I push aside the tears and wait for the spell to do its work.

I don't honestly know what will happen. The fire will either die or consume me.

It's too late to run; the burning vortex swirls about me, rising up, and for a moment, I fear I'll be lifted off my feet and that'll be the end of me. I shudder as my toes leave the floor only to be set back down on it once again. I fall to my knees, worried the flames will overwhelm me, but they don't. The fire no longer rages.

It's working. It's actually working.

My words harness the flame, but it does not vanish, so I say the words again: "*Erehem oc lewton erauoy!*"

For an instant, I lock eyes with the terrible creature. Its irate gaze seems to scorch right through me. Then, like being sucked into a vacuum, the fire elemental shrinks into nothingness, leaving only a shower of sparks. Scattered papers settle around me, and the chandeliers stop swinging from their chains. Soon, the only sound is the gentle *drip-drip-drip* of spilled ink leaking to the floor. Smoke still chokes the room.

I lower my hand, realizing what just happened. I read a spell from a grimoire. I did it! Magic! I'm filled with pride.

There's a noise from behind, and I turn, seeing Aspen stepping out from behind the shelter of the stacks. His clothes are ruffled, his hair a mess, his mouth gaping. His skin is smeared with ash. His eyes go to the book in my hand, and then to me, looking like he's seeing a ghost.

"You banished it?" he asks. "All on your own?"

I'm out of breath. I can only nod.

"Wow," he says. "That's incredible."

In the chaos, the professor comes upon us. "Aspen! Oh, thank goodness. Did you get rid of the spirit?"

He's about to explain when I interject. "Yes! He did! He was amazing!"

Aspen shoots me a confused look, but I shake my head, and he keeps his mouth shut. Our little white lie.

14
ATTICUS

Silence is safe.
—*Wilkie Collins,* The Woman in White

TODAY CALLS FOR pizza. Lots of pizza.

When Dorian and I heard about what happened at the Rosette—word spreads fast on campus—we were sick with worry for Raven and rushed to find her. We found her safe and sound outside the library, where a group of advanced wizards were reassembling the broken stained-glass window, the tiny fragments sparkling like glitter as they floated up into the air. Good as new.

We spend the rest of the day at my place, sprawled on the window seat, gorging on extra-large pepperoni pizzas, just like old times. A fire demon can set a friendship back to rights, who knew. Raven explained what happened, the evidence—ash and the smell of sulfur—still on her clothes.

"I found out more about your mystery woman, too," Raven says to Dorian. His eyes widen, and he freezes, a slice raised to his lips. "Her name was Adelina Ward."

"Ward," he repeats.

"Aspen mentioned she was the daughter of some rich family who donated to the school, but I don't know anything more than that. The Rosette doesn't have any more info."

"How'd Aspen know about her, then?"

Raven shrugs. "He's good with the archive. He remembered seeing her name. But it seems like her files are missing now. He invited us to St. Ad's Halloween party, by the way."

I nearly fall out of my seat. "You mean St. Adolphus Hall? The secret society?"

Raven smiles at me curiously. "Yeah, you've heard of it?"

"Professor White warned me that they were trouble, but I'm dying to know what those rich kids get up to."

"So you're coming? Both of you?"

"Aspen will be there?" Dorian asks. He can't hide the edge in his voice, no matter how casual he tries to be. I don't have to be able to read his mood to know that.

"He's my . . . date." She tiptoes around the word as she averts her gaze, raising it slightly to look at me, gauging my reaction. I'm not sure how I feel. She's moved on. I can't be surprised. I shouldn't be. What went down between us, on this very window seat . . . Maybe it's best we don't mention it again. Pretend like it never happened.

"Sure," Dorian says after a long moment, watching me. "We'll come."

Raven beams. "Oh, and it's a masquerade," she says. "Atticus, think you can paint us some masks?"

Dorian is still staring at me, unaware of the vast sea of unsayable things between me and Raven. When he looks at her, his eyes soften. We're almost back to normal. Almost.

"Sounds fun," I say, and pop a rogue pepperoni in my mouth. "Can't wait."

Professor White clicks her tongue. "Shame," she says.

"What?" I ask, momentarily confused as I look up from her schematics.

For a fleeting, heart-stopping second, I thought she was talking about me, but Professor White is frowning at the collapsed scaffolding inside Arches. "It seems that our efforts are stymied once again."

Right. Back to work.

Apparently during the night, more of the scaffolding fell. No one knows how it happened, but Professor White suspects shoddy craftsmanship this time, although she is still looking for the saboteur on her team. Now she shakes her head, as if she's disappointed in the scaffolding. "I'll have to complain to Warden Stone about the people he hired. If he's not taking the restoration seriously, then I'm not sure why I'm here."

She runs a frustrated hand through her hair and whips the pencil out from it. Over her shoulder is a single-strap musette made of faded brown leather. She opens the flap, retrieving a notepad. I spy a black book in the bag made of darkened leather, with gold foil glinting on the spine.

"What book is that?" I ask.

Professor White is so busy writing in her notebook, she starts as if she's forgotten I was here. "What? Oh, this? It's an old reference text. I found it in the archive." She turns her attention back to her notes, writing and speaking at the same time. "Arches was originally built to house a new department of magic dedicated to the art of creation. But it was never used. It's been largely empty since. I'm pulling every book I can find on the subject." She sighs as if burdened by a great weight. "Bindings were once common practice in architecture. They attached certain elemental forces to the structures. Arches contains some unique bindings related to living things, creatures from other planes, demons and such . . ."

I'd felt those spirits when I first visited the site, but I had no idea how they were used to build Arches. "May I take a look?" I ask, hopeful. "Maybe I can research the subject for you."

"Of course, I will lend it to you when I am done. Although be careful, the spells contained in this book are quite powerful. Using them without the proper training can be dangerous. Sometimes"—she glances in the direction of the Rosette—"magic is dangerous even in the hands of our staff."

Raven had told us how the lesson had gone wrong. The professor's incompetence led to student injuries and the building being damaged, but she didn't get fired. Average teachers would kill for that kind of job security, I bet.

"Now," Professor White says, straightening herself. "Shall we inspect the damage?"

She climbs the scaffolding, and I follow, the ramp wavering beneath me. It creaks and groans, and I throw my hands out to steady myself. I'm worried about the soundness of the structure, but Professor White doesn't seem bothered at all. Five floors of scaffolding have collapsed into a heap of twisted metal and wood, and yet she strides onward confidently.

"We'll have to rebuild everything," she says, marching ahead. "Have the workers install the beams into the putlog holes *properly* this time."

"You think they weren't installed properly?" I ask. The putlog holes are little slots in the wall where the building supports the scaffold.

"Of course not. I'm under a tight deadline, and I know the assembly crew had only a day to get it done. Warden Stone trimmed the budget, forcing us to accelerate the timetable. If he didn't have the final say in my tenure, I'd give him a piece of my mind."

I allow myself to smile, since her back is to me. She's fighting the bureaucracy, one scaffolding at a time.

“I can oversee the repairs, if you’d like,” I say. “I’ve had experience with these kinds of things.”

Professor White looks me up and down. “Sounds like a plan. Follow along.” At the top of the remaining scaffolding, we survey the work. She’s prattling about how much this will set us back when I notice something peculiar about one of the putlog holes. I kneel close to the hole, letting her ramble while I inspect it. My skin goes cold when I realize what’s wrong.

“Um, Professor White?” I ask.

She spins around, her mouth half-open as if she’s about to make another point, when she sees what I’m looking at. “My goodness!”

The hole where the beam sits is crumbling, the stone turning to sand.

“This wasn’t an issue with the scaffolding,” I say.

“No, it’s the building itself,” she says thoughtfully. “We need to work faster.”

15
ATTICUS

Our true passions are selfish.
—*Stendhal,* The Red and the Black

I FIND RAVEN hunched over the writing desk at the apartment. It's been a week since Professor White discovered that the building was crumbling from the inside. We've been working day and night on the problem, and I've barely had time to sleep, let alone talk to my friend. Raven has one knee drawn up to her chest, her toes curled over the seat of the chair, the other knee bouncing nervously as she writes. She doesn't hear me come in. It's the first time we've been alone together in the living room since we messed around. I hesitate, not sure how to start. In the soft lamplight, a small halo frames the top of her head, and when she tips it to the side, her hair shifts to one shoulder. Something about seeing Raven in a natural state, unfiltered, makes my chest hurt. My heart can't handle everything that's been thrown its way recently. When I shut the door behind me, she practically jumps.

"Sorry," I say.

"I wasn't expecting you." She takes a breath and settles back into her chair. Her eyes narrow; her shoulders tense.

"You seemed busy. Who are you writing to?" I ask.

"My parents. It's nothing." She hastily finishes up her work, folding the letter into thirds and stuffing it into an envelope.

She's nervous.

We've been missing each other even though we both live here. After our trio—the full Oneiric Society—bonded over Raven surviving the Rosette explosion, it felt like we were back to normal. But I'm still a little wary. The past few days, she's always busy, and now it's like there's a wall of TV static between us, electric, tangible. And I'm afraid if I poke it, I'll get shocked. So I don't pry.

"Are you still up for the party tonight? St. Ad's? Aspen?" I ask instead of the questions that are really on my mind: *Do you hate me? Are we good? Are we still friends?*

Raven nods. She notices that I'm holding a box. "What's that?"

"Special delivery," I say. "I gave Dorian his when I ran into him leaving Old Bones."

"Our masks?" she asks.

"As Oscar Wilde once said, 'Give him a mask, and he will tell you the truth.'"

Raven doesn't react like I hoped she would, with barely a smile. It stings a little.

She comes over to the table where I set the package down. It's the size of a shoebox, the contents neatly wrapped in red tissue paper.

"Oh, will you look at that," Raven says as I pull the wrappings away.

"Plaster and papier-mâché, just like the artisans in Venice," I say. "It took me ages to smooth everything out, but I think they came out beautifully. Yours is a full mask in the volto style." I hand it to her. The plaster face is pale with red lips and touches of gold on the cheeks, courtly and striking, just like she is. I wanted to capture her as best I could.

Mine, I painted black and gold with a curling filament sculpted around the eyes and lips. It will stand out spectacularly with the black robe I found at a thrift store.

"You truly outdid yourself," Raven says.

I press the mask to my face and try to read Raven's expression. Her eyes are bright with excitement as she puts on her own mask and strikes a little pose.

"How do I look?" she asks.

I want to say she is beautiful, that I've always found her beautiful, and that I will always love her but can't be her lover, but the words get stuck halfway down. I swallow thickly and manage to say, "Great."

WHEN THE HOUR arrives and it's time for the party, we walk side by side to the old cemetery, passing Arches and all of its mysteries. A yellow plastic tape prevents anyone from going too close. I make sure we keep our distance, but I'm nervous and my senses play tricks on me. As we pass, I think I hear a screaming howl coming from inside. I stop walking.

"Did you do that?" I ask Raven.

"Do what?"

"Make that noise."

"Um, no," she says, furrowing her brow curiously. "Freaky."

I stare at Arches, scanning for movement, and hold my breath, listening.

There's only the quiet sounds of the campus and the soft rustling of leaves, and a part of me thinks I must be imagining things. It was probably just the wind slicing through the tower. There's no one in Arches; no lights illuminate the interior, just as it should be.

The tower is empty, but I'm left with a troubled feeling in my gut. This has been happening to me more and more. I'm hearing things that don't seem to be there.

Raven doesn't seem bothered, or maybe she's just lost in her own thoughts.

Campus is mostly empty, and there's a crispness that makes it feel as if the air could bite you. The breeze nips at our cheeks and sends brown leaves skittering like rodents across the cobblestones. The clouds passing overhead blot out the moonlight, and the air grows colder. I lift my shoulders toward my ears, wishing I'd worn something a little warmer. "I hope the party isn't outside." This black robe is thin cotton. I should have tried to find a wool cloak.

"I wouldn't worry. If it is, this is a school of magic–right?" There's a twinkle in Raven's eye. That's the Raven I know. Maybe she's forgiven me fully.

"Right, magic. I'm sure everything'll be perfect. We're just slipping into a party with all of the kids who did the one thing we couldn't do–they were admitted to Sibylline."

"Right, those wizards." She snorts. "Not one of them could banish that fire demon . . ." She trails off, and the aura around her head glows an angry red.

We turn the corner and stumble upon the old cemetery.

An iron gate made of angel wings sits propped open in the high stone wall, the bars rusted, the paint peeling. Most of the headstones are weathered and cracked, covered in ivy, the names having faded with time. We take a winding dirt trail toward the very center of the cemetery, where a stone cottage sits atop a hill. Its windows glow warmly from within; the party has already started. I spot that familiar symbol, the eye and the pentagram, that I noticed on my first day of work. It adorns the cottage roof and several of the nearby tombstones.

Waiting for us beneath the drooping branches of a leafless tree, Dorian stands dressed in a robe and holding his own Venetian mask in his gloved hand. He smiles when he sees us, his teeth glinting in the moonlight. I want them to bite me. He waves at us with his mask, one that will cover half his face in swirls of red and gold.

"The artist himself," he says, making me blush.

"You like it?" I ask.

"It's perfect." Dorian's eyes stay on me, lingering maybe a little too long.

Raven gives me a sidelong glance, then clears her throat. "Right," she says, slipping her mask over her face and pulling up her hood. "Shall we?" Raven steps up to the door and knocks. A slat in the aging wood slides open, and a pair of dark eyes peer out.

"Speak the password," says the person on the other side. We see only her lips, painted red and luscious.

Raven traces an X through the air as she says, *"Omnes una manet nox."*

Sparks trail after her finger.

The slot slides closed and the door flies open, the music booming.

Inside, I'm overwhelmed with noise, both auditory and psychic. The party is staged inside a vast empty sepulcher. Marble busts line the walls, and a single floating chandelier flashes with multicolored lights. It's the only source of illumination and turns the space into a dizzying whirl of rainbow and shadow. The room is packed, everyone gathering around a tall and intimidating figure, a man in a glittering jacket and black face mask. He yells something unintelligible into a microphone. The music thumps, surrounding me in sound, but there are no speakers in the room. Then I realize the busts that line the tomb are all singing, acting like magical speakers. With a wave of his hand, the figure in the glittering jacket controls the music, raising the volume.

Students float through the room, laughing and talking. Their emotions wash over me like a great ocean wave, and it makes my world spin. Raven and Dorian brighten visibly, their spirits lifted as they take in the scene. Everyone's dancing. People cheer and holler, screaming for more as the bass booms.

I want to be happy. I really need to enjoy tonight. Everything has been so tense. Raven, the Rosette, work, Dorian, desire. I need to dance, and drink, and forget. But I can't.

I'm starting to regret ever coming to the party. I didn't think it'd be this bad. The heightened emotion of the room is nauseating. There's too many things happening at once, too many voices, too many feelings. I squeeze my eyes shut and think about the digits of pi: *three-point-one-four-one-five-nine . . .*

I want my thoughts to be my own, but my internal voice is pushed out by someone wondering if there's Elysian mead in the punch bowl. I gather it's some sort of drink brewed magically, but the voice vanishes before I can hear the rest, replaced by some girl wondering if she's going to get lucky tonight.

Half a dozen voices hit me at the same time: *I . . . bathroom—beautiful night—sweating so much in this mask—oh my God, he's so funny! . . . Who's that golden god, is he in Sorcery 101? No, I think he works here. At Old Bones. Always wears gloves.*

"Raven!" A voice cuts through the cacophony, and a guy—Aspen, I assume—appears at Raven's side, beaming, with a red, possibly Venetian, mask in hand. He lights up, literally—his aura glows when he sees her. Raven's right, he's like a Labrador as a person. "You made it," he says, yelling over the music, which has, once again, increased in volume.

Raven doffs her mask, but when she smiles, it doesn't reach her eyes. "Hey, Aspen! These are my friends Dorian and Atticus."

Aspen shakes Dorian's gloved hand, but I only manage to

wave. I'd remove my mask, but my hands are shaking too much, and I worry I'd drop it. I'm a mess. My stomach is tied in knots, and there's a tense feeling climbing up my throat. I'm going to puke. I know it. My chest tightens, stomach convulsing.

"It's nice meeting you guys," Aspen says to Dorian and me, then turns to Raven and extends an elbow. "Come on. I want to introduce you to some people."

Raven offers us a fleeting look, but I manage to give her a thumbs-up. Donning her mask again, she lets Aspen escort her deeper into the party.

"You look amazing," I hear Aspen say to her, his voice fading into the music.

"He seems nice," says Dorian flatly, but I'm not really paying attention.

I spin around, searching for somewhere quiet. I don't even bother to tell Dorian where I'm going. I stumble into the kitchen, but it's worse in there. They're doing some kind of drinking game with magic, levitating shots of vodka and dropping them into people's mouths. The voices in my head are drunk and loud. I wave my hand through the air, trying to bat them away, but I can't. I find a stairway and rush up the steps, scaling them two at a time. I stumble down the upstairs hall, searching. For what I don't know. I can't breathe. This mask is suffocating me. The voices threaten to drown me in the cacophony.

At the end of the hall, I find an empty room. I throw the door open, whip off the mask, and take a deep, relieved breath. No more voices, no more images.

It's quieter here, and I feel like myself again.

"Finch?"

I turn to see Dorian peeking into the room, his brow knitted with concern. He's taken off his mask and lowered his hood.

“You all right?” he asks. “You rushed off.”

“I just needed a minute. I got overwhelmed, that’s all.”

“Anything I can do to help? Do you want to leave?” he asks.

Massaging my throbbing temples, I say, “No, I’m doing better now. Crowds are always difficult. Parties are almost impossible. I should have known better. I ought to have thought of this in advance or maybe just prepared myself. Like I waded into a vast ocean when I ought to have been just dipping my toe.”

It’s a sloppy metaphor, but I’m still feeling flushed, my thoughts jumbled. I can still hear the thumping music of the party, but it feels less violent, less invasive now that Dorian is here. He shuts the door, muffling the noise. Then something catches his eye, and he crosses the room to stand before several easels with half-finished paintings. “This must be an art studio,” he says. “You always seem to find your way to them.”

“Maybe it’s another one of my gifts,” I joke. “Don’t let me keep you. If you want to go back to the party, I don’t mind.”

“It’s not as fun if you’re not there,” he says, smiling, finding the most casual way to make my insides turn to jelly. “Besides, with Raven being Aspen’s date, I felt awkward being alone.”

He’s still looking at the paintings, and I can’t stop watching him. We used to go to art galleries together. Rather, *I* used to go to art galleries, and Dorian *just happened to be* working there. I would bring him food, and he’d take a break from his docent duties to walk around the gallery with me, and we’d look at all of the exhibits. Most of the time, though, I would be looking at Dorian instead. Looking at him, just being with him, really, helps calm me down. He’s a stabilizing presence.

My eyes follow the angular slope of his nose, the cut of his jaw, the way his hair drapes just against his eyebrow. He brushes it back, unaware of my gaze, then points to a painting on the wall.

"Hey, look," he says. "Doesn't this look like the reading room in the Rosette?"

I crane my neck to look. "Yeah, I think so." I'm reminded of the night we snuck into the Eastern Archive. How close he'd been when we hid from Warden Stone. I think often about that moment and what might have happened if we'd been alone and Warden Stone hadn't dropped the book, startling Dorian. I've even pictured it in my head, imagining in elaborate detail everything he might have done to me, everything I wanted him to do.

"It's a Hubert," he says.

"Is it?" I ask. I was so distracted by him, I didn't even notice.

I lean in and get a better look. He's right, the style matches perfectly. Dorian would know, of course—he's the expert—but this painting is different, outside of his usual subjects. "Why would he have painted the Rosette?"

Dorian doesn't answer. He's transfixed by the painting. The stained-glass eye on the Rosette is its focal point, glowing with an internal light that looks as natural as seeing it in person. The magic of the portrait is subtle, but once you see it, you can't look away.

"Something moved," Dorian says.

"It's a Hubert. Of course something moved."

Dorian frowns as he stares at the painting. "No, it was, like, a shadow or something . . . there." He places his gloved finger on the canvas, right on the eaves of the cathedral-like structure.

"It can't be real, can it?" I ask. My question goes unanswered. Dorian seems hesitant to investigate.

I don't see anything, though. It must have been a blink-and-you-miss-it detail. Dorian doesn't seem to see it again either. After a long moment, he takes a deep breath and turns his gaze to me, his features softened, and then he glances to the door when he hears a burst of laughter coming from outside.

"How are you feeling?" he asks me.

"Better," I say truthfully. He looks pleased, but there's something else in his face. His aura is a somber color. "You?"

He sighs, as if he knows that I know, and bites his lower lip before admitting, "You know, it's funny. I thought I'd enjoy this." He gestures to the party behind the closed door. "Instead, I just feel so out of place here."

"How so?"

"Wearing this mask . . . I thought I'd finally feel like one of them." He runs his hand through his hair again and glances to the door, laughter drifting through the cracks. "But we're just pretending, we're frauds. Sometimes I don't even know what we're doing here." He sighs as he gets to what's *really* bothering him. "It's strange seeing Raven with a date."

"Yeah, Aspen. I'm not really sure how she feels about him," I tell him. "I know he's a third-year. But he does have a silly name. Like a ski resort."

"So—he's an apprentice wizard," he says bitterly. His aura is a worrisome red, so similar to Raven's.

"You're a thousand times more of a wizard than he will ever be," I say.

"It doesn't matter," he sighs. "I'm not good enough for her. I never have been."

I shake my head. "Dorian. That is so far from true."

Dorian almost laughs, a self-pitying kind of chuckle. "I mean, I can't even touch her, can't hold her, not without . . ." He trails off, flexing his gloved hand. "And now she's with some guy named Vail."

"Aspen," I correct him.

"Yeah, Mr. Telluride." He snorts.

"Monsieur Beaver Creek," I say.

"Jackson Asshole." He laughs.

Then we're both laughing.

He drags his hand through his hair again, an endearing nervous habit. "I don't want to be jealous, but I can't help it."

"For what it's worth, I don't think she cares about Aspen." I try not to giggle. "You know she's always preferred Deer Valley."

Dorian swallows, nodding as his aura turns pink, indicating embarrassment, perhaps. I'm never certain.

"Maybe you just need practice," I say, trying to be helpful. "Right now, you don't know what will happen if you touch someone, but maybe, with some experience, you can learn to control it. Perhaps it's time to stop letting *it* control you."

He runs his hand through his hair again, and it makes me crazy with desire. *I* want to do that to his hair. And I wish he would just give up on Raven, since I'm right here.

"Why don't you just try?" I ask, offering my open palm. "When's the last time someone held your hand, not just your glove?"

A twitch shivers through Dorian's lips, and he tries to hide it with a smile. "You really want to?" he asks.

Yes, yes, yes, I think. "Why not?" I say.

"Because it's . . . Are you sure?" he asks.

"Sure as sin."

"If we touch, I'm just worried I won't be able to stop what's happening. I can't seem to end the visions once they start . . ."

"So don't try to stop it. Are you afraid of what you might see in me?" I prompt.

He swallows again. "You aren't worried? You don't care if I know everything?"

"I have nothing to hide. Besides, if it doesn't work, well then . . . there are worse things that can happen." I don't want to hide my feelings for him anymore. I am tired of hiding. I squeeze my hand on his, feeling the warmth of the leather. His fingers squeeze mine, a gentle assurance. Heat rushes to my face. Slowly, I tug on his glove, pinching the tip of it with my fingers. He lets me take it off, and it falls to the floor.

All it takes is a touch. Just one.

His bare hand slides up my arm, slowly at first, and then he's touching my face, touching my cheek with the tips of his fingers, so light it sends goose bumps down my throat. His fingers are warm and soft.

"Okay?" I whisper.

He nods.

So I grab his hand, holding it tight. I guide him, pressing his palm solidly against my cheek, letting his fingers dig into the back of my head. His touch sends ripples through my body. I can't breathe.

He frowns, and I feel it, a tension, a buzzing in the air not unlike the coming of a storm. The air around us is electric. He doesn't say it; he doesn't have to.

I can hear the words pouring out of him. My magic, it's piercing his mind. Instead of simply feeling his emotions, I can hear his thoughts as well. And what does he see? What does he know of mine?

His inner dialogue cuts in and out, but it's his voice. I'd know it anywhere. *His skin is so soft. I wonder what it's like to kiss . . . Kiss . . . Do it . . . Should I?*

He wants to kiss me? My pulse races with excitement. His hand is still on my face. I move closer, and to my relief, he doesn't move away. But the longer he looks at me, the more his aura swirls with pink. Orange and pink like the setting sun, vibrant and demanding to be observed.

He wants me.

His desire is tangible. My heartbeat thrums. This is so new, so exhilarating. He's so close, I don't want to move.

Kiss . . . His mind echoes. *What will happen?*

"You can kiss me if you want to," I tell him.

I sense his fear like it's my own, a flutter of trepidation, but it passes. It's replaced by a burning question. A desire to know.

Slowly, he leans his head down, and he closes his eyes. I tilt my head up, meeting him in the middle. At first the kiss is tentative. His lips brush mine, featherlight, the softest embrace. He pulls back a millimeter, waiting, and I wonder if he saw something. His breath curls around my cheek, and it takes everything in me not to close the gap again.

"Still okay?" I ask.

All he can manage is a nod. He doesn't answer out loud, but I sense it, his nervousness, his anticipation, his desire. It's a jumbled mess, coiling around him like a storm cloud. It was his first kiss. I know it. Alas, it was not mine.

"Do you want to try again?" I ask.

He doesn't answer with words. He doesn't need to. It pours out of him like a dam broken, all of his emotions, his wants and fears, swirling in my thoughts. Then he moves in, pressing his mouth against mine. I melt when we touch, my pulse thumping hard in my ears. I give in and reach up, threading my fingers into his hair as we kiss again. His hair is soft, exactly how I thought it would be. I've wanted this for so long it hardly seems real.

My eyes slide closed, and I swim in the emotions we share.

Tentative but curious, afraid to handle this fragile thing between us.

"You're okay," I say against his lips.

He sighs into the kiss. Our kiss. He's holding me so close, I can finally touch his muscles I've so admired. His arms, his shoulders, his tight Captain America ass. I squeeze it. A small moan escapes me, and his breath hitches at that, but he doesn't stop kissing me. Our mouths open, deepening the kiss, and I shiver beneath his touch. The taste of him makes my head spin, and for a moment, it feels as if I might be dancing.

His desire overwhelms me, and I'm lost in the moment.

Our jumbled thoughts intertwine. He's a searcher, like me; he's trying to find something real to hold on to. He wants so much out of life, and so do I. He yearns for what he cannot have, and he wants things that he's afraid of losing.

I ride his thoughts like ocean waves, letting them move through me.

This is more than just a kiss. It's two minds melding together, two souls touching for one brief moment. My tongue darts out, licking his upper lip, and this time he's the one who moans. It's soft, and it comes from somewhere deep inside his throat, and it makes me so hard.

I don't need magical powers to feel his excitement, too. I'm practically sitting on his lap. I want him so badly that I might risk everything to have him.

Then I hear the words: *But Raven . . .*

He pulls back, and I let him. It's as if all the air has been sucked from my lungs. The unsaid thing hangs between us. Raven. The one person he truly loves.

Fuck.

"Sorry, I–" He starts to say, but I cut him off.

"So did you see anything when you touched me?" I ask, fighting to keep my voice level. This was supposed to be an experiment. That's all. I can pretend that's all it was, but he doesn't answer.

He doesn't need to answer. He's still thinking about Raven.

Just like I was thinking about him when Raven kissed me.

His lips are pursed. Mine are hot. He holds his breath and stares at me, his eyes pinpricks of light. I still feel his emotions, though they're fading now that we're apart, the way we're meant to be. His aura glows orange and pink, just like when he looks at her. And then it's gone.

Our minds are no longer joined.

He takes a step back and lifts the glove from the floor. He tugs it into place, and it's as if he's placed a wall between us.

"We're cool, right?" he asks. I can't read him anymore.

It's taking everything in me to keep the tears at bay. I nod. Of course. We'll always be friends. But I gave myself over to him, let him into my head, let him see the deepest parts of me, and still . . . he doesn't want me. I'm practically standing naked in the cold.

The kiss is already a memory when he turns to leave the room.

16
DORIAN

There is no bombast, no similes, flowers, digressions, or unnecessary descriptions. Everything tends directly to the catastrophe.
—Horace Walpole, preface to the first edition, The Castle of Otranto

I RUSH THROUGH the doors of the museum, straightening my hair and readjusting my tie to look somewhat presentable. It's been a week since the Halloween party, and I haven't slept well since. I think of how Atticus's day-old scruff brushed against my skin, his face so different from a girl's, and the way the memories flowed out of him, letting me see his life through his eyes. I became him. I saw his childhood, and his mom, and the drawings he taped on his bedroom walls. I felt eraser dust under his fingers as he sketched a new building's façade, smelled the cinnamon rolls he always ate at the Acroteria, heard the sound of Raven's laughter after he told her a joke. And I saw myself, and how he looks at me, sees me. How much he's wanted me for years. Kissing him unlocked something inside me I never knew was really there. I've cared for Raven for so long, probably before I really even knew what love was, and Atticus was just a friend. But now all I can think about is him. I think about him when I wake up, when I brush my teeth, and on my way to work.

Raven and Atticus.

I'm being pulled in two different directions.

What the hell?

I find Professor Evander in his office, a room full to bursting with souvenirs and knickknacks he's picked up over his travels across the world. He's sitting with one of the other curators, an old man with Coke-bottle glasses and a frizzy white beard. Reams of paper, parchment that's so old it's yellow and cracked, sit in tall stacks. The office, usually pristine, is crowded with boxes haphazardly stacked in every corner of the room.

"There's tardiness and then there's truancy," the professor says gruffly.

"It won't happen again," I say.

"That's what you said yesterday and the day before. Come with a peace offering?"

I'm holding a paper tray from the Acroteria. A to-go latte and four pastries of differing varieties. I set it down on his desk.

"Hm," he says. His mouth is pressed into a thin, flat line. He looks me up and down, as if he's trying to see through me. "At least you knew enough not to arrive empty-handed."

I suppress a smile. I learned that from Atticus, who always takes care of us. "If I'd known you had company, I would have brought more."

The other archivist, whose name escapes me, picks one of the papers up and sniffles as he reads the elegant penmanship. He doesn't even seem to notice the coffee. He's muttering to himself and peering through his glasses as if he's looking into a telescope, lost in the beyond.

"No bother," Professor Evander says. Without getting up from his desk, he points to a large binder situated on one of the guest chairs in the office. "The gala is almost upon us, so it's all hands on deck. There's a list of all of the donors and their addresses. I need you to write and mail thank-you letters to each and every one."

The binder is heavy when I pick it up. There are a ton of names in here. It'll take me ages. I keep the groan to myself. "Can I work on this at home?"

"Of course. I hope your penmanship is as good as these look." He takes a croissant and a sip of his coffee before saying, "Oh, and I need you to gather a collection of admissions essays from famous alums, so you are to go to the Rosette to fetch them."

The Rosette. Raven will be there. I haven't seen her since the party. I've avoided both of them while I try to sort myself out. It's been too long. I miss them. I miss her.

"Be sure that you deliver the essays to me *on time*, by the end of the day," the professor says. "No more distractions."

WITH PROFESSOR EVANDER'S heavy binder tucked beneath my arm, I stride through the doors of the Rosette. Passing beneath the restored stained-glass windows, I make my way past the long rows of oaken tables and carved wooden chairs. Everything is back in its place, every piece of vintage furniture restored. Students and staff move about the library carrying stacks of books or studying at long rows of tables, hunched over candlelit texts. It's as if the disaster never happened. There isn't a single scratch on the floor or a bit of broken glass hiding in some corner. The library is pristine, immaculate in every way, and I find myself feeling envious once again of the students and teachers. Truly, there are marvelous things that can be learned at a place like this, and I still want to know all of them.

I need an archivist to let me into the records room, so I search for Raven, scanning the stacks, walking up and down the long rows. When I come up short, I make my way to the circulation desk, where I find a blond girl twirling a lock of her hair as she stares off into the distance.

"Hi," I say, smiling as the girl's eyes slide to me. "I'm looking for Raven."

"She's not here," she says, inspecting me. She must be wondering how I know Raven's name. "Can I help you? She's with Aspen."

At the mention of his name, a stab of jealousy shoots through me. After I left Atticus in that study, I went looking for Raven—to confess? I don't know. I found her, even though I wished I hadn't. She was making out with Aspen in a corner. Seeing the two of them together like that, I wasn't even shocked, just numb. So I guess they're together now.

I brush it off as best I can. This must be Pippa, the girl that Raven has talked about. "I need to get into the archive," I say. "I have to see some records."

Pippa's nose actually crinkles, as if I'm bothering her by asking. "That's restricted."

I flash her my badge. "It's for Old Bones."

Pippa's eyes linger on it. "Oh," she says. "Sure."

She places a sign at the desk announcing that she'll be back in five minutes, then she turns and heads off toward what I assume is the records room without saying another word. At the door, she hands me a candle before making her way back up the stairs. "Come find me when you need to lock up," she says as she goes.

"Thanks," I say absently, listening as her footsteps fade.

Shrugging off her cool indifference, I drape my coat on the back of a chair at a reading desk and set the mailing binder down before I light every candle I can find in the records room. Some are fitted in lanterns or sconces, and with all of them burning, there is enough light to comfortably read. The candlelight flickers, and the shadows dance across the floor, giving the room a sinister air that seems to press down on me from all sides. Dark shapes move out of the corner of my eye, and the hairs on my arms rise up, even though I know it's only a trick of the light.

Raven told me that the Rosette once served as a cathedral, and remnants of the old days still linger in this room. Here and there, instead of tiles, the floor is made of actual grave markers, large granite slabs with names and dates inscribed into the surface. Out of respect, I do my best not to tread on any headstone. Intellectuals, leaders, even some wardens have been laid to rest here, quiet and peaceful. Once, this was a tomb, I suppose. Now mahogany filing drawers stretch deep into the walls, filled up with old records. I set the candle down on a table and locate the files. It appears the old ones have been collected into leather-bound books with the dates pressed into the spines. Each book is heavy and thick. There are hundreds of pages in each of them and probably a thousand books in the section. Evander didn't give me a list to work off of, and searching for the most exemplary names from Sibylline's alums will take hours.

Without magic, that is . . .

There's no one here to see me use my power, so I slip off my glove and flex my fingers. The cool air kisses my bare skin, and I ready myself for the rush of memories. I walk down the long rows of shelves, running my fingers lightly over the spines until I feel something intense, a kind of spike, a strong emotion that I hope will reveal something of importance lurking inside. I take the book to the table and sit down, tempering the heavy beating of my heart. I breathe deep and focus, then I place my hand on the cover.

Thousands of whispers echo in my head, overlaying each other, revealing doubts, fears, worries, hopes, dreams . . .

Among all of these things, there's one particularly strong memory, and it catches ahold of me, taking control of my thoughts, dragging me down. I'm falling, and when I land, I'm not in the records room anymore. I'm in an oak-paneled rotunda. I recognize it almost immediately as the assessor's area, the place where we applied to Sibylline. A large semicircular table occupies the center of the room, where twelve men are seated. Reflexively, I try to apologize for my sudden intrusion, but my mouth makes no sound. Everyone's eyes are downturned, reviewing papers in front of them. No one looks up at me, as if they don't notice me standing in front of them. I'm struck with a sudden wave of déjà vu. In some ways, this is just like the day I applied, but then I notice the details. Their suits are different, with high-collared shirts and cutaway coats, and their hairstyles are all wrong, parted in the middle and slicked down—old-fashioned even for Sibylline. Most of the men are smoking, but what really gives it away is the Model T trundling down the road. It passes beyond an open window, and that's when I realize: I'm a ghost. A ghost in a memory from the past.

These men are in the middle of an assessment. This must be another test day, and they're going through a list of names to be either approved or denied entry into Sibylline.

One of the men, a stout gentleman with bright red hair, speaks up. He holds a cigarette clamped between his index and middle finger, lazily waving his hand through the air as he talks. "Several confirmed reports indicate this applicant is a natural psychokinetic. He can levitate small objects across the room at will—"

"Denied," interrupts a tall man with a monocle. He walks to the window with his hands clasped behind his back. His three-piece suit is jet-black. A red earring glimmers in his ear.

At first, I think it's Warden Stone. But no. When he turns, it's a different man. He's thin and dour-looking, with slicked-back hair and dark eyes. This must be one of his predecessors.

"His arcane test was off the charts," the man with the cigarette says. "He scored higher than any of the other applicants, Warden Kerrigan."

The warden turns to the rest of the group and repeats, "Denied."

The word is like a door slamming shut. The man with the cigarette makes a note on the page. Stamps it with the Sibylline seal, then signs it. With a flick of his wrist, he whisks the page away, and it evaporates into thin air, to be delivered to its recipient.

"Who else?" the warden asks.

The twelve men rattle off names, the warden shaking his head almost every single time. Until someone mentions a name I recognize.

"Alistair Dorsia. Poor grades, subpar entrance exam—"

A man with a pair of pince-nez glasses says, "But his family has provided several significant gifts to the foundation, as well as privately funding the renovation of the student dormitories."

Another assessor, one with a mustache so large he looks like a walrus, speaks up. "He's exhibited very little magical ability . . . but he *is* the son of one of the founders."

Babbling agreement circles the room.

Dorsia Hall must have been named after his family.

The warden nods. "Perhaps that's safer," he says. "After all that's happened, we very well can't have another incident, can we? The *chaos* that unfolded . . . We will not risk it. Never again. Approved."

The man with the cigarette stamps and signs the parchment.

But someone speaks up, a man in a gray suit. "If we keep this up, we will run out of promising applicants. And the school will suffer."

The warden cuts him off. "Sibylline will survive without those with unpredictable natures. Given what happened . . ." His gaze turns somber, then resolute. "The decision is final. I forbid you from speaking of it again."

The man in the gray suit swallows any argument he might have, cowed into silence.

My stomach lurches when the scene fades.

The smell of cigarette smoke still lingers, but the vision is over. I'm back in the records room, and it takes me a moment to reorient myself. I remember to breathe and lift my hand from the book as the warden's words echo in my head.

We can't have another incident, can we?

What incident? What happened?

Part Two

We know what we are, but know not what we may be.

—William Shakespeare, Hamlet

17
ATTICUS

It is one thing to mortify curiosity, another to conquer it.
—*Robert Louis Stevenson,* The Strange Case of Dr. Jekyll and Mr. Hyde

THE BLACK CAT follows me to work again, winding its way down the sidewalk, flitting between my boots and purring. It's been weeks since the Halloween party, and I feel like I've been worked to within an inch of my life by Professor White. We've spent every waking hour tending to Arches, repairing what we can, and trying to find the root of the problem. It's been slow going. Even Professor White seems to be at a loss for what to do. For hours at a time, she paces in her office, talking to herself and writing in her notebooks. Consumed by my work, I haven't seen much of Dorian since the party.

Since that kiss.

His kiss.

Everything I've wanted and everything I'll never have. He wanted and still wants Raven, while I want him, and Raven wants me, and the circle goes around and around without anyone getting what they want. Our dependable trio has splintered. What is it that people say? They don't want to risk any romance for the sake of preserving the friendship? Well, we have risked and lost, it appears. Dorian's at Old Bones all the time, and Raven has been seeing Aspen more and more, often leaving me alone in the apartment. She comes back looking satisfied, even if it's unclear whether she really likes him or is just tired of liking me. I'm happy for her, though—at least she has somebody.

Unlike me. Like this cat, I'm craving attention.

"Are you trying to tell me something?" I ask. "Or are you having fun trying to make me late?" Of course, the cat can't speak, but it hooks its tail around my leg, almost like it understands me. "I have a meeting first thing," I tell it.

The cat winds around my legs, as if pushing me in the opposite direction.

"I have to go," I say. "I promise I'll do whatever you want after I meet with Professor White. She needs me."

The cat lets out a mournful kind of yowl, and it stops in the middle of the sidewalk, watching me go with its bright yellow eyes. "Sorry!" I call again, waving.

I'm busy looking at the cat, and I nearly stumble into Professor White.

"Good morning, Atticus," she says, scanning me up and down. I think that's the first time she's called me by my given name. "Follow along," she says, starting off at a quick pace down the street toward Arches.

"What's the rush?" I ask, but the answer is staring right at me.

Giant cracks weave their way up the exterior walls of the building, splitting and fracturing like lightning. "Oh, fuck," I whisper. "How did it deteriorate so quickly?"

Professor White has no answer. She simply shakes her head, hurrying toward the doors.

The block is fenced off, with security guards at every sidewalk redirecting curious onlookers away from the site. "I fear we don't have much time," says Professor White. She looks a little gray in the face, like she's just seen a ghost, and she clutches her satchel slung over her shoulder, white-knuckled, as if she's bracing for the worst.

"What do we need to do?" I ask.

"I've developed a theory. I believe the errors in the renovation, things like the saw marks you found, interfered with the invocations that bound living spirits to this structure at its creation. I've been reading all about some of the magic that was used at the time." She taps the leather-bound tome that's poking out of her satchel.

"Here's the book I told you about the other day. Please be careful with it," she says as she hands the grimoire to me. I almost say something, but I keep my mouth shut. Am I allowed to have this? I'm so thankful. "Maybe study it and see what you can discern that might be of help. You will need a dictionary to translate."

I already have the world's best dictionary. I can't wait to show Raven. We climb the stairs to Arches, and she pushes open the doors. Inside, there are half a dozen architects from her staff, some standing around a small table, studying drawings, the rest standing in a circle.

"What are they doing?" I ask.

"Taking readings, trying to determine the extent of the damage."

The architects have their eyes closed, so I assume they aren't searching for physical damage to the building. "They're measuring magic, or something like–"

The ground beneath my feet shakes as if a tractor trailer is rolling by, but there's no truck to be seen.

"Yes, something like that," says Professor White as motes of dust fill the air. "I'm afraid the spirits of the natural world bound to this structure are departing it, and I'm trying to get a sense of how many may have been lost." She stares up at the tower, the structure she's committed everything to restoring. All her work for nothing. "I doubt it will last the night. It's only a matter of ti–"

The ground trembles again, and there's a deafening crash. Louder than anything I've ever heard. I stumble, trying not to fall, then plant my feet and wait for the shaking to end. It doesn't stop. Professor White throws out her arms, staring up at the tower in horror.

"Everyone out!" she yells as the trembling intensifies and the floor buckles underneath our feet.

The tower shakes as all the architects hurry to gather their things.

Dust hangs in the air, filling the room with gray clouds that billow downward through the scaffoldings, obscuring my vision. I lose track of Professor White. Through the haze, I catch sight of the others trying to find their own way out.

I spin, searching for the exit. It was behind me, I think, but now I'm not so certain. As the dust thickens, my surroundings become a blur. I turn and stumble into something hard and broad. It's a heavy wooden pole, one of the supports that make up the scaffolding. I grip the wood for support but realize it's moving, shaking; then it splits and I recoil, stumbling backward to avoid the whole thing falling down on me.

The tremors intensify, sending shivers lancing upward through my heels. The tower is going to fall. No, it's already falling, and I'm still inside it.

A muffled scream tears through the air. I'm not alone.

I follow the sound. The haze of dirt and debris is so thick, I can barely see my hand in front of my face. I cover my mouth to stop myself from choking, but it's too late. The dust is already in my throat and in my nose. My eyes burn, and I squint just to see. Someone else is here. I can't leave without them.

But it's so hazy all around.

I can't see.

I'm trapped.

18 RAVEN

It may be, of course, above all, that what suddenly broke into this gives the previous time a charm of stillness–that hush in which something gathers or crouches. The change was actually like the spring of a beast.

–*Henry James,* The Turn of the Screw

I'M WALKING TO work, Aspen at my side, when the ground begins to shake.

"What's that?" he asks, his brows furrowed. He places a hand on my elbow, protective as always. I lean into his support.

"Don't know." I stare at the trembling cobblestones beneath my feet and know that something is wrong. An earthquake? It's unusual, especially for Vermont.

In the distance, sirens blare.

Screams cut through the air. "Arches is collapsing!"

Aspen and I turn around to look at the tower, which is still standing, but the ground all around us is rumbling, shaking.

And then it happens.

The upper floors crumble like dry sand, brick by brick, everything reduced to dust. Layer by layer, foot by foot, it falls. Arches' finials, columns, spires, tracery, all of it surrenders to the mercy of gravity. The tower crashes downward into a great plume of dust and debris, blocking out the sky with a gray haze that spreads quickly from the site. A wall of dust rushes over the pavement like liquid smoke.

The cloud crashes into us. I barely have time to cover my face as it buries me from head to toe, caking my skin in a second layer of silt so fine it leaches into my pores. The rumbling stops, but my ears are still ringing.

When the dust subsides, we get a view of the destruction. The tower is mostly gone. Where the upper floors once stood there is now a hole in the sky. A gap. A missing limb. All that's left is the jagged lower half, jutting out of the ground like a broken sword.

"Oh my God," Aspen whispers in shock. All I can do is stare at it as, all around me, people are panicking, crying.

Then it hits me.

Arches. Atticus.

He was supposed to be at Arches early this morning, and a thick wad of panic lodges itself in my throat. *No! He can't have been in the tower! He had to have gotten out! I have to see him, I have to be with him. I have to know if he's okay.*

Sirens wail. Red and blue lights flash.

Police. Fire truck. Or an ambulance.

"Atticus!" I break into a run toward the tower.

"What are you doing?" Aspen yells, trying to pull me back.

"My friend was in there!"

I fight my way past police cruisers and fire trucks that crowd the narrow street in front of the rubble and stone that's all that remains of Arches. *Where's Atticus?* My mind is racing. *Where is my friend?* Is he dead? Alive?

I see his supervisor, Professor White, stumbling through the crowd, but no Atticus.

Police push the bystanders away, telling people not to look, but it's too late. I catch sight of it, and shock grips my insides like an icy claw.

"Is that . . . a hand?" Aspen asks.

It's a human hand underneath a pile of stones.

"Is it a student?" a girl in a blue sweater asks.

Oh God, please let it be a student and not Atticus. My thoughts are a jumbled mess, a buzz of bees, growing angrier and more panicked by the second. Why don't our stupid phones work in this place?! I can't call Atticus. I can't call Dorian.

"What were they doing in the tower anyway?" another person asks. I don't know who. The voices are untethered, disembodied.

To the side, a student, one I've seen dozens of times at the library, is talking to the police. His face is swollen with tears as he says, "We were supposed to meet here at midnight, to do the freshman trial, but I fell asleep . . ." He bursts into more tears, unable to finish his sentence.

A group of students is already talking. "One of the freshmen, they're saying."

"The trial to join St. Ad's? Trying to fly?"

"Yeah."

Aspen holds me tight, but I still feel like I'm floating.

"Aspen," I say. I'm dreaming. I have to be.

"I have to do something," he says. "Stay here." He lets me go as he navigates to a policeman.

I can't think, I can't move. I'm transfixed by the sight of the limp hand, a glimmer of something red and shining dripping from a fingertip. Police move onlookers out of the way, to clear the area for the fire trucks. People in yellow coats barrel past me, telling everyone to vacate. I don't move. I can only watch as the firemen retrieve the body; the crowd whispers, a quiet murmur rising up, the bystanders wondering just who it could be.

One of the firemen has ahold of the body and makes his way out of the rubble.

Don't let it be Atticus.

Don't let it be Atticus.

It's not.

Because Atticus is walking out of the fog and the smoke, holding a book. "Raven!" he cries, and we fall into each other's arms. He's alive. He's alive. He's covered in dust from head to toe, and he looks like he just climbed out of hell, but he's alive.

We hold on to each other as the fireman carrying the body walks closer to us. Atticus and I both turn to look and catch a glimpse of the figure's face.

"Pippa," I say.

Time slows down, filtered through fractured moments. Her blond hair is matted with blood. Her eyes are clouded over, sightlessly staring. Her arms hang limp in the fireman's hold. Someone screams. No, I'm the one screaming.

She's dead. She's actually dead. This can't be real. This can't be happening.

Atticus holds me. "Shhhh," he says. "Shhhh."

The fireman lays Pippa's body down on the stairs, where paramedics draw a sheet over her. The police officers try to make the crowd disperse, but none of us move. "There's nothing we can do."

Without thinking, I yell, "You can't just leave her there! You have to help her!"

My words make no sense. I know that, and Atticus keeps trying to soothe me. Taking me by the arm, he leads me away from the body, patting me on the back, doing his best to console me.

People run, both to and from the scene. There's shouting. And crying.

"What was she doing at the tower?" a student asks.

The police won't say, but rumor has it that it was part of a traditional hazing ritual to join St. Adolphus Hall.

"You knew her?" Atticus asks quietly.

I nod. I didn't like Pippa. She wasn't a friend, but she was someone I knew, a face I saw each day, and now she's dead.

"You saw, right?" he asks.

I nod again.

I saw.

There were claw marks on her chest. She was mauled. Ripped apart, as if by an animal. It doesn't make sense. Everyone thought she was crushed by the building. But that's not what happened.

She was dead before it fell.

Dorian

Death takes the good, the beautiful, and the young—and spares me. The Pestilence that wastes, the Arrow that strikes, the Sea that drowns, the Grave that closes over Love and Hope, are steps of my journey, and take me nearer and nearer to the End.

—*Wilkie Collins,* The Woman in White

WHEN I RUSH into the Acroteria, I spot Raven and Atticus, and an immense wave of relief washes over me, soothing the ache in my chest. They're both alive. Raven's head hangs low, her hair a curtain around her face. Atticus draws soothing circles on her back, saying soft words of encouragement.

There's a nervous energy in the air. Everyone in the coffee shop is whispering to one another, their faces pale and ghostly, their lips tight with worry. Fire trucks and police cars roll down the street. I throw myself down in the booth across from Atticus and Raven. "You guys okay?"

"Yeah, we're okay," Atticus says. "I got out just before it crashed." His eyes are haunted, and like Raven, he's covered in a fine layer of dust—it's all over his hair and his jacket. His hand trembles beside his coffee cup.

"About Arches—" I hesitate before I ask. "Is it true? It's gone?"

"Someone died," Raven says, cutting me off. "It was Pippa. They found Pippa—" Her voice hitches. "Supposedly she was up there at the tower trying to perform the ritual to join that secret society. They found her underneath the rubble—"

"I–I met her once, briefly. She's dead?" I ask.

Atticus nods.

Raven tightens her grip around the mug. Like him, she's shaking, so I reach for her hand but stop myself. I don't know if touching her will hurt or help, so instead, I grab my great-grandfather's old pocket watch and clench it.

Atticus meets my eye, but I don't know how to help him either. I don't know how to make any of this right. The rational part of my brain knows that I can't fix any of this, but the rest of me wants to do anything I can. "Raven, how can I . . ."

Slowly, she wipes her wrist under her nose. Her eyes are puffy, and her cheeks still shine with tears. "I'm okay," she says. "I'm just–in shock, you know?"

Both Atticus and I nod.

"We saw her body . . . We saw–" She gulps in a shuddering breath. "They're saying she was crushed when the tower fell, but . . ."

Atticus finishes. "She looked like she was murdered."

"How do you know?" I ask.

"There were these gashes on her chest. Like a knife or . . ." Raven curls her hand into a claw shape and scrapes the air, as if she's tearing at her own flesh.

"Like an animal," Atticus adds.

Raven lifts one shoulder, all the strength she has to shrug. "What kind of animal could have done that? Maybe a bear, or a tiger? But what would a wild animal be doing on campus? It has to have been a person, right?"

I frown. "So someone caused the tower to collapse to cover up a murder?" Sibylline, lying, covering something up. Now, that's something I can believe.

The scene I witnessed in the records room still echoes in my thoughts. *Can't have another incident . . .* That's what the warden said. I wonder how many secrets lurk in the school's past. I think about the vision attached to Hecate's wand, and I wonder if maybe, somehow, that was just one more incident that no one knows about. I can still see it: the sigil and the screaming. My stomach clenches at the thought.

"What is it?" Raven asks when she sees me wince.

"Remember when I touched that wand?" I ask.

She nods, waiting for me to continue.

"Maybe this isn't the first time the school's covered something like this up."

"Why? Is there something else we don't know . . ." Atticus trails off.

Raven prompts me to continue. "What is it?"

"A few weeks ago, I was in the records room, in the Rosette, looking through admission records for Old Bones, and . . . I found a book from a hundred years ago." I tell them about my vision. "The warden back then, he said something about an incident with a student, how they can't have it happen again."

Atticus lets out a huff. "What are they so afraid of?"

"This is just a guess," I start, "but do you think it could have anything to do with the vision in Hecate's wand? The conversation I witnessed seemed to be from a similar period in time. It could explain why the school is so secretive. I think something happened a long time ago, and it changed how they admitted students. They hid some secret, some event, and it's linked to everything that's going on right now. We just need more information."

"I have something," Atticus says, lifting a book from the chair next to him. It's a leather-bound tome covered in dust. "Professor White gave this to me just before Arches fell." He flips the book open and places it on the table. "Told me to study it."

Raven's eyes dance over the cover. "It's in Akkadian," she says, her words muted. "A language spoken in Mesopotamia."

"I knew you'd want to see it," Atticus says gravely. The leather-bound cover is imprinted with straight, grid-like cuneiform.

She reads, and her dark eyes sparkle with light. I listen while she mumbles the words, taking characters written in a long-forgotten script and speaking them aloud, casually, as if she were reading a comic. Her magic is a beautiful thing to witness. Sometimes terrifying, too.

"The text describes the trapping and binding of magical creatures," Raven says.

"That makes some sense," Atticus says. "Professor White mentioned that Arches was built with ancient spirits of the natural world, ephemeral creatures that were somehow bound to the original structure at the moment of its creation." He pauses. "I wonder what happened to those spirits when Arches fell? Maybe there is some clue in the book, some text that will tell us what happens to a spirit bound to a structure that's destroyed. Maybe you can search for that? There's something here, some mystery in these old books and buildings, and I want to understand it."

"Me too. I think something happened a long time ago, and it's the reason why we weren't admitted. Maybe I can search the museum for more information, and Raven, perhaps you can use this book or the library or both?"

Raven smiles, and her grin brightens the whole cafe. "I'll get right on it." She gives us a thumbs-up. "Thanks, guys. For being here."

"Just say the word," I remind her. *"Nil sine magno labore."*

"Nil sine magno labore," Raven echoes.

Atticus nods, agreeing. *"Nil sine magno labore*—oh! Professor White, are you all right?" he asks as an older woman in a tan overcoat and long skirt, covered head to toe in dirt, walks into the cafe. She has gray hair and a pencil sticking out of a bun.

"Atticus! Good! Just the one I'm looking for. Come with me," she says. "We need to save the tower."

The three of us exchange confused glances. The tower is destroyed–there's nothing to save. But Atticus leaps to his feet to follow her anyway.

20 ATTICUS

Would you like to live with your soul in the grave?
—*Emily Brontë,* Wuthering Heights

PROFESSOR WHITE WALKS at a breakneck pace through the empty campus, forcing me to jog at her side just to keep up. Her face is set in a determined stare, and she curses beneath her breath, barely looking at me.

"What's going on?" I ask.

"Taken everything from me," she mutters. "Everything."

My stomach lurches. "Taken what? Who?"

She doesn't answer; she only grinds her teeth, lost in thought.

I stretch out my mind, searching hers, trying to piece together the fractured mosaic that makes up her emotions. But she's always been difficult if not impossible to read, and today her thoughts are no different. I capture only fragments: *I'll find . . . Rubble . . . Life's work . . . Find a way . . . Down . . . Nothing left . . .*

Police tape cordons off the area, with security patrolling the perimeter of what used to be Arches, making sure no one unauthorized can enter. There are no students around. Everyone's taken refuge indoors elsewhere. The tower rests in a crumpled heap of shattered brick and stone, a far cry from the majesty that once was. Amid the rubble, workers sort through the debris, and bulldozers wait to clear the rest. Fire trucks still linger, though there's no sign of fire, and people with hard hats and high-visibility vests climb up and down the rubble, shouting to one another. One figure stands out from the others, overlooking the work with his hands on his hips and his head held high, his ruby earring glinting in the light.

A certain sharpness emerges in Professor White's mood, and it's directed at him.

"Warden Stone," Professor White says, marching up to him, not even a little breathless. "I told you, I need more time."

Warden Stone gives Professor White a cursory glance, as icy as the color of his eyes, before he returns his attention back to the site. "We need to start demolition immediately, Anna. It's a danger to the students. The rest of the structure could collapse at any moment."

Professor White stands firm, her head high, holding her ground. "I need time to investigate. I want to know why—"

Failing to hide his annoyance, he interrupts. "Was that not what you were supposed to have been doing this entire time? Investigating? Understanding the structure and what needed to be done to maintain it? Was this not your responsibility?"

Professor White bristles, her thoughts aflame with anger, burning like a sparkler on the Fourth of July. "These things take time. My associate here"—she gestures to me, and I would beam with pride when she calls me associate, not assistant, if not for the circumstances—"has found irregularities in the renovation. We were in the midst of analyzing the damage, but the rate of deterioration was much faster than we realized. If you just give me a week, I can investigate further."

Warden Stone barely looks at me, which is a small relief. When I reach out and touch his mind, I sense frustration. I search deeper, expecting grief, but find nothing. There is no sense of mourning for the dead student or the lost building. I sense only rigid determination. It's like he wants both messes gone and he needs it done yesterday.

"You've had plenty of time. I cannot offer you more. My decision is final." Without another word, he walks away, addressing a man in a hard hat as he leaves us behind.

"What an ass," she mumbles, her head shaking, lips curled up in indignation. Apparently, his word is final.

I sense her mood hovering over her head like a storm cloud, thick and dark. "I tried reasoning with him, but he won't . . . he won't listen."

"Is there something–*anything* I can do to help?"

She studies me, looking me up and down, her tongue pressed against the inside of her cheek as she does.

"Really, I'm here if you need me." I want to prove myself to her, but I don't want to come off as desperate, but then again, what else am I?

"I always knew I could count on you," she says, a renewed spark of determination in her eye. "Come with me."

Being deemed worthy lights something inside my chest, a warm glow, but I don't have any time to bask in it. She beckons me forward, toward the site. We duck under the police tape, and no one stops us, especially when Professor White flashes her badge, proclaiming that she's the lead architect and she's more qualified than any of them to understand how to handle a magical building's collapse. A smattering of pride warms my heart, seeing her work. I want to be just like her someday.

"By eight in the morning tomorrow, all of this will be covered in bulldozers," Professor White says, sweeping her hand over the mound of debris. As she walks, she parts the sea of workers, guiding me around the ruined tower, then up and over the rubble, kicking away bricks and tattered beams. "The collapse exposed a series of century-old offices and archives deep underground. I had no idea they even existed. I am guessing they were used by the staff who were setting up the school of magic when Arches was first built. This is an unexpected and important find. If Stone demolishes it, he'll be burying history along with it. It really is a tragedy."

I know what she means. Forbidding access to knowledge is forbidding access to the past, and subsequently the future.

"There's no way we can get to it?" I ask.

"The chambers are half-collapsed. It won't be easy," she says. "Given time and sufficient preparation, I had hoped to search the site myself, to learn more about Arches and why it was made. There could be old books and important relics down there, but if Stone has his way–" She cuts herself off when she spots a figure lingering in the rubble nearby.

"Excuse me!" she calls. "This area is off-limits!"

I recognize him. It's Aspen, Raven's, uh . . . friend, from the archive. He doesn't look startled to be shouted at, though. Instead, he glares in our direction, a complete change from his Labrador appearance when I met him at the party. His aura is a hazy yellow–curious, intrigued. Is he looking for something?

After a moment, Aspen skulks off. What was he doing here?

"St. Ad's boys . . ." Professor White grumbles. "Always lingering where they don't belong."

I recall Professor White had warned me about St. Adolphus Hall when we first met. I wonder if it's for a good reason. I don't have the guts to ask her about it, though. She's lost in thought.

Her gaze drifts toward the rear of the building, where a fallen wall forms a kind of ramp leading down into the ruins. She contemplates it, wondering if it's stable. From my point of view, you would have to be insane to climb down it. Nothing about any part of the rubble looks truly trustworthy. No wonder Stone wants to demolish it.

"There's no other way to access it, a way around?" I ask, thinking about the network of tunnels under our feet.

"There might be," Professor White says. "If someone could just get down there and save all those books . . ." She shakes her head. "Otherwise, everything in it will be lost."

She circles the site, falling silent as she goes. I try to sense her thoughts and get only her frustration. I suppose that's to be expected. This is her life's work crumbling beneath our feet.

I touch her thoughts again, and her despair washes over me, like fresh paint on a wall, obscuring my own psyche. I sense regret, layered within something below I cannot grasp. I drift, plunging farther into her mind, and I have to force myself to pull back, counting to regain control of my own head. *Zero, one, one, two, three, five, eight . . .*

I take a deep breath as Professor White's energy fades from my grasp.

"Atticus, someone should save those books," she says intently.

Then I realize. It's me. She's asking me to save them.

Underneath the rubble is a chamber full of old and powerful books of magic . . . and Professor White has given me tacit permission to take them. The chambers below Arches are exactly what the Oneiric Society has been looking for.

RAVEN

Be with me always–take any form–drive me mad! only do not leave me in this abyss, where I cannot find you!

–*Emily Brontë,* Wuthering Heights

IT'S MIDNIGHT, AND the darkness feels oppressive. Even with Dorian and Atticus at my side, it's like the night itself is conscious of our movement, observing as we cross the diamond quad and slip beneath the police tape, moving from shadow to shadow, as we keep our steps light and our breaths quiet. The watchful eye of Sibylline glows bright in the Rosette's window, lighting our path.

When Atticus told us what we were doing, I couldn't contain my glee. Books are my specialty, and he promised a whole room full of them. Of course, that room is buried beneath the fallen tower. Sweat blooms on my palms as we stumble upon the outermost ruins of the crumbled tower. Seeing it up close now, even in the dark, I'm reminded of how majestic it once was and how untouchable it had seemed when it still stood. Now it's practically a tombstone, a crumbling memorial rising out of the broken ground.

I'm about to ask how much farther when Atticus brings us to a half-collapsed wall surrounded by police tape.

"In here," he whispers.

All I see is wreckage. "In where?" I ask.

Atticus slips around the brick wall, sliding into a gap hardly big enough for him to squeeze through sideways. I hesitate. Tight spaces and I don't get along, and I'm not sure I want to do this anymore.

"Is this the only way?" I ask, but he's already nodding.

There is no other way.

The thought of going into a narrow tunnel without a map or a known way out strikes me as unnecessarily dangerous, and my breath catches in my throat. I picture myself climbing through tunnels with millions of tons of rocks over my head, and I can't breathe.

Dorian pauses in the slender gap between the walls. "Are you okay?" he asks. "You don't have to come with us. I know you're claustrophobic."

"You're not leaving me behind again," I tell him sharply.

"Course not," he says. He's dressed all in black, so his fair face and golden hair float in a sea of darkness, comforting me. "Come on." His words are quiet as the night, his smile warm. He holds out his gloved palm and I take it. It helps ground me.

I take a deep breath, and Dorian turns, leading me down into the darkness.

Moving through the ruins, I squeeze my eyes shut, trying to convince myself that I'm not walking under a precarious half-fallen tower, and I nearly trip on a hunk of rock.

"Raven?" Dorian asks. "Are you okay? You weren't–"

"Looking where I'm going? Yeah."

"Trust me, you want to see where you're headed," he says, pointing to a place where the path ends in a sheer drop. "This way." He indicates a stone spiral staircase curving downward, and we descend in absolute darkness. Atticus's footsteps echo in all directions, as if they are coming from ahead of and from behind us, making it seem as if we might be lost. The air here is dusty, and

I fight the urge to cough. The scent of smoke fills the air, and the temperature grows colder with each step. Dorian's hand in mine is a steady guide, my only comfort, as he pulls me over rocks and debris. Unseen objects crunch under my boots.

Ahead, Atticus lights a lantern, and the glow casts flickering shadows on the stone walls as it kindles to life. At the foot of the staircase, he pauses, the light held high above his head illuminating a massive wooden door with brass tracery laid across the surface. His face is caked with dust, and motes hang suspended in the still air, but his eyes are bright, and he flashes a smile when we approach.

"First door of probably many," he says. "Shall we?"

Then he turns the knob, and the mechanism inside clicks. It's open.

He pushes it wide, exposing yet another corridor. Before us, the tunnel gapes, the gentle slope leading downward. Dorian's hand gently squeezes mine once again, and he catches my eye, giving me a small, comforting smile as we follow Atticus deeper into the tunnel. He leads the way, the lantern swinging on its hinge, the silence almost unbearable.

I tighten my grip on Dorian's glove. "Is this the arm I burned?" I ask, just to break the quiet and make a little conversation.

"Yes," he says.

"It doesn't hurt?"

"No, not so much anymore."

I know he isn't hurt, but I still like to hear him say it. "You know I would never do anything to hurt you," I say, worried just a little that I'm stating the obvious, but somehow I have the urge to say it anyway.

"I know," he whispers softly.

Atticus pauses in the corridor, and we gather around the

lantern. "I don't think this is part of the original tunnel system," he says. "I studied that map we used the first time, almost memorizing it, and I don't recall any of these tunnels."

"Maybe they were never connected to the rest of the school," says Dorian.

"Or they were walled off and erased from the map?" I ask.

Atticus nods. "Professor White said that the school had originally intended for Arches to house the department of creation magic, but the plans changed for some reason. The building was never used, so maybe these passages were closed. I don't know."

No one has answers, so we continue onward, winding our way around one turn and the next, the air heavy with the scent of decay, a thick layer of dust covering everything. We stumble upon a gate. Iron bars crisscross the width of the tunnel, and a single massive lock holds them in place, barring our path.

"What's this?" Atticus asks, his tone playfully curious.

I drop Dorian's hand and step forward, noticing the ironwork inlay on the lock, forming sigils and hieroglyphics illegible to me at first. And then it clicks.

"It's cuneiform. These markings are just like the ones we found in the book Professor White gave you," I say.

"Really?" Atticus asks. "But you said that book is all about binding spirits."

"It is," I say.

"Is it open?" Atticus asks.

"I don't know . . ." I step back. "Are we sure we want to go in?"

Dorian takes off one of his gloves and places his hand on the bars, tracing it over the ironwork. His eyelids flutter closed, his face screwed up in concentration.

"I . . ." he says, opening his eyes. "I don't think there's anyone inside. This hasn't been used in a long time."

"Do you see anything else?"

Dorian doesn't answer. He pulls on the lock, and the gate swings wide with a heavy groan. "The lock's broken," he says.

It's true. With the door open, the bent latch is clearly visible.

Dorian looks worried, his eyes darting.

"It's old. Maybe it was just rusted," says Atticus. He raises the lantern and leads the way again, deeper into the tunnel, into the unknown.

Dorian watches me carefully as he tugs on his glove. "No one's been here in a long time," he says, his way of assuring me.

"It's still creepy."

"It's just a door," he says.

"If you say so . . ."

Behind me, I hear something, a soft hiss, and I whip around. Darkness stretches behind us, an inky-black void that seems to go on for infinity.

"What is it?" Dorian asks.

"Did you hear that?" I ask.

"No, nothing," Dorian says. "What was it?"

I don't know.

I certainly don't believe in ghosts, but I *am* afraid of rats.

And what if Warden Stone appeared out of the darkness and caught us trespassing? I cock my head and listen as the seconds tick. It's the hollow sounds of the wind wailing in the distance, and I wonder if my imagination is working overtime. Something about this whole place doesn't sit right with me.

"Never mind," I say, spinning around to follow after Atticus. He's ten paces ahead, and I rush to catch up, Dorian right behind me.

"If we don't find anything soon, maybe we should head back," he says.

Atticus looks over his shoulder at us. "This will all be sealed off tomorrow. We won't have another chance."

"I know, but there is something about this place that worries me. What kind of school, even a magical one, would need a gate like that?" Dorian asks, stopping yet again. "And by the way, there aren't any books down here. Not that we've seen."

Looking at our surroundings, Atticus lifts the lantern high and illuminates the ceiling. High above us, covering the stones like a cage, is a grid of iron bars and grates, layers of thick metal. Moss hangs in strands from the straps, like fingers poking through the gaps. The image reminds me of a novel I once read, *The Count of Monte Cristo,* and the Château d'If, the isolated prison at the heart of the story.

It's then that I realize: "What if these bars weren't meant to keep something out? What if they were designed to keep something in?"

22 Dorian

Against the new masonry I re-erected the old rampart of bones. For the half of a century no mortal has disturbed them. In pace requiescat!

–Edgar Allan Poe, "The Cask of Amontillado"

"A PRISON, YOU mean?" I tug at my glove, making sure it's covering my skin. When I touched the door, I didn't see anything like a prison, but then again, the memories tied to this place have mostly faded, leaving behind vague mirages of an empty and forgotten chamber.

"There's no other explanation. The heavy doors, the iron bars. I'm just guessing, but it feels like a prison. What else could it be?" Raven asks.

"I don't know," Atticus says. "Professor White said nothing about a prison. It was supposed to house the school's department of magical creation. Perhaps, when it was abandoned, someone found a new use for this place? Maybe there are answers down here and we just haven't found them." I can only see the back of his head, the edges of his face limned in the golden glow from the lantern.

At the end of the tunnel, there's a heavy wooden door. Smooth dark oak, with an iron latch. He gives us one final glance, fire in his eyes, and a wide smile, and then he opens it.

Inside is a small room with broken tables and chairs, crumbling with disuse and time, the chamber as windowless and dark as a cave. What anyone would be doing here is beyond me. There are doorways leading into other rooms equally dim and dingy.

"What is this place?" asks Atticus, holding the lantern high as he takes everything in.

"It sure doesn't look like a classroom," Raven says.

"We should split up," Atticus suggests. "Light any candles you come across. Let's see if we can find anything."

There are wax candles in wall sconces, and we light them one by one with the lantern. Some have been burned down to nubs; others have never been lit. It's as if whoever used this place intended to come back but never did. Maybe they abandoned these chambers in a hurry?

There are several antechambers, one with a small library full of rotting books beyond salvaging, and another with a bed, the fabric reduced to moldering rags. I guess this was a workshop of some kind, with a sagging wooden table and broken glass bottles and fractured crystal balls littering the floor. The ground is filthy, but so is everything in this place. No one's been here for probably a hundred years.

I light the remaining wall sconces in the workshop, illuminating the rest of the room as best I can. It looks like the lab was the most well-used room in the complex. It still has a rug, a broken mirror, and an old lace dress hanging on a hook, but now there are tree roots growing down from the ceiling.

I hear Raven and Atticus moving about in the next room, shifting what sounds like furniture. I'm about to join them when I notice there's a book on the desk, and I flip it open. It's written by hand in a flowing script, and I slowly turn the pages. There are hundreds of entries, so I turn back to the very first page. On yellowed parchment, written in blood-red ink, are the words *The*

Life's Work of Adelina Ward. The vision returns to me, the images of terror flashing in my mind's eye.

"Atticus, Raven?" I call out, my voice shaking.

The two of them are standing in the doorway a moment later. "What did you find?" Atticus asks.

The book in front of me looks like it could fall apart or crumble in the slightest breeze. "It's Adelina Ward. I think this is her study. This is her . . . stuff," I say, gesturing to the room.

"Adelina Ward, as in the wand you touched, the one that knocked you out?" Atticus raises his eyebrows.

Raven hovers by my side to take a better look, and I get the urge to touch the book with my bare hands, but I hesitate, remembering what happened when I picked up the wand. Raven flips the page, revealing a wall of cuneiform text.

"Akkadian?" I ask.

Raven nods. "Just like this one." From her bag, she pulls out Professor White's book. The cuneiform script in it perfectly matches the handwritten letters in the book we've just discovered. With a shudder, I realize what we've found: These two texts are written by the same hand. The books are bound in the same leather and filled with identical weathered parchment.

"It's a matched set," says Raven, stunned.

"How'd Professor White get her hands on that one?" I ask Atticus.

"She was using the book as part of her research," he answers. "She thought the entries in it might be important or somehow relevant to the restoration of Arches. If that's true, then Adelina Ward must somehow be equally relevant."

"So Adelina Ward, the woman from my vision, is somehow connected to the history of this place," I say.

"That's the only explanation, right?" asks Atticus. "Ward's work must somehow be related to Arches. This was her lab, but why would she place it here?"

"It is strange . . ." says Raven. I touch her shoulder, and she jumps, as if she'd forgotten I was here.

"What's wrong?" I ask.

"Just a strange feeling. Like I've seen this book or maybe this handwriting before," she murmurs, slowly placing both books in her bag, safely storing them away. She's lost in thought.

Atticus circles the room. "We should keep searching. Maybe there is something we have yet to find." He stares at the iron bars and the strange markings that cover the walls.

I run my hand through my hair and try to stop the chill sliding down my spine from making me shudder. But then I realize the chill isn't my imagination. There's a breeze. It flutters over the skin on the back of my neck, like a breath.

I spin around, but nothing's there. I take a deep breath to calm my nerves, but then I feel it again. That breeze. It must be coming from somewhere.

I slip off my glove and hold out my hand, reaching to the air. The breeze flows between my fingers. The wind is coming from a crack in the wall, and I follow it.

"There's something back there."

When I press my hand to the cool brick, I sense it. It's faded with time but still legible—a memory from a distant past. I watch a ghost, nothing more than a hazy shape, drifting through this same room. The phantom's hand moves to the sconce on the wall, polished and new in the past, rusted and old now. I slide my hand into the ghost hand's place, and my solid form merges with the spectral one. Our hands tug at the lever at once.

The sconce grinds against the wall as it turns and something shifts.

The wall opens up, revealing yet another tunnel. Raven and Atticus stumble backward.

"A hidden passage!" Raven cries.

"Surprisingly common in Sibylline," Atticus says.

Fresh air fills the room, and the temperature drops even more. The tunnel ahead is dark, and even the candlelight can't penetrate it.

I take Atticus's lantern and lead the way.

The passage is just like the others, with the same carved sigils, but the pattern is more frequent, more compact, the characters resembling the stars gathered at the center of a galaxy, the markings dense and jumbled, piling on top of one another until they're almost unreadable. The air here buzzes with magic. I can almost taste it. Powerful magic was once at work in this place, and the lingering effects are still tangible.

After about fifty paces, the tunnel opens into a large, circular room, with high ceilings made of the same gray stone as the floors and walls. Patches of moss grow in cracks, and there's a faint sound of dripping water. The walls here are thicker, too, the stones seemingly heavier. The smell of stagnant water and wet stone caresses my face. Every brick is marked with the same Akkadian sigils. Binding spells.

Making our way to the middle of the room, we find a large metal structure about the size of a small garage. Its iron bars are woven into a lattice cube. It has one door, and it hangs open.

"It's . . . a cage," says Atticus, slack-jawed.

There's something on the floor inside the cage. Bleached white, covered in rags, a toothy grin.

A skeleton.

23
RAVEN

There was everything.
—*Henry James,* The Turn of the Screw

"JESUS CHRIST," ATTICUS blurts out.

"I don't think that's him," Dorian jokes.

I shush them both. I've never seen a real skeleton before. It isn't anything like the plastic models I recall from high school science class. The bones are yellowed and rotted, and clumps of hair still dangle from the skull. Here and there, hints of flesh cling to the bone.

"You guys, it's real," I tell them. "A real dead body."

It takes a second for it to sink in. This isn't some Halloween decoration. This isn't a prank.

Someone died down here.

Atticus moves as if to scream, but Dorian clamps his hand over his mouth. Atticus stares at him with panicked eyes, his voice muffled. He tries to jerk away, but Dorian holds him tight.

"Don't," Dorian says, shaking his head. Atticus's nostrils flare as he breathes hard against his glove. "I know, I'm freaked out, too, but people can't know we're down here."

Once he's sure that Atticus won't scream, Dorian lowers his hand. Atticus still looks terrified, but he swallows it down. Dorian turns to me, eyes hard. "This is a bad idea. We need to leave. Now."

He pulls Atticus toward the door. But I don't follow. We need answers, and I know where to look for them.

I pull out the book from my bag.

The Life's Work of Adelina Ward.

I stare at the cover as if it might spring open and devour us whole.

"Raven, what are you doing?" Dorian asks. "Come on, let's go."

"Maybe the book will tell us something about what happened here." I open it to the first page. Just to see. Just to read. The script is delicate, if a little hurried. Some letters are smeared, and the pages are thick and sometimes tattered. I'm transfixed by it.

"We can read it later, let's just go!" Atticus hisses through his teeth. I ignore him. He doesn't see the potential here.

"It's a diary," I say. "The first entry, it's dated from 1917." Then I read the first line, "'Everyone said it couldn't be done.'" I pause. The rest of the page is smeared, the ink faded. "I can't read the rest." I move to flip the page, but Dorian puts a gloved hand on top of mine, stopping me.

"It's just a dead body. It's not going to hurt us," I say, tempering my annoyance.

I'm right, and he knows it. He glances at Atticus, who looks like he might vomit.

"We came all the way down here. Let's see this through. This might be our last shot here, Atticus," I remind him. "Do you really want to run away now?"

Atticus swallows thickly. "Dead people freak me out," he says, but he stays put. I've won.

Dorian sighs. "Fine, Raven, wait. I want us to try something," he says.

"Try what?"

He takes off his gloves and holds out his hand. "Do you trust me?"

I stare at his bare fingers, at his skin. We've never touched before. And somehow, the prospect feels oddly intimate. I glance in Atticus's direction.

Atticus stares at Dorian, battling himself, before he comes over. "I'm going to hate this."

"I know," Dorian says.

He places one hand on the book, and Atticus places his hand on Dorian's, and they wait for me to do the same. I reach out tentatively, wondering what we'll see. Too late to stop myself, I join them, and I'm sucked into inky blackness.

I'M TELEPORTED SOMEWHERE else . . . another time, another place.

We're not underground anymore. Sunlight streams into large windows, casting puddles of light onto a polished desk. Students dressed in black robes sit at attention. We're in a classroom. At Sibylline. The school crest hangs on a plaque above the door, a single eye watching over everyone.

I'm in the middle of the classroom, still holding on to Dorian's hand. It's as solid as the new world around me. Atticus is here, too. We stare at each other, wondering if this is really happening.

I try to ask where we are, but I can't. My mouth moves, but no sound comes out. I'm simply an observer. We're shades traveling through history, haunting another time. His power has pulled us into the journal, into the memories imprinted when it was held.

Dorian looks at me, nodding, assuring me that this is okay, and I turn back to the scene in front of us. A teacher lectures a classroom of students.

"–elements require balance," he says, finishing an elaborate alchemical circle on the chalkboard. "The natural world requires an equilibrium. Much like Newton's laws of motion, there are laws of magic. For example, Newton's second law states that the acceleration of an object is directly proportional to the force applied to it. In other words, the stronger the spell caster, the bigger the result. Finally, Newton's third law dictates that when there is an action, there is always an equal and opposite reaction. When a spell caster exerts his will, the world itself pushes back. In this way the balance of forces is maintained. Let me show you how this works."

The professor writes a series of equations on the board, prompting everyone in the room to open their journals and take notes. One student stands out among the rest. She's sitting at the front of the class, her head bowed as she writes in a leather-bound book. It's the same book Atticus took from Professor White.

Adelina.

She's small in stature, her auburn hair cut into a short, wavy bob, stylish for the time. A smattering of freckles dots the bridge of her nose, and her bright green eyes look like emeralds. Like the other students, she's wearing black robes. Around her neck is a delicate silver chain, and she keeps one hand wrapped around the pendant as she writes furiously.

I notice she has a graded test tucked under the journal. She aced it.

But she's not writing down what the teacher is saying. She's scribbling a mixture of Greek, Latin, and . . . Akkadian, almost like a secret code. In fact, she's not paying attention to the lesson at all; she's working on something else entirely.

The teacher drones on about the balancing force of nature until Adelina raises her hand. "Yes?" the teacher asks curiously.

Adelina looks up from her journal, her face bright with anticipation as she asks, "What about chaos?"

"Chaos?"

"Yes, primordial chaos. The chasm from which the universe was born."

The professor furrows his brow. "I'm not sure I understand what you mean, Miss Ward."

"Do the same laws apply for the manipulation of chaos?"

Students in the class glance at each other, confused.

The teacher looks somewhat uncomfortable, but he answers the question anyway. "Some early mages believed that chaos was the fifth element, yes, but they found that it was impossible to apply the same mechanics to it. The equations fall apart, leaving us unable to manipulate it."

"So then you're wrong," Adelina says.

The professor's jaw drops. "Excuse me?"

"You said that the laws apply to everything. But not to chaos. So you're wrong." Her tone is matter-of-fact, almost haughty.

Whispers rise up in the classroom.

The professor's eyes dart left and right, studying the students' reactions. He takes a deep breath and says, "In this instance, we're looking at the applied mechanics of spell work. Since we do not understand the mechanics of this fifth element or the magic related to it, there is no point in discussing them. Chaos is not relevant."

"Then how did the universe begin? All of the elements we are discussing rose out of the primordial void of chaos, so they must somehow be related to it. The laws of these elements must relate to the laws of chaos in some as yet undetermined manner. Correct?"

The class buzzes with nervous anticipation, the students glancing from the professor to Adelina and back. The teacher maintains his calm. "Nothing can come from nothing, Miss Ward."

"Not unless you have the right tools," she says, her speech quickening with excitement. "Like a powerful wand–"

The professor cuts her off with a raised hand. "That's enough for today. Thank you, everyone. Class dismissed."

The students file out of the room, and the vision shifts, the classroom fading from sight, replaced by a different scene. We're in an apartment, though not one I recognize. There's a record player scratching out an old song, a velvet chaise in the living room, and an old-fashioned radio on the floor. Books upon books upon books stand like leaning towers beside it, with loose papers and rolled parchments and fountain pens dipped in ink scattered about the floor.

A young woman I don't recognize storms into the room. She has flowing brown curls wrapped with ribbons in a neat bun atop her head. She's wearing a long silk skirt, a blouse with wide sleeves, and heeled boots, looking like a proper Edwardian-era socialite. She marches in, a book clutched in one hand and a wide-brimmed hat full of flowers in another. She looks at the mess of the living room and groans.

Adelina follows the woman. She is dressed in a similar style, but she's wearing a pleated skirt that's a little wrinkled, and her hair is messy. It's as if she's been up all night studying. Deep shadows are beneath her sparkling green eyes.

"You don't understand, Mary!" she cries. "This will work!"

"No, Adelina," says Mary, spinning around in front of us, oblivious to our presence. "You're only going to make trouble for yourself. These equations are dangerous."

Adelina scoffs, rolls her eyes, and moves about the room, gathering her things. She takes a book with a green leather cover from the shelf and stuffs it into her schoolbag. There is something familiar about the book, like I've seen it once before on a shelf when I was a child, but I can't remember where. Before I can get a better look, it's already gone from sight. Adelina's readying herself for class. She grabs two more books and a stack of papers from a nearby desk.

Adelina is insistent. "I am telling you, Mary. Creation, *real* creation, is possible. The magicians who made Arches, they materialized it out of thin air. But we can do more than that. I can do more."

"You need to sleep," Mary says. "Look at this place. Please. This obsession of yours is going to make you sick."

"Chaos is the key. The creation of the universe from nothing. If we can harness the primordial essence, bend it to our will, just like any of the other elements they teach us about in class, we can do the impossible! I just want to borrow the wand, just for a little bit. You can get it for me from Old Bones, I know you can. Please, just do it for me."

Mary rubs her forehead. "What are you rambling about?"

"*Life,* Mary! I can create life!"

The room fades to black, and the vision shifts again.

WE'RE IN THE Rosette. It hasn't changed. Even after a hundred years, it's as if it's been kept in a time capsule. The same bookcases, the identical marble floor and stained-glass window.

Adelina sits at a table, awash in the red light of the colored glass, hunched over her journal. Several books lie open on the table in front of her, and I recognize one. It's the tome we stole from the archive: *Evocations and Invocations in Theory.*

A boy carrying a stack of books arrives at her table, smiling shyly. He's slender, handsome in a soft way, with a kind smile. His hair is brown, slicked back, and parted on the side. He even wears suspenders over his white button-down shirt. There's a small ink stain on his sleeve, and more on his hands. He's an archivist.

"Here you go, Adelina," he says, setting the books on her table. "The spells you asked for."

She jumps from her seat and rushes to him, kissing him passionately. He stumbles when she embraces him, but he doesn't pull away. Are they dating? When she breaks the kiss, her eyes sparkle with energy. "I did it. I solved it, Henri," she says, breathless, wild. "The spell, it will work."

"Th-that's great!" Henri says, still smiling. "I knew you'd figure it out."

She kisses him again, clutching his shirt tightly, and he kisses her back. He draws her into a hug, and Dorian's fingers twitch around mine. His expression is strained, his mouth pressed into a worried line. When he locks eyes with me, a frightened look creeps into his features. What's wrong with him?

Adelina pulls away, and when she looks at Henri, there's a frantic energy in her eyes. It makes my stomach drop.

"We should celebrate," she says. "Meet me in my workshop, below Arches. At midnight."

The scene fades once more into murky darkness.

THEN WE'RE IN the tunnels beneath Arches. We're in that same large room where we found the cage, but in this time, there's no cage. The room looks as if it is new, the marble floors are polished, and hundreds of lit candles illuminate the space.

Adelina clutches a wand with mother-of-pearl inlay. Her black robes are disheveled, hanging off one shoulder. She circles the room, smiling with her head thrown back, as if she's enjoying a spring shower.

There's a body on the floor.

It's Henri.

He's laid out on a pentagram drawn in blood. A steady stream of red drips from his forehead. His eyes are closed, and he's barely breathing. His chest rises and falls in fits and starts.

Dorian flinches.

This is his vision. This is what he saw on his first day at the museum. He's frantic, glancing around, knowing, perhaps, what comes next, and dreading it with every ounce of his being. I want to say something to him, to remind him that this isn't real, this is just a memory, but I can't. This has already happened, and I can't do anything to stop it.

Adelina lets out a little sigh. She's so happy and so relieved, like a weight has been lifted from her shoulders. She stares at Henri's body on the ground with a smile so twisted, it looks like she's holding the corners of her lips up with her fingers.

Then I notice something: Tears glisten on her cheeks.

"Thank you," she whispers. "Thank you."

Hurried footsteps echo down the secret passage. Mary emerges, cheeks flushed and hair wild. She ran all the way here. And when Adelina sees her, she is delighted. "Mary! You came!"

Mary sees Henri.

"Adelina, what are you doing?" she cries, and runs to Henri's side. "What happened to him?" She kneels down, and her hands begin to glow. She's trying to heal the boy.

"I just needed a little blood, that's all," Adelina says.

Henri doesn't wake. Mary looks up at Adelina, angry tears swimming in her eyes. "What did you do?"

"I did it. I created life. Like I said I could."

"Stop this, Adelina."

"It's already done. The malum is free."

A shadow flickers in the candlelit room.

Mary whips around, horrified. "A malum?" she asks.

Something moves in the dark. No. It *is* the dark that moves.

"Everything they taught us was a lie, they said it was impossible," Adelina says.

"Please. Adelina. No. Don't do this." Mary stumbles back, hands up.

"My creation needs more magic, I think," she says absently, ignoring Mary's plea. "It needs to feed, like all of us do. It wants to live."

Mary lets out a sob as the shadow approaches. It moves like liquid smoke, melting over the ground, taking shape, growing tall. Arms, legs, head, a warped humanoid.

"You have magic in your blood, too, Mary. Just like Henri. Just like me." She holds out her hand, showing a cut in her palm, fresh blood spilled. "It just needs a little," she says. "Just a little more."

The malum towers over Mary, slowly descending as it hisses with pleasure. I don't want to look, but I can't turn away. She's frozen with terror, eyes wide. No one can help.

Then the shadow envelops her, consuming her in darkness.

Her screams echo around the chamber. And all Adelina does is laugh.

THIS DREAM ENDS and another begins, but the sound of Mary's screams still reverberates in my mind. Dorian is shaking, so is Atticus, and so am I. Henri and Mary, they're dead. The shadow took their lives, feeding off the magic in their blood.

I want to run. I want to leave these memories, but I can't.

We're back in the large chamber where we found the cage, though everything is different. There's no pentagram, no candles, no bodies, and we're *inside* the cage. Adelina sits on the marble floor, wearing nothing but rags. She's got her knees tucked up to her chin, her arms wrapped around her legs. She rocks back and forth, muttering to herself, as a man with a ruby earring stands at the entrance to the tunnel, watching her. It's the same ruby earring that Warden Stone wears.

Men in dark robes move about the room, summoning iron bars and sigils, and sealing away all the entrances.

They're imprisoning her in the cage.

They're building the prison beneath Arches.

Adelina doesn't seem to notice. Her gaze is distant, like she's living in some dream.

"Two students are dead because of you," the warden says.

Adelina makes no indication that she's listening.

"That malum is no longer a threat. It is imprisoned in these walls like all of the other spirits," the warden continues. "Your possessions have been confiscated. Your life is forfeit."

Still, Adelina mutters to herself.

"No sorcerer like you will ever set foot on these grounds again. No one will be allowed to do what you have done."

With that, he turns, departing the chamber. The door slams closed with a hollow clang, and the lock slides into place.

Adelina stares at the door from behind a curtain of hair, matted and dirty. The warden disappears down the passage with the men in darkened robes, and Adelina is left to rot in the cell. Her head drops to her knees. Her shoulders bounce, and her laughter echoes.

The vision ends, and we're thrown back into the present.

Atticus nearly falls to his knees. Catching himself on his hands, he pants, gasping for breath as if he had just sprinted a mile. My thoughts are spinning.

Dorian puts his hands on the top of his head and paces. "It was the wand! She used Hecate's wand! I saw it that day!"

Atticus leaps to his feet and grabs Dorian by the shoulders, steadying him.

"I saw it, I saw it," Dorian repeats, eyes glistening. Atticus doesn't let him go.

I look down on the bones, at the skeleton. "After what Adelina did," I say, thinking out loud, "they turned this place into her prison and closed it off from the rest of the school, hiding what happened. And she died here, trapped in the base of the tower with her creation, the malum."

"But the tower was destroyed," says Atticus. "If this building was a kind of prison, a place where spirits were held, what happened when the tower fell?"

It hits me. I know what he's thinking.

I look over at Dorian, whose hands are still shaking. He gets it, too.

We all sense it, but I'm the only one who says it aloud. "The creature from the vision . . . It's alive."

ATTICUS

Truly there is no such thing as finality.
—Bram Stoker, Dracula

IT'S NOT JUST a prison cell. It's a tomb. I should have known from the moment we set foot in this place. I sensed it in the air, a sick and twisted feeling. It's in the walls and in the stones. This place is evil.

The malum . . . it survived, trapped in this prison for a century. When the tower fell, it was freed. For all I know, it could be close. My heart pounds, my skin goes cold, my vision narrowing to a pinpoint focus. I don't like this. I don't like this at all.

I take a step back, and then another. Dorian and Raven stand motionless, as if transfixed.

"We have to get out of here," I say, fear burning hot in my veins. I grab Raven and Dorian, my hold viselike on their hands. "Come on. Please. We need to go. Now!"

We turn and run, sprinting back toward the passage that leads upward to the surface.

The light from the lantern bounces, making the world spin, but I keep running. Raven and Dorian are right behind me, their feet pounding the rough stone, their breathing hard and ragged. We hurry toward Adelina's office, and we don't bother closing the secret passage. We rush through her abandoned chamber, and—

Something stands in our way, maybe twenty feet ahead.

My eyes don't quite believe it. My brain is convinced it's a trick.

It's impossible.

In the soft candlelight of the lab, a shadow drifts through the room.

It's here. Adelina Ward's malum.

Raven lets out a little shriek, and we stop.

Every muscle in my body seizes up. I can't move. It's like I'm made of lead. My knees tremble, my hands, my body.

Dorian shifts, trying to process what he's seeing.

Maybe *shadow* isn't the right word. It's almost as if a void has materialized right before our eyes, a kind of black hole that consumes every photon of light that touches it, creating a dark and shimmering illusion that makes my mind desperately try to fill in the gaps around it.

The shadow moves, twisting, revealing its true form.

It's just like what we saw in the vision. It's taller than a person, with elongated arms, spindly legs, and a long and slender thing atop its shoulders that only vaguely resembles a head. But it's not a person. If it were, I could tell. I could feel it or sense its thoughts. But there's nothing. The shadow grows as it moves, expanding until it occupies the width of the corridor, blocking the only exit.

It just stands there. It doesn't seem at all surprised to see us. Or frightened.

It's motionless, like it's waiting.

Slowly, it tilts its head, and a soft hissing echoes in the chamber, growing louder. I don't know how I know—it doesn't have a face, or eyes—but I know it's looking at us.

And then it takes a step forward. Soundless. Long strides. Coming toward us.

I don't know what to do. My mind goes blank. Completely, utterly blank.

Raven–

Dorian–

Oh God–

Silently, the malum stalks forward. Wisps of shadow drift from its body like smoke from a candle that's just gone out. Long appendages slither out of its arms, twisting like ink-black roots into fingers . . . and claws.

I snap out of my trance.

All at once, I'm moving before I realize it. I shove Dorian and Raven back.

"Go!"

They sprint in the opposite direction, toward the cell, and I turn to follow, but the malum hisses, and searing pain hits me.

I scream, but I don't stop running.

The shadow is right behind me. It's hungry. It wants blood.

Dorian and Raven run ahead of me, and I stumble to keep up.

It's coming.

We crash through Adelina Ward's office, back into the secret passage, back into the cage. Raven is the first to arrive, then Dorian. They're screaming my name. The hissing and snarling of the malum drown out the world and grow closer–

I stumble, overcome with pain, dragging myself into the cell.

Dorian slams the door shut, and the malum crashes against the bars.

The iron, it's protected, or so I guess. Maybe this magical prison can keep something out just as easily as it can keep something in.

The wards hold. For now.

Dorian stumbles back as the shadow drifts about the cell, its strange and spindly head turned toward us as it paces around the perimeter of the room. As it goes, it melts into darkness, into a place the light cannot touch, but we still hear it, that unsettling hiss, like air being let out of a tire. I'm reminded of a shark circling an underwater cage. Only a few bars separate us from the predator.

Then the pain of my wound hits me. It cuts through me like a knife, and I cry out, falling to my knees.

"Oh God, Atticus! You're bleeding!" Raven cries.

The back of my sweater is wet and warm. It sticks to my skin. My flesh burns, my nerves on fire. I know it's bad. Raven's hands fly to her mouth, and Dorian whips off his sweatshirt to press it against my back, hoping, perhaps, to stanch the bleeding.

My whole world is pain.

My vision blurs.

Raven and Dorian are yelling, but I don't understand what they're saying. I want to tell them to stop, to leave it alone, but I can't. The pain prevents me from speaking. The hurt overwhelms me. Hot tears dribble down my cheeks as the sickly sweet tang of blood fills the air. I taste it on my tongue.

I try to move, but the agony prevents me.

I think I'm going to die.

"No, you're not," says Raven.

Did I say that out loud? I don't know, my mind isn't my own.

"Hold on, Finch," says Dorian. "Hold on."

I feel Dorian's warm embrace. His bare hands are touching me.

The world is slipping.

The pain, it's fading . . . but so am I.

"Hold on," says Dorian again. His voice sounds far away. "Just let me . . ."

And I fall into darkness.

25 RAVEN

Odi et amo.
(I hate and I love.)
–Catullus

ATTICUS LIES SPRAWLED on the stone floor, his eyes glassy and distant, and all I can do is fall to my knees and grab his hand. Dorian's tearing off his gloves. "Dorian, what are you doing?"

"Hold on," he says, speaking to Atticus. "Just hold on."

Dorian's hands are touching Atticus's flayed skin. The malum's claws sliced through his clothes, revealing flesh. His back is wet with blood, and I don't know how to stop the bleeding. Dorian's sweatshirt is already soaked through with it. The blood is almost black, and it covers the floor. There's so much . . .

Dorian lays Atticus down on his side, murmuring for him to keep holding on.

The malum prowls the chamber, stalking, visible sometimes in the scant light of the lantern lying forgotten on the floor. Everything about this is wrong. It's so wrong, I don't have time to process it. So much is happening all at once.

"Atticus," I cry.

He doesn't answer. He just lets out a low moan.

"We've got to get him out of here!" His hand is limp, he's fading, his skin growing colder under my fingers. He's dying. My love is dying. *Atticus, no.*

Dorian's hands are still moving, still pressing hard on his back. He's up on his knees, throwing his whole weight down. And now, I realize, his hands are glowing.

"What are you doing?" I ask.

He screws up his face, concentration pulling his features taut. "Let me try—let me just . . ." He doesn't finish.

"Dorian?"

As if yanked, his head is thrown back, and his eyes roll upward. He goes rigid like he's being electrocuted.

"Dorian!"

His whole body seizes up, and I fear he might snap in half. He grimaces, agony spreading across his mouth, his eyes unnaturally wide and pure white. If he could scream, he would. I move to push him, to snap him out of it, but that's when I notice the gashes in Atticus's back are closing.

I jump to my feet and stare as his skin folds itself back together, mended by invisible sutures. The bleeding slows, and Atticus's breathing evens out. At first, I think Dorian's healing him, but then bright red blotches appear on his own back, soaking through his white shirt.

I put my hand to my mouth to stop from screaming.

He's taking his wounds. He's absorbing them into his own body.

I didn't know that was possible.

His eyelids flutter, tears stream down the corners of his eyes. He's doing too much. He's dying, too.

"Dorian, no! You need to stop, or I'll lose you, too!"

He doesn't. Maybe he can't.

"I said stop!"

I hit his chest, and his hold on Atticus breaks.

With a yelp, he stumbles, falling heavily on the stone beside Atticus, the two of them unconscious. What did he just do? I want to scream. I can't lose both my best friends, not here, not now—

I flip Dorian over, pulling at his shirt, expecting to find his back flayed, just like Atticus's. There's blood, but there's no open gash. All that remains are three bright pink scars, looking freshly healed. Atticus's back is the same.

They have identical marks. A shared wound.

He did it. Dorian saved him. They're both alive.

They're both breathing.

The malum hisses, drawing my gaze upward. It circles us, prowling like an animal, looking for any way into the cell. It stretches its claws, as if desperate to use them.

I stare at the beast. This creature, was it the same one that killed Pippa? The wounds on Atticus's back, now Dorian's . . . they match what I saw that day. The malum seems to watch us, with an unnerving, intelligent patience.

It's not of this world. A deep, dark magic created this thing. And my shock and fear is replaced by a fuming rage.

"If this cage could keep you in then, it can keep you out now," I say.

If the creature understands me, it gives no indication. It simply melts into the darkness, hissing. The shadows lengthen. The lantern provides some small amount of light, but it won't burn forever. When the oil is expended, the room will darken, and we'll be left alone with the malum, unable to see it.

The bars shake.

I'm reminded that the demolition will soon begin. If we don't find a way out before it starts, we'll be crushed beneath the rubble.

DORIAN

Behind every exquisite thing that existed, there was something tragic.

—Oscar Wilde, The Picture of Dorian Gray

THERE'S A LIGHT glowing faintly in the distance. Warm, inviting, safe . . . I wonder if I'm dead. My body feels heavy. My limbs are like stone. There's a comforting finality to dying, a relief in knowing that it's over, that it's done. There's nothing left for me to do. No more effort needed. No more scraping by. No more trying. And failing.

The last thing I remember is trying to save Atticus.

I hope it wasn't all for nothing.

I have no answers.

I wonder if this is how death feels: trapped in a body forever, unable to move, sensing them burying you, thinking, feeling, knowing . . . ?

I wonder, what will my mom do? What will happen to her now? I want the coroner to tell her it was quick for me, that it was over before I realized what was happening. Then something hits me.

I can still smell things, the scent of iron and copper—blood. I remember what happened.

There's sunlight. Faint through my closed eyelids. I slide them open, aching from head to toe. I'm lying on the stone floor, and my back feels as if it's been cut to pieces.

Sunlight shines through cracks in the stone ceiling, fissures that illuminate the narrow cell where I lie. The lantern light is gone, replaced by the dim and hazy rays of the early morning sun. Am I dreaming?

I try to sit up, but when I shift, pain shoots through me, and the world snaps into focus. Faces hover over me. Atticus. Raven.

They're pale, and worried. They're covered in filth and blood, but they're alive, and still frightened. I recall everything that happened: The malum. Atticus. His bleeding wounds.

I don't care about the pain. I grab Atticus by the shoulders and pull him into a hug. "I'm so glad you're okay," I tell him.

"Me? Never better." He's pale and weak, but he wraps his arms around me. He's warm and in my arms, safe. I close my eyes and breathe in his scent, burying my nose into the slope of his neck.

"How long was I–" I start to ask, but I cough, which makes the ache in my back feel like a solid punch to the ribs.

"You've been unconscious for a while," says Raven. She wipes her nose on the back of her bloody wrist. Atticus's clothes are stiff with dried blood.

"What happened?" Atticus asks, pulling away. "You healed me, but injured yourself . . ."

"I know," I say.

"How did you do it?" Raven asks. She holds out my gloves to me, gifting them a second time. I slide them back on. My skin still tingles, as if I've been shocked by static electricity.

"I told you the story. When I touched that man on the subway, the one who was in cardiac arrest, I felt like I was in cardiac arrest. I almost died. Maybe I did die for a moment, but I lived, and the man survived. *I* survived. Somehow my power allows me to absorb more than just memories."

"You never told me that," she says, sounding hurt.

"Oh, right–I told Atticus."

Atticus blushes, and Raven looks at us keenly. Then she sighs. "Whatever. Go on."

"Anyway, I had no choice. I just acted . . . and it worked. We're alive."

"You saved me," says Atticus, "and you risked your own life to do it."

"We're not out of this yet," I say, noticing the malum.

It's still here. The creature paces, slinking like a silent cat. Its faceless head turns toward us as it walks on all fours in a grotesque prowl. My blood turns to ice when it looks at us.

"I had hoped that sunlight might banish it," says Raven. "It hasn't."

I try to stand, but I'm too weak. I can't run, not yet. And even if I could, what would be the point? The malum has us trapped. If we leave this cell, it will tear us to pieces.

Then there's a low rumble from above.

The whole chamber shakes. Dust rains down from the ceiling, and I cough, choking on the debris. Through the gaps in the ceiling, there's the unmistakable shape of a bulldozer.

The demolition. I almost forgot.

"Help!" Atticus calls. Raven and I join in, screaming, but the roar of the heavy equipment drowns out even our loudest cries.

We're alone with the malum, and soon this whole chamber will be demolished.

"We have only one choice," Raven says.

"Choice?" I ask.

"Yes, we can't run, can't stay here, so we fight."

"The malum?" I ask. "How?"

Raven's eyes glitter, cold and hard like diamonds, when she says, "With magic."

RAVEN

Life, although it may only be an accumulation of anguish, is dear to me, and I will defend it.

—Mary Shelley, Frankenstein

A BOOM RATTLES the floor, sending Atticus and Dorian crashing together. I stand firm, not taking my eyes off the malum. I refuse to die here. I refuse to die, period.

"With magic?" Atticus asks me. "Are you sure?"

I have to be sure. "Dorian saved you with it. Maybe I can save all of us."

I remember the spell, and what we needed to cast it. I have summoned fire before, and I know I can do it again. Unceremoniously, I spit on my hands, still red with Atticus's blood, and smear it around in my palm. Kneeling down, I draw the symbol for fire—an upright triangle—on the floor.

"Is that a good idea? Using my blood to write?" Atticus asks warily.

"It's all I have," I remind him. "Do you have any other medium? Ink? Or a pen?" It's a rhetorical question, and Atticus bites his tongue.

From memory, I write the inscription on the sides of the triangle. While I work, the malum prowls, its eyeless face turned to me. Its body scrapes against the cage. It rams our prison with its shoulder, and the iron bars shudder. I'm so focused, I barely flinch.

"It's trying to break in," says Atticus, sounding way too calm.

Does it sense what I'm trying to do?

Is it worried?

The ground shakes again, and the chamber walls tremble. The demolition has started. They're tearing down what's left of Arches, causing parts of the ceiling to crumble, dust and rock raining onto our heads.

We're going to be buried alive.

The beast rams the cell again, and it feels like the whole world is going to come crashing down.

The clamor of the demolition crew echoes like a gong in my head, threatening to drown out my own thoughts as I concentrate on the spell. The malum throws its full weight into each hit, and for the first time, the bars bend. The cage is failing.

"Get down," I tell Atticus and Dorian. They drop to the floor, shielding each other. Dorian covers Atticus's head with his body, and a hunk of stone strikes his back. He lets out a yelp, but he doesn't leave Atticus. A rock hits the floor inches from Atticus's head, shattering on contact. Soon the stones are falling all around us, and dust fills the air.

The iron bars slowly crumple with each of the malum's attacks.

My heart is beating so hard and fast, it hurts. I hold out my hands over the sigil, and I sense something, a vague tingling in the tips of my fingers. I welcome it, this power. Mine. The air gets warmer.

If I'm not careful, I could burn out all of the oxygen from the room. I could burn us all to death. I could hurt Dorian and Atticus . . .

My hands shake.

Concentrate.

I know this spell. I know how to do this. I won't be stopped.

Magic surges through my bones. My hair floats above my shoulders. I'm so light, I wonder if I could fly. The malum pounds furiously, each hit bending the bars more. The metal flexes and buckles, slowly tearing apart.

"Raven!" Atticus cries. Stones crack and break, metal warps, and the roar of the bulldozers echoes in my ear. Dorian yells something, but I can't make out the words. I ignore all of it, focusing on the sigil.

The malum rears back, ready to strike.

I inhale. There is power in words and in books. But there is power in me, too. Wild, unleashed elemental power. All I have to do is cast one spell. One simple phrase, two words, from an ancient and powerful text.

"Vocare ignis!"

My voice booms, and a great burst of wind rushes through the room as the sigil ignites in a blinding white light.

Then I tear my fingers into the air and *break* it.

Lightning flares in front of my eyes, blinding me, illuminating the room briefly before a fireball materializes in front of us. At first, it's no bigger than the palm of my hand, but as the magic surges through my bones, the fire grows bigger, and bigger, rolling toward the malum. The spell expands, gathering power, feeding off the oxygen in the room, feeding off of me. The orange flames churn and roil, a bubbling concoction of heat and flame.

The fire blazes hot and bright.

It's wild and untamed, but I lash it and bend it to my will.

I have no real training to guide me. I know the words and how to speak them. I know the symbols, but I am not yet a student of Sibylline. But my magic is building, growing, and it's *mine. I am* control. *I am* power.

The fire is everywhere, or so it seems; a churning tornado of hot air and flame surrounds us. Fire licks at our clothing and hair; it wraps the bars of the failing cage. Through the flames, the creature retreats. This is no normal fire. It is magical, just like the malum.

The fire climbs the walls, it spreads across the stone, singeing the sigils that line the prison, and the malum's howls are silenced by the roar of the inferno. Sweat drips down my face, down my spine. A great crack echoes through the chamber, and the ceiling crumbles. It drops straight down, striking the malum and most everything else in the room. But the cage holds. Apparently, the enchanted bars aren't damaged by the mundane force of falling rock.

There's no sign of the malum. I lift my hands from the sigil. With a swipe of my foot, I erase the symbol I drew in blood. The fire goes out instantaneously, leaving us trapped in a cloud of smoke. My ears ring, and I can barely stand. Exhaustion makes the world spin.

Through the smoke, a buttery glow penetrates the chamber. A sunbeam shines down on me. Like a God ray. I bask in the warmth of the light and wipe the dirt from my eyes.

I blink, unsure of what I'm seeing.

Shadows move in the distance; muffled voices filter down through the haze.

I can't hear what they're saying, my ears are still ringing.

Atticus and Dorian stand, brushing debris from their hair and clothes.

Men with hard hats and high-visibility vests stare down at us from above, their mouths open in shock.

"Stop the demolition!" someone cries, and the work comes to a halt.

He calls for a ladder, and I bury my head in Atticus's shoulder, squeezing Dorian tightly around the chest, sighing with relief.

28
ATTICUS

You will think me cruel, very selfish, but love is always selfish; the more ardent the more selfish. How jealous I am you cannot know. You must come with me, loving me, to death; or else hate me, and still come with me, and hating me through death and after.

—Joseph Sheridan Le Fanu, Carmilla

THE PARAMEDIC'S HANDS are cold as he takes my pulse.

"Can you tell me your name?" he asks.

"Atticus Garcia," I say. He's checking if I'm in shock. I might be.

My back may have been healed, but my body remembers. With a shudder, I recall the way the claws sliced my skin and how cold I felt, like I'd never be warm again. I think . . . I think I almost died. The realization hits like a hammer.

We sit outside the perimeter of the Arches demolition area with the paramedics. Raven is talking while an EMT bandages a small wound on her arm. Dorian lets another paramedic check his blood pressure. I'm seated in the back of an ambulance, draped in a shiny shock blanket. There's yelling from people in yellow vests, and the sound of construction equipment rolling out of the way, and a crackle of static from a radio. I feel hollow, small, and fragile, like a porcelain doll with a crack in its body.

The paramedic attending me asks something else, but I don't hear him. He asks again, and the world snaps back into focus.

"What?" I ask, dazed.

"Your heart rate is elevated, but that's to be expected. Are you hurt?" he asks.

"No," I say, shaking my head. Because of Dorian . . .

"What's all this blood, though? Are you injured somewhere?"

He gestures to my hair and to my hands, finding nothing that would cause it.

"It's . . ." I don't know what to say. I don't know if I should tell anyone about Dorian or what he did for me. I don't know if he'd want me to. I don't quite understand it. Maybe Dorian doesn't understand it either. I spot him again, leaning against another ambulance, and my urge to be with him surges.

He's standing with a blanket wrapped around his shoulders, his gaze distant. He almost died. Maybe he did die, or was close to dying.

Raven is talking to a police officer who just arrived. She's holding herself tightly across her chest, looking like she climbed down a chimney. Soot covers almost every inch of her. Her magic saved us all. Raven showed us just how strong she is. She twisted her hands into empty air and conjured fire, tearing the fabric of reality as easily as tearing paper. Beautiful. Terrifying.

"All this blood," says the paramedic. "Are you sure you're not hurt?"

I sense his growing concern for my lack of answers.

His thoughts swirl with worry, medical jargon overwhelming me. *Concussion . . . ? Possible internal bleeding . . . ? Acute stress reaction . . . ?*

He might take me to a hospital, or worse, he might call my mother. I don't want her to worry, and I definitely don't want anyone to know about what just happened to us. It's a miracle that we made it out alive . . . No, it's because of Dorian and Raven that we're alive.

"I'm fine, I swear," I tell the paramedic.

He seems to believe me. There's nothing wrong with me, physically at least.

Before he can say anything, I leave the ambulance and head straight for Dorian.

When he sees me coming, relief warms his eyes. "Hey," he says.

"Hey. Are you all right?"

He nods, swallowing thickly. "Yeah, they checked me out. They were pretty confused by all this blood, though."

"Same," I say, eyeing the nearby paramedics, who are speaking to each other and looking over at us suspiciously. But this is Sibylline. A lot of weird stuff happens here all the time. They must be used to it.

"Are you . . ." Dorian trails off, and his gaze lowers, toward where the gashes would be in my back. I pull my shock blanket tighter around my shoulders.

"I'm fine," I say. "Thank you."

Dust from the tunnels has turned his hair gray. I like it. It gives him a kind of mature, regal appearance. I have an urge to run my fingers through it, combing it back into place the way he likes it, but I stop myself when his gaze shifts to Raven. She's still talking to the police officer, holding her own against his questions. Dorian's gaze softens when he looks at her. He may have saved my life, but his heart still lies elsewhere . . . I swallow down the hurt that threatens to creep up my throat. He'll always want her over me. I was never in the running.

"What you did was . . ." I clear my throat, keeping my voice low. "That day on the subway you told me about . . ."

Color drains from Dorian's cheeks.

"You said he woke up after you touched him. So am I the second life you've saved?"

There's silence between us as Dorian sits with the realization.

"Maybe," he says with a slight smile.

Over his shoulder, I spy a man swiftly approaching. A familiar face stalking toward us through the crowd of people who have gathered at the demolition site. Warden Stone. He's flanked by two police officers, parting the sea of onlookers. He spots the three of us, unmistakably the ones responsible for all this.

He points to us. "You three. My office."

WARDEN STONE'S OFFICE is a mess. Papers are stacked in teetering piles on his desk, and boxes litter the floor. Brochures for Old Bones's new exhibit lie haphazardly on a chair. The room is cold. He's thrown open the windows, admitting the freezing late autumn air. But the cold isn't what makes me shiver. I'm still in shock, I think. Raven hugs herself tightly, eyes downcast, but rage and anxiety hum around her, making my skin itch. On my right, Dorian stands tall, his back straight. It's like he's trying to reach through the ceiling with the top of his head.

I want to touch both their hands. I want to feel them, to know they're here, even though they're right next to me. Warden Stone looks out the window. The sky is gray and the leaves have fallen from the trees, leaving the branches empty. Like skeletal claws they scrape at the slate-colored sky.

"Care to explain to me why you were down there?" Warden Stone asks us.

Dorian catches my eye, as if asking permission. I offer him a single nod, knowing what he's going to say before he says it.

"Sir, there's something under the ruins of Arches," says Dorian. "It tried to kill us."

"A malum," Raven adds. "A creature of darkness that was brought to life by magic."

"A malum?" The warden still doesn't turn to face us.

I would have liked for him to wheel around, confused, asking us to tell him more. Maybe we could be lauded as heroes who saved the day. But Stone doesn't even flinch. His hands are clasped tightly behind his back, and the only movement he makes is the slight squeezing of his fingers around his wrist.

Raven continues, unabashed, unapologetic. "We found a chamber, a workshop covered in sigils, and a prison cell. I think someone summoned the malum and bound it to the underground tunnels years ago, but now it's escaped."

Again, Stone doesn't move. I'm not convinced he's even listening, or maybe . . . "You know what we're talking about, don't you," I say, realization dawning on me.

"A malum hasn't been seen on this campus in a hundred years," Stone says languidly.

"We encountered one under Arches. If you go now, you'll find it," says Dorian.

"We'll investigate. It's what we do."

Why don't I believe him? Do I have to tear off my shirt to show him the mark on my back as proof? I catch Dorian's eye again, and I know he has the same thought. How else will we get him to listen?

The journal, of course, would absolve us.

I reach for Raven's bag to show Stone the journal, but she blocks me with her hand. She meets my eye, her expression hardened, then shakes her head, telling me to wait.

I want to argue, but I can't get a read on Raven at all; it's like she's closed herself entirely off from me.

Meanwhile, Dorian pleads with Warden Stone. "I know it sounds crazy, but I think the malum killed that student–"

"Pippa," says Raven.

"We ourselves barely made it out alive," he continues.

Warden Stone remains unfazed. "Thankfully, no one else was hurt." Finally, slowly, he turns. His icy blue eyes are as cold as the room, and he looks down his nose at us. "And yet somehow I can't help but be disappointed by the fact that you've violated almost every Sibylline policy."

"We're just staff members," I say. "We didn't do anything wrong."

"You've been caught trespassing in a restricted area, a place scheduled for demolition. It's a miracle you weren't killed. What were you doing? Looting?"

He is more right than he knows, so I change the subject. "Sir, please. You have to listen to us. There is something down there in the ruins."

"Yes, something that we are capable of handling. Thank you."

Anger rushes to my face. "Go do something about it, then," I say. "Stop the demolition and search the tunnels right now."

Warden Stone is uninterested. Then understanding dawns on me. I'm not a student or a teacher or a graduate of Sibylline. I am no one.

"What about Pippa?" asks Raven. "She didn't get crushed to death. We all know it. You're lying–"

Warden Stone's eyes flash dangerously. "I've read the investigation report. What happened to Pippa was an accident."

"I saw the claw marks on her body," Raven says flatly. "I know she was attacked."

"We need to call the authorities," I say.

"*I* am the authority," Warden Stone's voice booms, making me flinch. His thoughts are as strong as steel, his conviction unmatched. “For decades, the country has turned to us to handle matters relating to magical crime. As warden, I lead such investigations. Thus, if there is a malum in the ruins, I’ll be the one to handle it. Not you. You have no training, no knowledge of the art.”

Contempt rolls off of him like oil. I can taste it on the back of my tongue, bitter as bile. I try to rid myself of his thoughts, but it makes me sick. A lump forms in my throat. I try to swallow it down, but it’s stuck there. I’m choking on dread. I can’t bring myself to look at him, so I lower my gaze to his desk. There, buried amongst the pile of papers, is a familiar illustration: a body sprawled on a pentagram.

I’m so fixated on it, I almost don’t hear it when he says, “You have violated rules and ignored repeated warnings. I have no choice in the matter.”

“Sir, please–” starts Dorian.

“Therefore,” continues Stone, “you three are hereby unwelcome on this campus, even as staff members. This school is private property, and every inch of it is now off-limits. You are forbidden to set foot within these gates.”

I lift my head and balk. “What? But how are we supposed to–”

“You’re fired, Mr. Garcia. As are the rest of you.”

The world tips underneath me. Fired? Me? That can’t be right. How will I learn from the students and teachers at Sibylline? How will I ever understand my power?

The answer hits me like a sledgehammer: I won’t.

“That is all,” he says, not even bothering to meet my eye. Settling into his chair, he opens a large, leather-bound tome, dismissing us with a casual wave of his hand.

ATTICUS

Silence is of different kinds, and breathes different meanings.
–Charlotte Brontë, Villette

MY LEGS STOP working somewhere around the garden. I don't remember leaving Stone's office, I don't remember descending the marble stairs or passing under the ivy trellises. I don't remember anything. It's like I'm operating on strings. But now they've been cut, and I'm left hanging by nothing.

Fired. It's over.

I'm vaguely aware of my location—a garden in the quad, surrounded by Greek statues. In the middle is a stone fountain and cold-looking benches that might as well be carved out of ice. The fountain is empty, and the statues stare down on us, their gazes filled with reproach. Dorian collapses onto a bench, fists in his hair, elbows on his knees. Raven leans on a statue, her back to me, rigid, angrier than I've ever seen her. Me, I'm numb. I've been hollowed out. There's now a hole in my chest.

I start to pace. I still taste dirt, and ash, and my own blood. I'm chewing a hole on the inside of my cheek, and I welcome the pain. It's the one thing I can control now.

My mom is going to be so disappointed. I can't face her. I don't even know how I'll be able to break the news. Maybe I should just go into one of the steady magical trades. Being a psychic for the police department pays decently. Give up my dreams. They were stupid anyhow.

"But I don't want to go to Paris!" Raven wails, then looks at us in a moment of sheer self-awareness and starts laughing.

It's so absurd that for a moment Dorian and I laugh, too.

"Why do you have to go to Paris?" Dorian asks.

I raise my eyebrow. This is the first I've heard of this. I guess there are some secrets she can keep, even from me.

Raven sighs. "When we decided we were going to get jobs here, my parents tried to talk me out of it, but I wanted to come so badly, even if they disapproved. So I lied and told them I was taking a gap year in Europe. I wanted them to think that I was thinking about other schools. I've been sending letters to my cousin in Paris to mail home to my parents. Now I have to go there. Otherwise they'll kill me."

Dorian and I exchange a look. "They're not going to kill you," he says.

"No, they will," she says, laughing again. "So I'll have to go."

She's so spoiled, and she doesn't even know it. Unlike me and Dorian, she can bop off to Europe. Without a degree from Sibylline, I'll never get the kind of magical job I want. And what about Dorian? His mom's on Medicaid. That's the only thing keeping her alive. What is he supposed to do now?

"I just–I don't want to leave you guys," Raven says as tears form in her eyes.

And right then, I forgive her for still having the world at her feet. Seeing her sad makes me want to burn down the whole campus. Sibylline can hurt me all it wants, but it can't hurt Raven.

"We'll figure something out," I promise. All for one and one for all.

Dorian folds her into a hug. He soothes her with quiet murmurs, and she wraps her arms around his chest and cries into his shirt. I don't want to feel jealous of her, but I do.

My back aches, my head pounds. A migraine is coming on, and all I want to do is sink into bed, pull the covers over my head, and hope that this was all just a bad dream.

A figure approaches, wearing a gray uniform and a shiny badge. A security guard. "I've been asked to escort you to the public streets," he says. "This campus is private property. You need to leave."

"Yeah, yeah," I say, throwing up my hands. "Whatever."

Dorian and Raven walk ahead while I trail behind, determined to stay on Sibylline's stone path for a millisecond longer, as if hoping to absorb some last bit of magic from the atmosphere. But the security guard pushes me firmly in the back, making my wound twinge, urging me forward.

I turn, look up, and see Stone watching us from his office window. Backlit, his body stands rigid as if carved from marble. I sneer at him, and the guard shoves me again, harder. Stone watches as we're escorted all the way to the street and the gate closes behind me.

The clang of hard iron rings out in the cool autumn air as the lock slams into place, banging like a judge's gavel.

WE SLIDE INTO our favorite booth at the Acroteria, thankful that it's just outside the limits of the campus. I've done my best to wash off the dirt, filling the bathroom sink with sand, which still lingers here and there, in my cuticles and under my nails. I pick at them idly while Dorian orders a pot of tea to share. Raven sits across from me, her chin resting on her palm as she gazes out the large window. The streets are empty. Classes should be starting right about now. The morning is unusually dark, the sky crammed with storm clouds that refuse to give up their rain. Greedy.

I still can't get a proper read from Raven. Like the clouds outside, her aura is opaque, and the longer I look at her, the more frustrated I get.

"So you just wanted to keep Adelina's journal?" I ask, breaking the silence between us.

Raven's gaze slides to me. "I didn't want to give it up. I couldn't. It's the last book of magic we might ever get our hands on." She bites her lip, a prick of white flashing behind red. "It's important."

"That book is evil," I tell her. "It was used to hurt people."

"It's just a book."

"Is it?"

Raven scoffs. "There's so much more we don't know about this magic. You want to throw it all away?"

"Maybe some things aren't supposed to be known."

Raven stares at me. She's changed since we've come here. Sometimes it's like she cares more about magic than how dangerous it can be. But I can't bring myself to say it. She, of all people, should know how words can be used to hurt just as they can be used to inspire.

"We can't keep it," I tell her. I hold out my hand.

For an agonizing moment, she stares at me, her breath fluttering in her chest. Reluctantly, she slides the journal across the table toward me. I can tell it's taking a lot for her to give in, but I'm grateful she listens. She's right in a way, it is just a book, but it feels like a loaded gun in my hand.

I slide the book into my bag, lean back in the booth, and take a breath. A gust of wind kicks up wet leaves, splattering them against the window. Almost dying and getting fired in the same day has me feeling empty.

I can't stop thinking about what I saw in Warden Stone's office. "He knew what a malum was; he didn't ask us to define it. Stone *knew*," I say.

"You think Warden Stone's responsible for everything that's happened?"

"Didn't you see that illustration on his desk? The body on the pentagram?"

Her eyes widen. "What? No."

I don't want to believe that Warden Stone could be responsible for the malum getting free, but I don't know what to think anymore. Who would believe us anyway?

Dorian's voice cuts in. "Look at this." He's come back to the table, a ceramic pot of steaming tea in one hand and mugs looped around his fingers in the other. He carries a newspaper tucked under one arm, and he drops it onto the table. It's the school paper, *The Tyrian*. "I saw it on the counter."

The Tyrian is magically imbued and updates in real time.

"'Another mysterious accident ends in tragedy,'" Raven says, reading the headline aloud. Her eyes are round when she meets my gaze. My whole body goes cold.

"Another student is dead," says Dorian, jabbing his finger at the article. "Their body was found this morning. All classes are canceled until further notice."

It explains why the campus was empty.

Raven leans over the newspaper, her eyes moving across the page. I know she doesn't want to miss any detail. She scans the article three times before she leans back in her seat. "The malum . . . It has to be." She holds her head in her hands.

"Hey, it's not your fault," I say. "We did what we could."

Her jaw hardens, and I know my words give little comfort.

Another student is dead.

The student smiles at us from their picture. Nerdy, with square glasses, innocent. It feels like an ice pick has been stabbed into my chest. I know all too well what his final moments were like. No one deserves to die like that. No one. My eyes burn just thinking about it.

When I blink away the tears, I notice something in the photo. On his jacket, he's wearing a pin with an eye and a star–no, a pentagram. I recognize the symbol.

"He was a member of St. Ad's," I say. My mind revs like an engine.

Raven nods.

"And Pippa, the one who died from the archive, she was trying to join them, too, wasn't she?"

"Yeah, I think so," says Raven.

"You think the killings are related?" Dorian asks.

"Don't be ridiculous," says Raven.

Professor White always seemed suspicious of them, told me to stay away. Maybe it was for a good reason. But then I remember seeing Aspen that day at Arches.

"Aspen is a member," I say. "He has connections to all of the victims. I saw him lurking at Arches after it fell, like maybe he was looking for an entrance to the tunnels. He has access to restricted grimoires. Do you know for sure where he was last night? And the night Pippa died?"

Raven goes still, staring at me. She's rendered speechless.

"You think Aspen is involved?" Dorian asks me.

"Maybe he knows more than he's letting on."

"But what would Aspen want with the malum? Why use it to kill kids from St. Adolphus Hall?"

I fall silent. I don't know. I start crosshatching on a napkin in front of me, dragging my fingernail into the paper in neat, even lines. My back aches, and I try to hide the discomfort by shifting slightly in my seat. Dorian notices, though.

"What's wrong?" he asks.

"When the monster attacked me . . . it felt like it wasn't just cutting me open, but that it was taking something from me."

Both Dorian and Raven gape at me. "What do you mean, *taking*?" Raven asks.

"I don't know." I wince at the memory of the claws still fresh in my back. "I'm just telling you what I felt. Like it was feeding on me somehow. Not on my blood but . . . something deeper."

"Adelina said the malum needed to feed, that it required magic to live," says Dorian. "Do you think that's what it was doing to you, feeding on your magic?"

I shrug. "I don't know . . . maybe?"

"But you're fine? It wasn't able to finish–right?" Dorian asks.

"I think I'm okay. We stopped it, but this isn't over. It's still killing people, maybe taking their magic or something, getting stronger every time."

Dorian takes a deep breath. "What is it we're dealing with? Chaos incarnate? How do we even stop it?"

It's a rhetorical question. None of us know. And without access to Sibylline, we might never know. His words hang in the air between us. The gentle clatter and bustle of the cafe echoes around us. My tea sits long forgotten in front of me.

The gloom outside matches the aura over our heads.

"It knows our faces. Maybe it'll try to come after us again," says Raven. "If it needs magic, we're the obvious targets. We have power."

Dorian folds his hands over his mouth, his gaze distant. I can tell he's thinking a million things at once.

A small part of me, the part that hurts, wonders aloud. "Maybe we really should let Sibylline take care of things. They specialize in magic. They're the ones who have been studying the craft for centuries. They can handle the malum."

Admitting it hurts. But I miss home, I miss my mom, I miss my old bed and my old room. I miss the way things used to be. I miss when we were the Oneiric Society and things weren't so fucking complicated between us.

Once I'm on a roll, I don't stop. "I never wanted to be caught up in grand conspiracies or . . . goddamn shadow monsters!" I bury my face in my hands, mumbling, "Shit. The last moment I felt any kind of real joy, like everything was going to be all right, was when I kissed Dorian. And then everything got worse. So much worse."

When I lift my head from my hands, Dorian looks stunned. I almost don't know why, but then I realize what I said.

"You . . . you kissed Dorian?" Raven asks me, as if she's unsure she heard correctly. "When?"

My cheeks get hot. "At the St. Ad's Halloween party."

"Is this true?" she asks Dorian, shocked.

"We don't have to talk about it," he says, trying to change the subject. He won't look at me. I'm a monster. I just outed him without even thinking. I of all people should know how that would feel.

Raven blinks, eyes misting. She turns back to me, as if looking for the truth, and I sense her pain as my own. I never meant to hurt anyone, but I try to explain.

"You were off with Aspen," I tell her, "and Dorian and I wanted to test the boundaries of his magic."

“So what *we* did that one night . . .” She can’t bring herself to finish the sentence. “Did it mean nothing at all?”

Dorian stares at both of us—now it’s his face that’s flushed red. “You and Raven . . . you guys?”

Now I feel like *I’m* trapped in a cage. No way out.

Raven’s still waiting for me to answer her, so I do. “You didn’t seem like you wanted to talk about it, so I didn’t. You seemed perfectly happy with Aspen.”

“That’s not fair,” says Raven. “You made that very clear. You didn’t want to be with me. Aspen does. Don’t use that against me.”

Dorian finally interjects, raising a placating hand between us. “Please, stop. We’re all figuring things out. We’re still friends. The three of us—friends. Always, right?”

But Raven looks stony. “Not sure what kind of friend would use us like that.”

“That’s not fair,” I say, my voice wobbling. “I didn’t mean to hurt you—”

“Well, you did. Whether you meant to or not.”

I look to Dorian but find no sanctuary. He’s picking at the edges of his gloves, and doesn’t look either of us in the eye.

In trying to have them both, I’ve lost them both.

Outside, the storm rages. The rain comes down in sheets, coating the window.

I want to sink into the cafe booth and vanish. I don’t deserve friends. Maybe I deserve *this,* this air of hurt and betrayal.

“Right.” I nod. “Then I guess this is it, then. Have a safe trip home.”

Without another word, I walk out of the Acroteria, and no one stops me as I wade into the freezing rain, never once looking back.

30

RAVEN

Of course I was under the spell, and the wonderful part is that, even at the time, I perfectly knew I was. But I gave myself up to it; it was an antidote to any pain, and I had more pains than one.

—*Henry James,* The Turn of the Screw

DROPS OF RAIN pelt the gray pavement as I climb the stairs to the apartment door, thinking only of Atticus, hoping I'll find him waiting for me inside. When I come in, the wind rattles the windows, making the building creak and groan. The room is dark and cold. Lightning flashes and thunder rumbles. It's unusual, an autumn thunderstorm in Vermont.

I shake off the rain, but I'm already chilled to the bone.

"Atticus, can we talk?" I call into the apartment.

Nothing, no sound, no one answers back.

He's not here. I can't apologize. I said such hurtful things, and meant none of it, not completely. I don't know what I was thinking. I was angry, and hurt, and I lashed out. When I rushed after him, I lost him in the storm. I thought he was going home. Now I'm alone, and filled with regret. I hadn't meant to snap at Atticus. Not really. I was just jealous, thinking of him and Dorian together.

Shivering, I light a fire, put on the kettle, shower quickly to wash off the grime from the tunnels. I keep expecting Atticus to walk into the apartment, but he doesn't. So I wait. I drink tea and stare out the window, hoping to see him coming down the street, hunched over in the blustering wind. I promise myself that when he walks through this door, we'll figure out what to do next together. Like we always do. Maybe I'll take him to Paris with me.

When there's a knock at the door, I almost trip over the coffee table in my haste to answer. The second I fling it open, an apology dies on my lips.

Aspen, standing under an umbrella.

"I heard what happened," he says. His cheeks are pink from the cold. "They really fired you?"

"Oh, yeah," I say distractedly.

"Are you okay?"

I almost laugh. "Am I okay?" I repeat.

Aspen frowns. "Can I come in?"

Atticus's warning wedges itself into my thoughts. Can I really trust him? Can I trust anyone? My heartbeat flutters. "I just want to be alone," I say, slightly pushing the door closed.

"Raven–"

"What we had was fun, but I think it's best if we end it. I'm sorry," I tell him.

The look of hurt on his face is convincing, making me believe for a brief moment that I've ruined the last good thing I have in my life, but I close the door anyway. I wait, listening for his footsteps to retreat before I head back upstairs.

Why is it that whenever I open my mouth, I always make things worse?

I busy my mind with reading. I pull blankets that smell like Atticus over my shoulders to stave off the chill; he never comes. I add more fuel to the fire, always glancing out the window, but the streets are empty. I eat dinner in silence, staring at a door that never opens. I wake after an hour's nap when I think I hear it creak, but it's just the wind.

Atticus isn't coming home.

Dorian

It was not the thorn bending to the honeysuckles,
but the honeysuckles embracing the thorn.
—*Emily Brontë,* Wuthering Heights

MY CLOTHES HANG neatly in the closet, ready to be folded into a suitcase. I don't have much. One pair of shoes. One coat. One toothbrush. The apartment came fully furnished, so I don't have to worry about the rest.

While I pack, I think about Atticus. And Raven. And my future. I can't imagine going forward without them in it. I don't even have a plan. And Atticus—Atticus just stormed away. Raven tried to catch up with him, but he was gone. I wish I could explain, but all my thoughts are so murky and confusing, even I have a hard time seeing through the mess. The line between friend and lover has blurred. I like them both. They're both so smart, so ambitious. They know what they want. I admired them the moment we met. Loved them, though I didn't know the right words to say it. I don't know how to label myself; maybe I don't have to. Not now, at least.

But now they're gone.

A pathetic laugh escapes me when I throw my suitcase lid closed.

What will I do now? Move back to the city. And do what? I have no idea. Start over, I guess. Seeking comfort, I touch my great-grandfather's watch in my pocket. He started over, once. It's never too late to start again. But it's a lot scarier doing it without my friends.

I really can heal with my touch . . . Maybe I can help my mom with her cancer. But would I just be making myself sick, too? How does my magic work? What can I do? How can I help? I have power I've only just begun to understand, but the truth is I don't know anything about myself. Not really, not yet. Without Sibylline, I'm just stumbling in the dark.

I distract myself by cleaning my desk, throwing everything into a cardboard box, until I come upon the binder from Old Bones, the one with all the donor addresses I was supposed to mail thank-you letters to. I brought it home, promising Evander I'd complete my work before the gala, but I completely forgot about it. Granted, I had other things on my mind. I only got through mailing thank-you notes to surnames that began with the letter *R*.

Idly, for old times' sake, I open the binder and riffle through the pages, scanning the contents.

Inside are the lists of names and the donated articles. Every artifact that comes into the museum has a paper trail. It's the only way items can be verified in their origin by ordinary staff. Sometimes the names have hundreds of donations under them, but my attention snags on one name.

Stone, Jeremiah.

Warden Stone. My blood turns to ice in my veins when I read what he donated. I sit on my bed as I read and reread the entry to make sure I'm not hallucinating. I've seen them before. I remember them all too well. I can't not.

Warden Jeremiah Stone donated three artifacts to the museum.

One necklace made from carved beetles.

One onyx ring with snake detailing.

One wand made of wood and mother-of-pearl.

"SAY IT AGAIN," says Raven, her eyes hard. "Warden Stone donated a wand, as in . . ."

"Hecate's wand, yes. The same wand Adelina Ward used to raise the malum."

Adelina needed a powerful wand to conjure chaos, and the only wand powerful enough to do it once belonged to the goddess of magic.

From her seat on the couch, Raven stares in shock at the document as I pace. I can't sit still, not after what I just found. I rushed over to Atticus's apartment and was thankful Raven let me in. I bet I sounded like a maniac pounding on the door.

"How did he get Hecate's wand? I thought it was taken from Adelina when she was locked away."

"His predecessor must have kept it in storage. Only now did Stone decide to donate it."

"Why, though?" Raven asks.

"I don't know. I just know that it's not a coincidence. Where's Atticus? He needs to hear about this, too."

"He hasn't come home yet."

"Yet?" I stop pacing. "What, you haven't seen him at all since yesterday?"

"No," Raven says, rubbing her arms for heat or comfort. "I thought he was with you . . ."

"He wasn't."

"You don't suppose he went back to the tunnels to find proof? Maybe the malum . . . ?"

"No." I cut my hand through the air, banishing the thought. "Maybe he just went somewhere quiet to sketch. Remember how he used to do that?"

Raven nods, like she's forcing herself to believe it, too. "You don't think Stone might . . ." Raven pauses, as if wondering if she should say it aloud. Then she continues, "You don't think Stone's responsible for the malum's escape, do you? You don't think he's picked up where Adelina left off?"

"I don't know," I say again. Dread sits uneasily in my gut. "I mean, wouldn't that jeopardize his position as warden? It still doesn't feel right. We're missing something. He may have known what was down there, but I can't imagine him setting the creature free."

Raven hums, staring at the page.

Without Atticus, the group feels incomplete. There's a gaping void in his absence. I go to the window and search for him in the distance, but all I see is gray. Late autumn has sapped all of the color out of the world.

Even if we could prove that Stone is behind it all, who would believe us? We're just a few disgruntled former employees, with nothing to lose and everything to gain from taking down the university's warden. We were fired. Who would listen to us?

"Raven," I say, my breath catching on her name.

She glances up at me, her dark eyes wide and curious. I admire the curve of her lips, the furrow of her brow. Being near her will always make my heart race.

I lick my lips and drag my teeth over them, chewing on the words I've always wanted to say but never had the courage to speak until now. "I . . . I know it might be too late, but I want you to know how much I care about you."

Raven's gaze softens as she stands up and joins me at the window. "I care about you, too, Dorian."

Her tone isn't at all what I expected. I don't think she understands. "No, I *like* you, Raven. Actually, that's not entirely true. I don't just like you. I've been in love with you since we first met. And I have to tell you before you go away, because otherwise I'll never move on."

There it is. The truth. Finally out.

Raven doesn't say anything for a moment. Then she places her hand on my gloved one. "Oh, Dorian, I know. I've always known. Just like you've always known Atticus has a huge, terrible crush on you, right?"

I guess I've never been that good at hiding my feelings for her; I'm practically a lovesick puppy. But Atticus—it was only recently that I knew it to be true. I'd been so preoccupied, so lost, I never really realized. But Raven saw it. She knew.

"How ironic," I choke out, "the guy who can see the truth through touch couldn't even see the truth in himself until it's too late."

"It's never too late," she says. Her dark eyes have captured mine. "I'm sorry I didn't mention that Atticus and I fooled around."

"I'm sorry I didn't mention it either."

She lets out another huff of a laugh and shakes her head. "I don't know why we're making this so hard for ourselves."

"Because we like making things complicated."

"We like challenges."

I allow myself a smile. "A challenge means it's worth doing, right? Nothing without great effort."

Raven smiles, too, and she takes a deep, steadying breath, eyes locked on mine. The urge to touch her is almost overwhelming, but I hold myself back. My other hand clenches into a fist to stop myself from doing it.

"I was jealous of Aspen," I say. "And then when I found out you and Atticus kissed, it felt like a punch to the gut. Like I was losing both of you."

"I'm right here, Dorian," says Raven, and there's something different in her gaze this time when she looks at me. She used to look at Atticus that way.

"Aren't you going to Paris?"

"Come with me."

Raven's eyes are soft and warm. They dance across my face, reading me like a favorite book. She tips her head forward, and I hold my breath. She pauses, the briefest moment. The scent of her honey shampoo sends my spine tingling.

"You're joking," I whisper.

"I'm not," she says. And there it is again. That look. With that curious twinkle in her eye, a glow so potent it could light up the universe. Her fingers tighten around mine. "Don't you think?"

My lungs constrict, my breath catching in my throat. I drop my head, lean in. *Do it,* I tell myself. *Do it, just kiss her. She wants you to.*

But I still can't. It's everything I want, and it's so close, even as I recall what she just told me—that Atticus has felt for me what I've felt for Raven this whole time. Atticus . . .

"Dorian," whispers Raven. "Are you going to kiss me, or am I going to have to throw myself at you?"

A groan escapes me. "Raven."

I close my eyes and press my lips to hers and take what I've always wanted.

32
ATTICUS

Beware; for I am fearless, and therefore powerful.
—*Mary Shelley,* Frankenstein

ONE, ONE, TWO, three, five—I'm counting to block out the noise. *Eight, thirteen, twenty-one, thirty-four*... I've been walking for so long, I've lost count of the times I've started over.

I haven't gone home yet. I haven't slept. All night and day, I've wandered the outskirts of campus, looking at the skyline, my heart burdened by an immeasurable shame. I can't believe I've been so stupid. My friends both hate me, and it's all my fault.

The gray clouds promise more rain, making the air feel colder. Wet leaves lie plastered to the cobblestones, and a murder of crows stares down at me from leafless trees.

It's starting to get dark, which helps me slip back onto campus. I keep my head low, just in case a security guard notices me. But I have a reason to be here.

Professor White heard about what happened and reached out, sending me a letter that appeared in my hand, just like the day Sibylline rejected me.

Her letter, on the contrary, was far more welcoming. She wants me to come by Mansart Hall so she can give me something, maybe a goodbye present, maybe a recommendation. Who knows? Either way, I have to pick up my things from the office anyway. Who would I be to decline?

A black cat sits on the stairs to Mansart Hall, watching me with vivid yellow eyes.

I look up and down the street, but no one else is around. The cat hisses when it sees me, and blocks my path.

"Sorry, friend, I need to get in there."

But still it doesn't move and tries to keep me from going further.

I keep trying to walk around it, and it keeps trying to stop me from entering the building. Finally, in frustration I pick it up and move it out of the way.

The black cat gives me one last baleful look before taking off at a sprint and disappearing into the night. Mansart Hall stands before me, dark and dreary. Warden Stone be damned. I trudge up the stairs and walk inside to see it one last time. But no one is here. The office is empty. There's the sound of movement from the back room.

"Hello!" I call.

A head pops out from behind an open door, dark gray hair and a pencil sticking out of the bun. Professor White. "Oh, Atticus, just in time!" she says. "I'm so glad you came."

I rush toward her as she emerges, closing the door behind her, clutching a leather-bound book. Her clothes are unkempt; there are bags beneath her eyes. I must look worse, though, because she grows concerned when she sees me.

"You look . . . Well, you look awful," Professor White says.

"I don't know who else to tell," I say, looking at the office for the last time. Then I pull Adelina's journal from my bag. I'm done with Sibylline. I've abandoned my dream. This is all I have left of it, and I just want to rid myself of it. I realize now why I came here to

Mansart Hall. For this to be truly ended, I need to give the journal to someone I trust. I hold it out for her to take, and her pencil-thin eyebrows rise.

"What is it?" she asks.

"Me and my friends, we found this in the tunnels, under Arches. It belonged to a wizard who did something terrible a hundred years ago. She created something she called a malum, a thing that needed magic to survive. It killed students, feeding off their life force . . ." I'm rambling. I must sound insane. "The malum is still alive. I'm sorry. I didn't mean to tell all of this to you. I just wanted to give this to someone. I thought it might somehow be better in your care."

Professor White stares at me for what feels like an eternity. Her aura is a jumbled mess, like a tornado–it swirls.

"Okay," she says. "I'm glad you came to me. I know what we should do now." She beckons me to follow her, taking me deeper into the office, toward a back room.

I follow, expecting to find others, but the room is empty. I thought she was taking me to meet someone.

Professor White locks the door behind us.

I swallow a lump in my throat. Why is my heart pounding so hard?

"You came here to give me the journal, so hand it over," she says, insisting.

I hesitate. Her eyes sparkle with something I've never seen in her before, something not right. She's always been passionate–maybe some would call it obsessed–when it comes to her work, but the look in her eyes now has a sharpened edge to it. Before I obey her, I take a breath and extend my power, reaching into her thoughts. I don't expect to have easy access to a seasoned magician's mind, but as she stares at me, everything comes into focus. It's as if I've wiped a dirty lens clean, and finally I can see what's been standing in front of me all this time.

I listen and hear her thoughts: *I can finish everything.*

My breath catches in my throat. "What did you say?" I ask.

Professor White looks startled, but she recovers, frowning. "I said, give me the journal."

"I never told you it was a journal."

Professor White stands frozen, her hand extended toward me. The look of urgency on her face disappears, and a frown takes its place. "Ah."

My heart pounds with growing panic, but I try to keep calm. "I just remembered, I have to go. My mom is waiting for me, she's picking me up," I say, reaching for the door. I turn the knob, but it's locked, not with a bolt, but with magic. The keyhole glows when I try to twist it. "Can you let me out, Professor White?"

I spin around, throwing my back against the door, holding the journal tight to my chest as her thoughts wash over me: *Atticus doesn't suspect me. He knows nothing.* They are as loud as if she's spoken them. *He doesn't suspect a thing. There's no evidence I tore down Arches. Calm him down. Get that journal.*

I'm still trying to turn the knob, but she's shaking her head. "Come now, Atticus. Let's be done with this."

But I know the truth. I know what happened.

"It was you. You were the one who sabotaged the project. You tore down Arches. You set the malum free. Why would you do that?"

Professor White smiles, though she looks somewhat surprised.

"Are you in here?" she asks, tapping her fingers against her temple. "Don't you know telepaths are banned from Sibylline? You didn't, did you?" She laughs. "The school doesn't let anyone like you in anymore."

I grip the journal with all my strength, my fingers going numb.

"I guess there's no use hiding it. You'll just read my mind anyway," Professor White says. "Yes, I orchestrated the fall of Arches to release the malum. I'd think you would understand. You are an architect. Like me, you are a builder and a dreamer. Don't you want to do wonderful, impossible things? Don't you want to explore the limits of magic? That's what I've done. The malum is just the start of my grand design."

It's like I'm in Arches all over again. Everything has come crashing down around me.

No no no, this can't be happening. Professor White has been nothing but kind, supportive! She's done nothing but help.

Then it hits me like a brick in the gut. She's been using me. I was an easy target. Desperate. I've been blinded by my own pathetic need to impress her. I didn't think . . .

I squeeze my eyes shut, blinking back tears. "Why? What's all of this for?"

"Want to know a secret?" Professor White asks playfully, like a schoolgirl. "When I was a student here, I barely passed my courses. I didn't have a natural gift of my own, not like you and your friends. But with a malum, I can absorb magic. From chaos comes everything. I can bolster my own magic, channel from the malum into myself, take from those undeserving of it and put it to better use." She steps toward me, her eyes alight with conviction. "I can make things, just like the great creators did. I can build *anything*."

"You can't do this," I say. "You have no idea what you're tampering with."

"Yes, Atticus," she says. "I do."

From behind her, a shadow moves.

Fear bolts me to the floor. I can't move.

The malum emerges from her own shadow.

"I just need a little more magic," she says. "Arches had to fall to set the malum free. But I have plenty of work left to do. Now . . ." White holds out her hand again. "Give me the journal, Atticus. And I can make this a little less painful for you."

The malum hisses, and my blood runs cold.

I squeeze my eyes shut.

My magic allows me to enter the minds of other people. I do it with ease. I slip into their thoughts and listen. Now I attempt something I have never done.

I reach out.

33
DORIAN

It was cold and barren—it was no longer the view that I remembered. The sunshine of her presence was far from me; the charm of her voice no longer murmured in my ear.

—*Wilkie Collins,* The Woman in White

RAVEN'S LIPS GLIDE across mine. Kissing her is so natural, so easy, we move in harmony. Her fingers run through my hair, her body close to mine. I narrow the gap between us, our limbs intertwined. It's impossible to know where I end and she begins. We stumble—me forward, her backward—into the windowpane. Her back thumps against the glass.

"What about your boyfriend?" I whisper.

"What boy— Oh, you mean . . ."

"Snowmass." I smirk.

"He's not my boyfriend," she says. "Not anymore. We broke up."

"When?"

"Yesterday. When I figured out what I wanted."

Her warm fingers skitter across my skin, touching my neck, my jaw. She traces the curve of my ear with the tip of her finger, and I'm instantly hard. The lightest sensation sends everything in me on fire. I may as well be electric.

I can't help it. I hunger for her embrace and melt each time we touch. Each kiss she places on my lips draws us closer and closer. We share one mind. I see through her eyes, hear her laughter, feel myself kissing her, my mind curving out and back into itself like a Möbius strip, over and over. I get dizzy, but I don't lose control. I'm learning to control my power.

One more kiss, another, and another. Then I come up for air. I breathe and my eyes flutter open. I don't realize there are tears running down my cheeks until Raven wipes them with her thumbs. I almost feel embarrassed, but I don't.

She pulls my shirt over my head, then takes hers off. "Okay?" she asks.

I nod, and we kiss as we make our way to the bedroom. What could I possibly say right now that would capture how I feel? Powerful, elated, free. No words seem good enough. Now she's unbuckling my belt, and I'm helping her out of her jeans. We're both breathing heavily, and I kiss her all over, on her collarbone, between her breasts, down her stomach.

Her body is splayed before me. Everything I've ever wanted.

"Dorian," she whispers. "Do it. I want you so much."

I can't reply; I'm overwhelmed with desire as I position myself at her entrance. But before I can move, my mind explodes.

I lurch back and cry out.

Atticus's voice rings in my head. It's as if he's screaming from afar. *DORIAN! RAVEN! HELP!*

The sheer force of his psychic energy paralyzes me, and I don't know what to do. Meanwhile, underneath me, Raven opens her eyes.

"What's wrong?"

Then Raven screams and holds her head.

Everything hurts. It feels like my head is cracked in two, an axe buried deep in it. Then the blade is ripped out just as quickly. The pain fades, but the words remain, echoing in my thoughts. The room spins, and I struggle to find my way back to myself. It's as if the world were a boat at sea, rocking violently, and I have no hope of standing upright on it.

"Raven?" I ask. "You heard him, too, right?"

"Atticus," she says, scrambling to her feet and putting her clothes back on. "He's in trouble." She tosses me my shirt and pants. "We need to find him!" she cries. "Where do you think he could be?"

"I don't know, but he's somewhere in Sibylline–let's just go back to campus and see if we can figure out anything. Maybe he'll send another message," I say as we hustle out the door.

The strangest thing. There's a black cat at the doorstep. It stares at us intently, as if trying to tell us something.

"It's just a cat," says Raven. "Ignore it."

I move to follow her, but something nags at me. "What do you want, cat?"

It arches its neck and curls its tail.

"Do you want us to follow you?"

It meows.

I remember how Atticus mentioned that he'd made a friend of a cat that hung around the architecture school. Was this the cat? Did Atticus send this cat?

"I think it knows where Atticus is," I say, kneeling down. "Do you?"

The cat meows again.

"Okay, we'll follow you."

We sprint across campus, following the cat all the way to Mansart Hall.

The rain returns, soaking us from head to foot. I don't care about the burn in my lungs or my legs; I only care about the terror in Atticus's voice, the panic, the desperation. I have to find him. We storm up the stairs and through the unlocked doors. Mansart

Hall is empty. There's no one here, not even a security guard waiting to escort us off campus. We search the offices where Atticus worked, all the desks, all the back rooms, until–

"Dorian!" Raven cries.

I follow the sound of her voice and find her standing in a hallway. She's looking at a puddle on the wooden floor.

It's blood.

"Something happened. I think something happened to Atticus," she says.

Searching for answers, I take off my glove and place my palm on the door.

The vision comes to me, fast and strong, like a punch to the gut.

Atticus. The journal. Professor White and the malum. The scene plays out in front of me. In the vision, the malum envelops Atticus as Professor White cackles.

I lurch out of the vision. "We were wrong," I tell Raven. "It's not Warden Stone. It's Professor White who's controlling the malum."

"Professor White? His mentor?" Raven is aghast.

"She took Atticus," I say. "They're in the tunnels."

"But where? They're hundreds of miles long."

"I don't know," I say. Desperation tastes like acid in my mouth. I don't want to believe that it's too late, but I don't know if Atticus is alive or dead. I don't know how we're supposed to help.

"Why would Professor White take him, unless . . ."

We stare at each other, the same thought running through our heads.

We bolt for Professor White's office, finding her name stenciled on a door. It's locked, but that doesn't stop me. I throw myself against the door, smashing it from the frame. My shoulder throbs, but I ignore the pain. The office walls are painted with strange sigils. Arcane summoning circles cover every surface.

The place bristles with magic. Pages ripped from grimoires are tacked haphazardly among the sigils. This is the work of an unhinged genius, the desperate scrawl of someone who's obsessed with the chaos . . . and she's taken Atticus.

"These are the same markings we saw in Adelina Ward's cell," says Raven, studying the symbols. "Oh God, Dorian. She's practicing chaos magic. She wants to continue Ward's work."

On her desk is the brochure for Old Bones, and an advertisement for the exhibit.

The revelation hits me like lightning.

"She *is* going to finish what Adelina Ward started," I say. "She's going to do it again, but White needs Hecate's wand."

Part Three

Omne trium perfectum.

(Every set of three is complete.)

–Latin maxim

34
ATTICUS

We learn from failure, not from success!
—*Bram Stoker,* Dracula

EVERYTHING HURTS. EVEN my eyelids ache. I try to open them, but it's like they're glued shut. My mouth is dry; my tongue tastes like iron. I try to swallow, but I can't.

I don't know where I am. I'm on my back, lying on something hard and cold. A chill rakes through me like tiny daggers. My shoulder throbs, a low, heavy pulse. *Ba-dump, ba-dump,* faster and faster. I try to touch it, but I can't. I manage to open my eyes to see why. My arms, they're raised over my head, and when I try to move them, a rattle echoes in the chamber. Something cold and hard binds my wrists. I move to wriggle free, but the iron cuts my skin when I struggle to pull my hands from it. I'm chained up. My legs are bound. The freezing cuffs clutching my ankles are like vises, holding me down.

I don't know what happened. One minute I was with Professor White; the next . . .

Everything comes back to me. My eyes snap open.

I know where I am.

I'm in Adelina Ward's cell. The cage, half-collapsed but still standing, surrounds me. Thousands of candles illuminate the room in an eerie glow. The sigils on the stones are just as I remember them. Rubble and debris from the demolition litter the floor, but the very center has been cleared out, making room for the spot where I'm bound. The demolition was halted when they found us in this room, and I thought they'd sealed off this place, preventing anyone from entering it.

Someone found their way inside it. I'm bleeding from my shoulder. The gash is shallow, but it aches with each heartbeat. I turn my head to see a smear of something red on the floor. Blood. Someone used it to draw a shape on the stones. A summoning circle.

A shiver runs through me.

Panic is a monster. It's all-consuming, a gaping mouth with teeth, and venom, and hot, wet breath. It has me, and it won't let me go. Again, I tug at my chains, but the metal tears at my skin. I cry out. I can't sit up. I can't move. I can't run, no matter how hard I try.

I am helpless. I might as well just lie down and die.

But then the rational, logical, calm part of my brain reminds me: Panicking will not help me get out of here.

I close my eyes and try to breathe. I focus on the Fibonacci sequence, reciting it under my breath. "Zero, one, one, two, three, five, eight, thirteen, twenty-one . . ." A sob escapes me, making me choke on the words.

"You're awake," says a voice.

Professor White peers down at me from above. She holds the journal clutched tightly to her chest. She looks unbothered, even as I pull on the chains. No empathy in her eyes, nothing.

"Why am I chained?" I ask, but she only shakes her head.

"You're stronger than I thought," she says blankly, as if observing a weed growing out of the sidewalk. "That's good."

"Professor White, please. Let me go."

She doesn't answer. She moves away from me, out of the cell

and around the room, to a table stolen from Adelina Ward's lab. It's covered in candles and books. She arranges the desk reverently, as if preparing an altar for a ritual.

I've seen this once before, in the vision with Adelina and Henri. I know what Professor White is planning to do.

"If you try to summon another malum, you may not be able to control it. I saw what happened last time. I know what Adelina Ward did."

Professor White turns. "Oh, you're mistaken. I'm not trying to summon a malum."

"You're not?"

"No," she says, grinning slightly, like I'm a stupid child who asked if the moon was really made of cheese. "You misunderstand me completely. No, malums—while useful creatures—are crude things. Like dogs. Singularly focused and insatiable. Throw a bone at their feet, and they devour it without a second thought, then ask for more. I believe that I can do better than that. I believe, with Adelina's foundational work, I can use her failure as a launching point for my own discovery."

I tense up. "What are you talking about?"

"I'll give you a little lesson, seeing as that's what you've always wanted at this school, isn't it? Sneaking around lectures and stealing books. Oh, I heard about a book missing from the restricted archives, I did. I know it was you and your friends."

My stomach plummets.

"I think we have a lot in common. So listen well. There are different fields of goetia. Conjuration, divination, evocation . . . I could go on. The foundations of this school are literally built on the summoning of spirits from another realm. Elemental spirits built Arches, just as they built the monuments of our school and our government."

Her eyes are bright, her tone triumphant. She's proud of her work and eager to share it with me. "It's all well and good, what the founders did back then. But the one subject that interested me the most was necromancy. The ability to speak with the dead, to learn their secrets. It's truly one of the most powerful forms of magic."

My hair stands on end. My body screams, eager to break free, but I can't. I'm a butterfly, pinned and trapped under glass. All I can do is listen.

"I believe I can combine the two, conjuration and necromancy. Ward focused on evocation as a measure of her practice. I intend to use invocation."

I struggle to recall how Raven defined these words, the memory hazy in my panic.

Professor White sees my confusion and clarifies what she said. "In evocation, we call a spirit into existence. An invocation is where you call a spirit into *you*."

My whole body goes cold, her words echoing in my thoughts. Professor White circles the room, her hands behind her back, like she's lecturing a class on calculus.

"Adelina Ward brought forth chaos, untethered it from its primordial basin, and called it into our world. Made it real. She was a visionary, but she was also impatient. That's why the malum is difficult to control. It needs the magic of others to exist, but in doing so, it kills people. It's well behaved, though, when you have the right spells. It often does whatever you want, though perhaps not in the ways you expect."

"I won't help you," I say. My wrists are raw with pain.

"Sadly, you don't have much choice in the matter."

Then it occurs to me—I haven't seen the malum. I search the room, but I can't find it. "Where is it? Where's the shadow?"

"It's needed elsewhere," she says.

I pull on the chains again, willing them to break, but they're solid iron.

"For now, you are my focus," says Professor White.

"What do you mean?"

"I tried experimenting on the spirits bound to Arches, but their dead essence made the magic brittle. I was missing a key component. A putlog hole, so to speak. A stabilizer."

"Tried doing what? You destroyed Arches for some experiment?"

"I was testing out the spirits locked in the tower. Through that process, I learned of the existence of the malum. They told me about the creature bound beneath the building. They taught me how I could control it, how I could free the shadow from its prison if I destroyed the tower."

"Why?"

"The malum is a tool, one of many that I intend to use today. You are yet another one."

"Please," I say. "Don't. You're not Adelina Ward. You don't have to do this."

Professor White moves to the desk. She sets down the journal on a stack of books, undoes a bundle of herbs, and lights a fire under a small cauldron.

A skull sits on the table. The skull from the cell. Adelina's skull.

"Adelina's spirit is bound to the skull. And with the right spell, I can call her back. I can invoke her, learn from her. I have many questions, and I can't wait to ask them."

"You can't mean . . ." I'm horrified at what she's implying.

Her eyes are fire bright. "I do. You're going to be perfect."

DORIAN

Our words are giants when they do us an injury, and dwarfs when they do us a service.

—*Wilkie Collins,* The Woman in White

SPOTLIGHTS CRISSCROSS THE night sky, like a beacon, guiding us forward. Lines of expensive cars queue up in the drive to Old Bones, letting people out to marvel at the decorative multicolored lights and glittering incantations.

"Why didn't Professor White steal the wand earlier?" Raven asks, breathless as she runs by my side.

"I don't know," I reply. "Maybe she wasn't strong enough. Perhaps after killing those two people, she'll finally be able to break through the protective wards." It's a guess, but I can't think about hypotheticals now. The one thing we know for sure is we have to get to the wand before she does. I just hope we're not too late.

Raven and I bound up the stairs to the museum, running across the red carpet lining the steps, past people in tuxedos and sparkling ball gowns walking to the front doors. The *Procession of Time* exhibit is in full swing as music pours out of the museum and into the night, announcing the start of the gala.

I couldn't care less about it. I can't think about anything except Atticus.

"Excuse me, coming through," I say as we push past the line of people filing into the front doors of the foyer. It's a packed crowd, and I grab Raven's hand to make sure she doesn't get lost.

At the front of the line, I flash my museum badge, still holding Raven's hand, and the security guard lets us in without question. He didn't even bother to check if it was valid.

Inside, the museum is packed full of people perusing the exhibit, holding flutes of champagne and eating canapés, admiring all of the pieces that I've spent the last few months meticulously curating. A string quartet plays music on a small stage, filling the room with sounds fit for a grand ball. Candles infused with magic cast a warm haze on the heads of beautiful guests, esteemed alumni, and current faculty alike.

Raven and I are forced to catch our breath as the crowd swarms ahead of us.

Hecate's wand sits in a glass display box, right in the open. "At least it's still here," I say.

"But for how much longer?" Raven says.

Her gaze roams the museum, taking in everything with wonder. She's thinking the same thing. "How are we supposed to steal it? There are hundreds of people here, witnesses. They won't just let us."

She's right.

"Come on," I say, pulling her deeper into the exhibit. Laughter and clinking glasses fill the air. I look left and right, searching for Warden Stone. I don't see him yet, but I know he's here somewhere.

Finding Professor Evander is easy enough, though. He's surrounded by a small crowd, men and women praising the exhibit. It's like he's holding court, gesticulating with a champagne flute at the museum around him to appreciative murmurs.

"Professor," I say, leaning in close and whispering. "I need to talk to you."

He looks startled at first, and then smiles at the other guests. "Of course! Excuse me, everyone, duty calls!"

I guide him to the outer perimeter of the crowd, and we hide behind a pair of columns. "What seems to be the matter, Mr. Winthrop?" he asks. "You're not supposed to be here."

"I need to take something from the museum. Right now."

"Excuse me?"

"There's an artifact here that is dangerous. Hecate's wand, remember, the one that knocked me out my first day? In the wrong hands—"

Raven hisses in my ear, "Stone is here." She motions toward the crowd, and I catch sight of him. He stands with a group of professors, looking right at us.

"Professor, please," I plead. "It's important. I believe someone intends to use it. We have to hide it."

"What are you talking about?"

There's a commotion. Guards have been called. Warden Stone is coming our way, directing security with a radio. They're going to arrest us.

"Professor, everyone here is in danger. Something terrible is going to happen, and Warden Stone—"

"He knows all about the danger," Professor Evander says.

"What?"

"The wand, it was his idea to store it here. It's the safest place."

"Not anymore," I say.

A strong hand grabs me by the arm, and I look up into the face of a security guard as broad as a building. Raven lets out a yelp as another guard grabs her arm, too.

Warden Stone stands behind us, talking briefly into the radio before gesturing for the guards to move in. "You are trespassing at a private event," Stone says.

"Warden Stone," Professor Evander says, "is this really necessary?"

"Professor Evander, please listen!" I beg, as the guard twists my arm painfully behind my back, making me wince, and pulls me away from the professor, through the crowd of curious onlookers wondering what's going on.

The guard's hand on my arm is solid as a vise, twisting my skin. I grind my teeth and check him like I would at lacrosse. This is all going wrong. I have to think of something.

But then, from the far end of the museum, there's a scream. High-pitched and wild.

The security guards stop pushing us to the exit to turn around and see what's going on. There's a rush of movement near the bar. Shattering glass and more screaming.

Professor Evander rushes toward the sound.

A hulking shadow rises up above the crowd.

The malum.

"What is that?" The guard holding my arm is frozen in fear.

There's more screaming, and people are running toward us. They crash into one another. Bodies strike the floor. A stampede in ball gowns and tuxedos.

I don't have time to be scared. Everything is happening so quickly.

The malum is larger than I recall. It's a whole head taller than everyone in the room. The guards forget about us. They turn to face the shadow. Warden Stone stands with us, inert with shock. Then the party devolves into pandemonium, people running in every direction.

Warden Stone comes to his senses and charges the malum. He

summons a spell, gathering the power in his hands, and throws it at the shadow. The creature howls as the spell splashes over it.

I grab Raven's hand and run.

We dodge blasts of explosive energy. They whiz past our heads like wasps. It's a room full of magicians. All eyes focus on the malum. No one is looking at us anymore.

Hecate's wand is still in its protective case. I grab a napkin from a table, wrap my fist in it, and punch the glass. Raven flinches, and the glass fractures like a spiderweb. I hit it again, and this time it shatters. All around us people scream and scurry toward the exits. Magic fills the air, and the malum's roars never cease.

Wand in hand, I run. At the exit, hundreds of people clog the narrow doors. Everyone is trying to escape. We can't get through.

A voice cuts through the noise. "Raven!"

We whip around to see Aspen standing behind a painting that's swung outward on hidden hinges. He waves us over frantically, and we have no choice but to follow.

36 RAVEN

But we are strong, each in our purpose; and we are all more strong together.

—*Bram Stoker,* Dracula

"ASPEN?" I ASK.

From the shadow of the tunnel behind the painting, the archivist holds out his hand to us. "Come on!" he shouts.

Can I trust him? What if Atticus's theory about St. Ad's was right?

But a fireball rockets past my shoulder, making the choice for me.

I take his hand and Dorian follows quickly. Aspen seals the wall behind us, and we're plunged into darkness. The commotion outside is muffled, but still audible. Warden Stone's voice rings out above the roar of the crowd, and the boom of an explosive spell rattles the floor.

My hands are shaking. Dorian's arm brushes mine, and I grab on to him for support.

In his hand, he holds the wand.

Aspen summons a handful of light in his palm, illuminating the corridor. We're in one of the hidden tunnels leading underground.

"The malum," Dorian says, breathless. "It's the same one, right? There aren't two?"

"I don't think so," I say.

"Are you two hurt?" Aspen asks.

"No." Though my heart is pounding so hard, it aches.

"Is that what Professor White is controlling?" Aspen asks. The battle still rages on the other side of the painting. Whatever they're doing, the security guards aren't able to slow it down.

"How do you know that?" I ask warily.

"I've been looking into the malum for a long time. I suspected Professor White when I found her trying to steal a book from the Rosette all about chaos magic. She's hated me ever since. St. Adolphus Hall has kept an eye on her for a while."

It all starts to make sense. That's why Atticus saw him around Arches that day. He knew Professor White was up to something.

Aspen moves to lead us away from the carnage. "I have to get you out of here."

"We can't. Our friend is in trouble," I say.

Dorian explains, "Professor White took him to the tunnels under Arches."

Aspen's eyes land on the wand in Dorian's hand, but something heavy slams into the painting hiding the entrance, making all of us jump. It sounded like a body.

"That wand is the only thing that can stop her now. Go," Aspen tells us. "I'll deal with the malum."

"You're sure?" I ask.

"The place is crawling with wizards, we'll handle it."

"Right."

"You've been there? To these tunnels?" Aspen asks.

I nod.

"Take this." He cups the lights from his hand and holds them out to me, transferring the spell from his palm to mine. The lights dance inches above my skin, floating like a cloud of fireflies. "If you know where to go, if you remember the place, the lights will be your map. Follow them. It's how we move around the tunnels to the archive."

"Thank you," I tell him. "And I'm sorry about, um, us . . ."

"Yeah, I figured that wasn't going to work out when I met your two friends. The three of you are kind of a throuple, aren't you?"

Before I can answer, Aspen's already pushed open the painting to join the fight. "GO!"

Dorian and I take off, traveling deep into the bowels of Sibylline. Our hurried footsteps echo all around us, and Dorian's haggard breathing is close behind me. "Nothing's following us," he says, checking over his shoulder. "But don't stop."

I don't intend to. I know what we left behind. I still hear those people's screams . . . They still echo in my skull. We pass through great atriums, winding corridors, chambers with vaulted ceilings, and ancient passageways, following the light as it guides us toward the tunnels under Arches. We find a place where the walls are covered in familiar writing. The sigils, the smell, the sounds, all of it is just as I remember. This is it.

My heart races as we approach the ruined chambers. My mind goes to the worst possible places, imagining how we'll find Atticus. I hope we're not too late. God, please let us get to him in time.

The lights lead us to the door of Adelina Ward's lab, where they vanish, snuffed out like a candle in a strong breeze. We're plunged into darkness. There is only the faint glow coming from under the door.

"We're here," I say.

In the dark, Dorian's eyes are mere pricks of light. He rolls up his sleeves, and together we push open the door and step into the lab. The candles in the wall sconces cast flickering rays of light across the stone. The alchemy table, full of vials and a simmering cauldron, bubbles with magic. There is no sign of Atticus or Professor White.

At the end of the tunnel, in the cell room, there's a golden light. Candles, hundreds of them. The air is rank with the smell of blood, sulfur, and smoke. The walls are half-collapsed but still standing.

Beside the iron cell, a body rests on the floor. It's Professor White. Her gray hair is splayed out around her head as she lies, her eyes wide open, a book on the floor beside her. Adelina's journal.

Then I see him. Atticus. He's chained up on the floor in the cell, dried blood marking a circle around his body.

Dorian throws open the iron door with a clang and rushes to Atticus's side.

He stirs, groaning, and Dorian scrambles to remove the iron cuffs from his wrists. "They're locked," he says.

I go to Professor White and check her pulse. She's still breathing, but she doesn't react to my touch. Her eyes are blank; they stare into endless nothing. In her pocket I find the key. I throw it to Dorian, and he unlocks Atticus's chains.

I grab Adelina's journal before returning to Atticus just as Dorian removes the last of the cuffs from his ankles.

"Atticus," Dorian says, gently pushing aside the hair from his forehead. It's stuck to his skin with sweat. He looks pale, almost sick, but he groans and his eyes open.

Dorian's face splits into a smile, and I throw myself into Atticus's arms. I hold him tightly, squeezing so hard I might break his bones. I kiss him, on the mouth, on the cheeks, on the forehead, relief making me shiver all over. He tastes like sweat and dirt, but his skin is warm, and he's alive.

Atticus pulls away, rubbing his forehead with an open hand. "Where am I?" he asks.

"Under Arches. We have to get you out of here."

Atticus casts his dark eyes around the room, looking confused. Dorian helps him to his feet, but he can barely stand.

"Can you walk?" I ask.

"I think so," he says, voice trembling.

I move to the cell door, but Atticus doesn't follow.

"Can I have those?" he asks, looking at the book and the wand in my hand.

There's something in his eyes, a flatness, that makes me hesitate. I pull back slightly.

Dorian doesn't seem to notice. "Come on, Finch, let's get out of here," he says, trying to lead him forward. But he doesn't move.

Atticus blinks slowly. He just stares at the room, at the book in my arms, at Professor White on the floor nearby. A befuddled expression covers his face, and he looks like he's waking up from a dream.

"Atticus," Dorian says, more forcefully.

"What?" he asks.

"Let's go."

"Dorian," I say, not taking my eyes off Atticus. "Wait."

Dorian stares at me, and then at Atticus, and it dawns on him. Something is wrong. He looks like Atticus, of course. He has the same dark hair, same dark eyes, same full lips. But something is off. I don't know what, but I just feel it.

His eyes are empty.

"You're not Atticus," I say.

37 DORIAN

The entire world is a dreadful collection of memoranda that she did exist, and that I have lost her!

—Emily Brontë, Wuthering Heights

NOT-ATTICUS SMILES AT us, and my whole world shatters. I don't believe what I'm seeing. It's Atticus, he's here, but—he's not. Not really. Same face, same clothes, same hair, but it's all wrong. It's like looking at a portrait and seeing a forgery. There's some element, some stroke, some touch that's missing. Invisible to an untrained observer. Invisible to someone who doesn't know him like we do.

"Adelina . . ." says Raven, standing in the doorway to the cell. "It's you, isn't it?"

Adelina steps toward us, wearing Atticus like a costume. She's stolen his face and his body. I don't know why I didn't see it. Maybe I just didn't want to acknowledge the strangeness of what was happening. Maybe I was too relieved to see Atticus alive. But now, as the ghost of Adelina Ward approaches, it's unmistakable.

"I know what I did wrong last time," Adelina says. "I know how I failed. And I know how to do it right. I've had a long time to think about it."

"Let him go," I say. Angry tears burn my eyes. "If you hurt Atticus—"

Adelina giggles. "Atticus isn't here right now."

No. It's not possible. It can't be true. He's in there, he has to be.

"Atticus! It's us!" Raven pleads, trying to break through, but Adelina smiles mockingly.

"Don't worry," Adelina says. "It was over quickly. He didn't want to be in this world anymore."

I don't know what to do or how to stop this. Is there anything I can do? This is magic that goes beyond me, beyond nature itself. Bringing someone back from the dead, it shouldn't be possible. And yet, here she is. Using Atticus's body like it belongs to her.

"So," she says, looking at the wand in Raven's hand, "let's stop wasting time, shall we?"

I step in front of Raven and slam the cell door closed, shutting Adelina inside.

She presses up against the bars, smashing her face against the frame, a grotesque smile on her face. "This won't stop me."

Adelina throws out a hand.

As if pulled up by invisible strings, Raven rises off her feet and goes flying toward Adelina's hand. With a bang, Raven slams hard into the cage.

"Raven!"

She drops the book and the wand and collapses into a heap.

I catch her just before her head can hit the floor, but Adelina grabs the book and the wand, grinning in victory.

Raven is dazed, but unharmed. Her eyelids flutter open, and she grabs on to my shirt, hauling herself back to her feet as she gapes at Adelina in fear.

"Thank you for bringing these back to me," Adelina says. "I've missed them."

She raises her wand, pointing it at us—

Then Adelina's head snaps back like she's been struck by an invisible fist. She stumbles, reeling. Blood leaks from her nose. She looks at us, and her eyes are somehow changed; they're different. They're *his*.

"Atticus!"

He's back.

38
Atticus

The world was to me a secret which I desired to divine.
—*Mary Shelley,* Frankenstein

"ATTICUS," DORIAN WHISPERS. He's the first thing I see when I wake.

The world snaps back into place. I'm in my body again, but everything feels wrong. Adelina is still here, in my body with me. I hear her whispering in my thoughts, growing louder. Raven and Dorian are calling my name, but my ears feel like they are stuffed with cotton. I shake my head to clear it.

"I'm . . ." It's like I'm standing on a rocking boat. It's hard keeping my feet under me. But they're my feet at least. They're mine again. "I'm fighting—" Pain shoots through my skull as blinding white dots fill up my vision. Blood pours from my nose and drips down the back of my throat. In my thoughts, Adelina thrashes, struggling to take control. I try to open my eyes, but tears blur my vision. I want the pain to stop; I want this to be over.

Raven and Dorian stare at me, terrified, and I know I need to fight Adelina. I do it for them. I screw up my face, push through the pain, through the storm of sulfur and smoke and ash that chokes my mind. I'm strong.

But she's stronger.

Like a hammer, she slams me down.

I'm falling, falling, *falling.*

"Don't you dare." Her words echo deep into my head. "I'll make you kill them if you interfere." She's using my mouth. She's stolen my voice, my body. I'm not in control. I'm a ghost in my own mind. I try to grab hold of something solid, anything I can reach, but it slips away from me, passing through my hands like fog.

"Atticus!" It's Raven's voice, but it sounds so far away.

I can see her, distantly, as if I'm looking through a telescope into the vastness of space. She's a star. A trillion light-years away. She's on her feet again. Dorian stands at her side. They're watching me, pleading for me to keep fighting. Dorian's mouth moves, but I can't hear him. I can't hear Raven either. I'm losing them.

"You are nothing," Adelina tells me. "You deserve nothing."

Her words consume me. Wash over me. Drown me.

I'm falling faster now. Sinking deep into myself. The darkness presses in on me. Folds me up. Adelina is moving my body, gathering her magic with Hecate's wand, using her old book. Raven and Dorian are almost gone. They're so far away. Everything is dark and cold. I only wish I could hold their hands one more time or feel the touch of their lips on mine.

God, I'm so sorry. For everything.

"You will know your place, and you will be happy there," says Adelina, shoving me deeper into my mind. Her words start to make sense. They enchant me. I want to spit in her face, but I don't. Her words are like a soothing balm, lulling me to sleep.

But Raven and Dorian . . .

I love them both. I always have, and I want to be with them. I think that's why I applied to this damn school in the first place, just so I could be with them. So they could be with me. So I could be in their life, and they could be in mine. Forever.

I'm so selfish.

I wanted us to always be together.

Us. Together. That's something solid I can hold on to. It's a handhold on a sheer rock face. I struggle to keep my grip on it.

I could let them go. I could save them that way. No—Adelina's trying to fool me.

Just let go.

But I won't. I can't.

I can't.

A part of me refuses to give up.

And maybe Adelina isn't as strong as she thinks.

I snap back into my own body. I'm in control again, and I'm holding the wand and the book. Raven and Dorian stare at me, frozen. I toss the wand and the book to Raven. She catches them. Adelina's voice echoes in my thoughts when she cries out, "No!"

Her words strike me like a fist to the face, and I stumble.

"The skull," I tell Dorian. "Destroy it. It's a tether."

Somehow, I know he must destroy it. Our minds are joined; I understand things that only Adelina knows, and I use her knowledge to my advantage. "Crush it," I say.

Dorian leaps to his feet and rushes to the table, where Adelina's skull rests. He lifts it above his head and smashes it to the floor. Shattered pieces scatter all around him, teeth and bone, and the voice in my head howls.

Adelina claws at my mind, biting and gnawing. Blood flows from my nose, and I fear I'll pass out. I look at the chains at my feet, and once again, I know what I must do. I drop to my knees and fasten the manacles around my wrists and ankles.

"What are you doing?" Raven asks.

"There's not much time," I say. I point to the books on the desk.

"You have to—" Before I can finish, my stomach twists. Adelina is taking control once again. "She's weak, but she can still control me. I can fight her, but—"

I'm too late.

Adelina takes my body, catapulting me back into the void.

Raven

Love will have its sacrifices. No sacrifice without blood.
—*Joseph Sheridan Le Fanu,* Carmilla

ATTICUS IS GONE once again. It's in his eyes. That shift, like a cloud passing over the sun. His face changes, and somehow doesn't change at all.

"No!" Dorian cries. He sees it, too.

Adelina tries to get up, but she can't. Atticus's body is chained to the floor, his hands and feet and head aligning with the points of the pentagram. Adelina tries to break out. She pulls hard on the chains, but they hold firm. She lets out a wild yell, and her gaze turns to us. The hatred in her eyes makes me and Dorian step back.

"How do we get her out of him?" Dorian asks. "What do we do?"

I can barely form a thought. I have no answers. All I see is my best friend, someone I love, and he's in pain. He's right in front of me and simultaneously a million miles away.

"I broke the skull," Dorian says, running his hands through his hair. "It was the tether, wasn't it? Why didn't it work?"

"What was Atticus trying to say? He was trying to explain something, but he never got the chance to finish. He pointed to the desk," I say.

Professor White's books cover the table. Some are flipped open, revealing spells written in different languages. "Dorian, Professor White used magic to bring Adelina here," I say, grabbing one and leafing through the aged pages. "She must have used an invocation spell. All I have to do is reverse it."

"You mean–"

"An exorcism, yes. I have to banish her."

"Do you know how to do that?" Dorian asks.

"I've already done it. In the library, I banished the elemental," I say. "I did it once, I can do it again. I can try. Help me find the spell she cast. She must have touched the book when she did it."

Dorian runs his hand over one book, then another.

"This one," he says.

On a page written entirely in Latin, I find the spell. It's the one that Professor White used to summon Adelina. "This will take time to complete," I say.

"What if it doesn't work?" Dorian asks. "Or kills him?"

I cast a worried glance at Professor White, who lies motionless on the floor as if in a trance, her chest rising and falling as her lips recite the incantation. "I don't know."

"Raven, it's a risk–"

Before he can protest, I say, "Trust me. Please. I need to do this. For Atticus."

We came to Sibylline to learn magic. And magic is power. It requires risk.

"Nil sine magno labore," I say. "Oneiric Society to the end."

Dorian swallows thickly, and then he nods. "Yeah, okay." Then he repeats, *"Nil sine magno labore."*

He lights the candles, and the sigil is already drawn.

A door was opened. I have to close it.

We walk into the cage together, staying just out of Adelina's reach. Fear lodges in my throat, but I give Dorian one last glance, and he assures me with another nod. If we don't do this now, we'll lose Atticus forever.

Adelina pulls at the chains, baring her teeth at me. I avert my gaze, studying the words on the page, the script shifting into a language I can understand. With a shuddering breath, I raise Hecate's wand and begin the spell. The second the reverse invocation leaves my lips, my mouth feels wrong. Like my tongue is made of lead and my teeth are made of cotton and my gums are pure iron. The wand grows heavier, and my arm shakes. I have to brace it with my other hand.

Adelina's eyes roll into the back of her head, and she groans.

I channel all of my energy into the wand, shape the wand's power to my will. I can't stop. Stopping now would mean failure.

My hair starts to lift into the air, floating, as power surges within me. Magic usually feels like coming home. A return. This time, it's like riding a hurricane. It swells deep inside me, like I might explode, and the only thing keeping me together is a thin layer of flesh. Sweat immediately seeps out of every pore. My body aches. My hands shake. I'm carrying the weight of the universe on my shoulders. Any second my body will give out, but I refuse to let it. I'm in control.

As the spell works, Adelina thrashes, writhing and bucking, her spine threatening to snap in two. Only her heels and her head are touching the floor, contorting Atticus's body into a grotesque arc.

Nearby, Professor White's eyes snap open. She's still speaking the words of the original spell, the one that called Adelina from the skull. She is fighting us with all her strength.

Dorian takes off his glove, drops to his knees, and clutches Atticus's hand, slotting his fingers into the spaces between his.

"Please." Adelina speaks with Atticus's lips, eyes shiny with tears. "It's me, Dorian. You're hurting me."

"It's not him," Dorian tells me. "Keep going."

I hope he's right. Please, God, let him be right.

Dorian bows his head and closes his eyes, his hands glowing.

I am magic. *We* are magic.

Professor White raises her voice. She is fighting us, too.

Adelina cries out. "Please, stop!" she says. "It's me! Atticus! You're killing me!"

Dorian bites his lips.

I fear I don't have the strength to banish Adelina and Professor White. Both of them studied at Sibylline. They are practiced and educated. They are true practitioners of the art. I can't beat them, not by myself.

Still chanting, I drop to my knees, and I press my hand to the body possessed by Adelina. She glares at me, cursing with Atticus's lips. "He's already dead," the voice says. "You're too late to save Atticus."

I fear she's right. Tears burn my eyes, and a sob bubbles up my throat. But then he gently squeezes my hand. His thumb brushes my knuckles. It's Atticus. He's still in there. I look at Dorian. There's a sliver of hope in his eyes. He feels him, too. Instinct drives me forward.

I drop the wand and grab Dorian's other hand. A rush of power surges through my arms. Our shared connection, our one soul. The three of us, we're all made of the same stuff. A trio of threads, woven into a single yarn. Stronger together.

"*Ema lfdna woda hsotkca bog.*" I continue reciting the spell.

Professor White convulses, her lips still reciting the words. My own voice cracks, my tongue as dry as sandpaper, and my own throat threatens to choke me out.

The practitioners of Sibylline's vaunted magical arts are fighting against us. They have knowledge and training. We have friendship and love, and raw talent.

I speak the words, and a gust of wind rushes into the room. One by one, the candles go out, extinguished in the gathering force of the magic. The glow from Dorian's hands is the only light in the room, but it is no longer his light. It's Atticus's and now mine.

I repeat the spell, its power somehow multiplied by our bond. The force of our magic burns hot like a fire, but it does not scald us. Our magic is warm and safe, a beacon in the night to banish the dark soul of Adelina. Professor White rages against that light, giving every last drop of her strength to fight us. She blazes white-hot.

The air is charged with potent magic. This is a contest of will.

Only one side will walk away.

"*Su otkcab emocem otkcab emoc.*" I say the words, and Professor White shouts over me, trying to drown me out.

So I say the words again, and Dorian speaks them, too, and I swear Atticus's lips move, joining us. At last, ours are the only voices in the room.

When the last syllable leaves my lips, I fall to my knees, still holding on to their hands with everything I have. Dorian's hand is loose on mine, as if he also has poured all of himself into the spell. The chamber is oddly quiet as the wind dies down, but my ears are still ringing.

Dorian rises up, sweat glistening on his brow. When he looks at me and realizes I'm okay, his relief melts into a smile. "Did it work?" he asks.

I don't know, and my voice is gone. It feels like I've been screaming for hours.

"Atticus? Are you there?" I ask, each word raw and calloused at the same time.

But Atticus lies motionless on the floor, his hand limp in mine.

Dorian

If all else perished, and he remained, I should still continue to be; and if all else remained, and he were annihilated, the universe would turn to a mighty stranger.

—*Emily Brontë,* Wuthering Heights

"ATTICUS?" I ASK. "Atticus." I shake him. Panic grows. He's not responding.

Raven stares, exhausted, stunned. What have we done?

My hands dance over Atticus's face and chest, searching for signs of life. He's not breathing, he's not moving. His heart's not beating.

No, no, this can't be happening. I unlock the manacles, and I pull him into my arms. Raven rushes forward, letting out a single strangled cry as the realization sets in. He's dead—Atticus is dead.

Searching for help, I spot a pile of ash on the floor outside the cell. It's all that's left of Professor White. She is gone, too, consumed by the power of her own magic. I simply shake my head, not knowing what happened. Maybe I'll never know. Perhaps I don't care. Atticus isn't breathing, and I press my ear to his chest and listen for the beating of a heart.

"No, no, come back, you can't go," I say. "Don't do this, please. Don't."

Raven shudders as a sob escapes her. She hasn't let go of Atticus's hand. She's holding it so tightly she might not ever let go.

"What about the cities you want to build?" I ask Atticus. "What about the places you want to see? What about everything you want to do? Come on, Atticus, you were never a quitter." I wait for him to wake up or crack a smile; I can't take a breath until he does.

But he doesn't move. Doesn't wake.

He's dead. This has to be a nightmare. It can't happen like this.

Raven plants a kiss on his lips. She whispers Atticus's name, asking him to open his eyes. "I love you," she says. "I *love* you. Please."

Then Raven looks at me tearfully, as if asking what else can be done, but I don't know. I don't . . .

She kisses my lips next. A gentle, assuring kiss, warm and sweet and too sad to bear. "Dorian," she says, "he's gone."

I shake my head. This can't be happening, not like this. Feeling her lips on mine, I sense Raven's feelings for Atticus. And I know her feelings for me. We're a twisted, knotted rope of love, and affection, and desire, tangled up and impossible to undo.

I love Atticus. I love Raven. I always have. I never had the chance to tell Atticus what he means to me. I wish I'd been able to say it. I wish I'd been able to tell him how I feel. And now he's . . .

Atticus rests limply in my arms. Raven rests her hand on my shoulder. I thought I had to choose between them. That's what I believed . . .

What if we don't take no for an answer? That's what Raven said that day we were rejected from Sibylline. Never give up. So why am I doing it now?

I will not let him sacrifice himself. I will not let the universe dictate what I can and cannot have. I didn't let Sibylline, and I certainly won't let Death itself.

Together, we break rules.

"Raven, help me," I say. "Help me do this one last thing."

I kiss her again, and she kisses me back, tears running down our cheeks. She nods against my lips. Through her touch, warmth spreads inside of me. Her power melds with mine, creating an undulating, swirling vortex of our shared love, our devotion, our will.

We are wizards even if the school will never admit us.

We are the deciders of our own fate.

We make magic, because we are magic.

And our kind of magic made the universe.

Raven's hair changes, from black to white, and I know, inexplicably, that the same is happening in mine, too. Raven lifts a hand, tracing it along my face, pouring everything she has into this moment. She's given everything for Atticus, and I'm giving everything back.

Then I kiss Atticus, telling him with that single touch to come back.

Come back to me.

Come back to us.

ATTICUS

But to die as lovers may—to die together, so that they may live together.

—*Joseph Sheridan Le Fanu,* Carmilla

THERE'S DARKNESS.

And then there's light.

Then both at the same time.

A warm embrace, a cool touch.

Inhale. Exhale.

Raven.

Dorian.

Raven.

Dorian.

I can feel Dorian's lips on mine and Raven's hands on my body. Someone is undressing me, and when I reach forward, I realize they are undressing themselves as well. Now Raven's breast is against my mouth, and I open it, licking her nipple. She sighs as Dorian's head brushes against my stomach, and now he's taking me in his mouth.

Is this a dream?

Is this real?

I don't know; I know only that I've come back to myself, and I feel myself lowering between Raven's knees as Dorian presses his erection against my back. I'm so hot, and the three of us are slick with sweat, and now Raven's hands are on my shaft, guiding me, and as I plunge into her, Dorian's thrusting into me. And the three of us are making love with each other, in a perfect, perfect circle. The arrows no longer point in the wrong direction, but toward each other.

Raven shudders first, then me, then Dorian.

An explosion of light and stars.

I'm alive.

I open my eyes to a new universe.

42
Raven

The moon, their mistress, had expir'd before;
The winds were wither'd in the stagnant air,
And the clouds perish'd; Darkness had no need
Of aid from them—She was the Universe.

—Lord Byron, "Darkness"

AS WE STEP out of the darkened tunnels beneath Arches, Warden Stone approaches us, flanked by men and women in flowing robes. "You three, come with me."

"Nope, we're done with this place," I say.

"Perhaps not quite yet," says Warden Stone.

We have no choice but to follow him to his office. I half expect to see a platoon of guards here to escort us away, but it's just us as Stone leads us inside.

His office is not as messy as we'd last seen it, and it's brighter, too. Candles have been lit, and the room isn't as cold as I remember. I stand between Dorian and Atticus as Warden Stone looks intently at each of us. He's always been an imposing figure, broad and tall, but now he stands as if a great weight has been lifted from his shoulders.

"A century ago, a girl named Adelina Ward, a student at Sibylline, created a malum. The shadow killed two students, but it was captured and contained by my predecessors. The shadow lay in a cell beneath Arches until the tower fell and set it free."

"We know," I say. "We figured it all out. Without your help."

Warden Stone presses his lips into a line, but he doesn't argue. It catches me off guard.

"What you don't know is that to prevent another incident," he says, "Sibylline denied admission to those with psychic ability. Sibylline didn't want another Adelina Ward. The ability to invade the mind, to read thoughts and feelings and emotions, was seen as dangerous. *Anyone* who was deemed remarkably powerful was seen as dangerous, too."

"So the school kept out people like us," says Dorian.

Warden Stone nods, his blue gaze no longer like ice. "Our hiring manager forwarded me your résumés. I knew someone was trying to free the malum—a faculty or staff member, I suspected—but I didn't know who. I couldn't let you in as students, but I thought if I let you work here, maybe one of you could help me figure out who was upsetting the magical balance in the atmosphere."

Numbly, I think back to that day we got our rejection letters. So they really wanted us after all? It's strangely vindicating.

Meanwhile, Dorian says, "Professor White was behind everything. She kidnapped Atticus to bring Adelina back."

"Where is Professor White now?" Warden Stone asks.

"Gone, somehow. Only dust remains," I say, not really knowing what happened when her spell failed.

"Sounds like telepyrosis," says Warden Stone. "She was consumed by the force of her own magic."

"What happened to the malum?" I ask.

"We were able to destroy it with St. Adolphus Hall's help. I've been working closely with them in secret. They knew those in their ranks would be targets. They have been studying the phenomenon for years."

Silently I give Aspen and his friends thanks. I'm sorry I ever suspected him.

"So why did you fire us?" Atticus asks. The memory still stings.

"It was a calculated risk," admits Stone, looking shamefaced. "My reasons were twofold. If I kept you on after what happened under Arches, it would look suspicious, and firing you would draw my suspect out of the shadows, so to speak . . . Professor White did exactly what I thought she would do. She was desperate not to lose a powerful magic user before her work could be completed."

It's all starting to make sense. "You knew we were the only ones who could stop her," I say. "So, then, why are we here now?"

"Don't you know, Miss Chen? You're so much more perceptive usually." Warden Stone gives us a thin smile. "I'm here to offer you admission."

"To Sibylline?"

"Where else?" he asks amusedly.

I'm floored. I look at Dorian, at Atticus—they're both as shocked as I am. Atticus looks a little haunted; his eyes have changed. They're still dark, still deep and warm, but they glitter with an unnatural shine, just like starlight, radiant even at night. Dorian's frowning, but his eyes are shining as well.

"It's time to make some changes around here," Warden Stone says. "Now, will you accept? We'll have the paperwork drawn up, and you will be welcome to move into the dormitory, of course."

"But—you—you fired us!" I shriek.

"I had to. I couldn't risk letting whoever was plotting against the school know that I was trying to expose them."

"So we come back as students?" Atticus asks tentatively.

"When the new semester starts, yes."

I look at my friends. We're at a crossroads, and they're my

guideposts. Atticus takes my right hand, and Dorian the other. Together, we answer.

CAMPUS IS EMPTY at this hour. No other living soul stirs. It's as if we have the entire world to ourselves. We leave Warden Stone's office, stepping into the predawn glow that washes Sibylline in rose light.

New students. Us. Who would have thought? Of course we accepted. It's everything we ever wanted. Where we're going now, none of us seems to really know. We walk only for the purpose of being together.

When we pass by the ruins of Arches, Atticus looks distant as he stares emptily at the rubble. It's like he's seeing something that isn't there.

"Finch?" Dorian asks.

His nickname jolts him out of the trance. He shakes his head, returning to himself. "Sorry . . ."

He died. Really died. And we brought him back. I squeeze his hand. "You're with us?"

The Atticus we know shines through, a smile on his face. "Right now, I just need a shower."

"Me too," says Dorian.

"Me three," I say cheekily. I'm not really sure what happened back there, the vision we all shared, together as one, but it felt so right. Looking at the both of them now, a swell of desire rises in me. I thought I'd lost them, and now I know for certain I never want to be without them. Shared, equally. It's a new feeling for sure, but one I can get used to. "Should we all just . . . ?"

I don't need to say it. They know. Atticus and Dorian exchange glances, color high in their cheeks, before they look back at me.

"Yeah," says Atticus, ruffling Dorian's newly white hair. "Why not?"

Dorian laughs. "Your place, Finch?"

"Who has the biggest bathtub?" Atticus wonders. Then, sotto voce, he says, "We're going to need a bigger tub."

I catch a glimpse of my hair as it falls from behind my ear. "Oh God, what are my parents going to think? I look like a ghost. I'm going to have a lot to explain."

"I think the white suits you," Atticus says, running his fingers through it. "It's soft, like moonlight through lace curtains."

I bring his hand to my mouth and kiss his knuckles as Dorian nuzzles my neck. There is no choosing–I love them both, and they both love me and each other. We are friends, lovers, a family, the three of us, forever.

I tip my head to gaze up at the velvet dark stretching overhead and breathe deeply as we walk in the slowly rising dawn. Let the future bring what it will. I can face anything knowing I will never be alone at Sibylline, or anywhere in the world.

That's right, Raven, you're never alone, says a voice.

"What was that?" I ask sharply. "Did you say anything?"

Dorian looks up. "Huh?"

Atticus shakes his head. "No. Did you hear something?"

For once, he's not the one hearing disembodied voices.

I don't tell him the truth; I'm too scared.

That's right, Raven, don't tell them. I will just be your little secret . . .

ACKNOWLEDGMENTS

THANK YOU TO my amazing editor Polo Orozco, my publishers Jen Klonsky and Jen Loja, my publicist Jordana Kulak, and all the lovely team at Penguin. Proud to be your author for so many years! Thank you to my agents Richard Abate and Hannah Carrande at 3Arts for keeping the lights on. Thank you to my friends and family and my loyal readers. Thank you to Mike, my husband and writing partner for more than twenty years.

Erehem oc
lewton erauoy
Vocare
ignis
Ema lfdna
woda hsotkca bog.
Su otkcab emocem
otkcab emoc.
Omnes una
manet nox
Dum spiro, spero.
Nil sine magno labore.
Omne trium
perfectum.
Call forth thee,
in thy name, to manifest,
in form, and freedom.
In thy name, thou
art free from this
summons.
Sibylline